Habitat for

A Novel

Donna McGinty

This is a work of fiction. Names, characters and incidents either are the product of the author's imagination or are used fictitiously. Any resemblance to actual events or persons, living or dead, is entirely coincidental.

ISBN: 1470085380
ISBN-13: 9781470085384

In loving memory of

My brother
Miles McGinty (1941-2006)
and
His soul mate
Dixie Dowis McGinty (1957-2009)

Author's Notes

I value and respect Habitat for Humanity's mission and how it operates at the local level (visit the brief history at the back of the book). I also respect and value law enforcement when justice triumphs. For these reasons and others, I seek to protect the good reputations of North Georgia's numerous Habitat chapters and many sheriffs' departments by setting the novel's main action in a fictional county—Creeks County (with apologies to Georgia's official 159 counties.) Also, I squeeze Creeks County onto the shoreline of Lake Sidney Lanier near Gainesville, putting it within easy reach of Athens and Atlanta.

The novel's various references to Lake Sidney Lanier (known to most as "Lake Lanier") are low key. While I could have chosen to use the lake as a "character" in the story, instead, I use the lake as a simple backdrop for Billie's desire to live on a houseboat and downplay her reluctant status as a multimillionaire-via-inheritance. To make amends to readers who would have liked for me to introduce clueless readers to the lake's size and grandeur, following are a few salient facts:

- 692 miles of shoreline

- 39,000 acres of water
- created from the Chattahoochee and Chestatee Rivers by the Buford Dam (lake opened in 1956)
- 68-plus parks and recreation areas, 12 campgrounds with 1,000-plus campsites*
- home to Lake Lanier Islands boasting resort hotels, golf, and a water park
- multiple full-service marinas
- recognized as one of the South's premier houseboat havens
- named for Sidney Clopton Lanier (1842-1881) because of the respect he showed for the Chattahoochee River in his poetry

Those readers who follow "water wars" will recognize Lake Sidney Lanier as being a primary source of water for Atlanta, which has produced a decade-plus-long confrontation with downstream neighbors, Alabama and Florida, both dependent on adequate water flow from the lake. As of September 2011, the 11th Circuit Court refused a request by Alabama and Florida for a new hearing to review a June 2011 decision by a three-judge panel, which essentially reinstated Atlanta's right to withdraw water from Lake Lanier, as needed. (Google Tri-state Water Wars Litigation for complete details.)

*These numbers fluctuate.

January 2012

Chapter 1

blotted my face with a sweaty shirtsleeve and leaned against a giant water oak. After quickly rejecting the laws of hygiene, I stuck a throbbing, dirty thumb in my mouth and willed myself to put aside the argument I'd had with Jake earlier.

A high-noon sun filtered through leaves and patterned the ground. Nothing stirred in the August heat except my hot breath. Across a 75-foot swath of cracked, red clay stacked with various cuts of lumber, bags of concrete, and boxes of nails and fasteners, I watched the volunteers gear down. Some wriggled out of heavy gloves; others unbuckled tool belts and stretched. Two disappeared into undergrowth, headed for the portable toilet. The aroma of freshly grilled chicken hung in the humidity.

I spotted Jake Wade, Habitat construction supervisor, and watched him fish a bottle of water out of a large foam cooler. He twisted the top off and poured half the liquid down the back of his shirt. Then he guzzled the rest of the water nonstop.

"You okay, Miz Billie?" Sam walked into the shade and mopped his black forehead with a crumpled red and white bandana.

Ruby waddled to Sam's side and shook a finger at me. "Honey, yo' face is beet red. And why you sucking yo' thumb?" She tugged the bandana out of Sam's back pocket and wiped pearls of sweat from her face and neck.

"Hit it—hammer," I mumbled around the thumb.

Ruby clucked and patted my arm. "Well now, honey, it's time for all of us to take a rest and eat. You come on over to the table, and I'll fetch yo' dinner and a bowl of ice for that thumb."

"Hold on, Ruby." Sam put a hand on her shoulder. "Maybe Miz Billie wouldn't feel right setting at table with the boss man. Their words is still stuck up in the air." He tucked his chin and cut his eyes at me.

"Nothing happened that Jake and I can't get over." My smile met with somber expressions. "Come on. Cheer up, you guys. I promise you'll get your house. Habitat always comes through. Now let's dig into that chicken."

Two vintage picnic tables set end-to-end in the shade of a pecan tree formed an uneven 12-foot long dining table. Those of us who regularly volunteered for the Saturday build claimed our places, as if they were reserved. Jake and I sat at either end of the table. To my left sat Sam and Ruby, Neal, a scrawny college student, and Pete, an older man with a gray ponytail and one earring. To my right sat Fred, a paunchy volunteer from a nearby rural church. He motioned for the newbies to sit beside him—Gloria, a rail-thin woman with wispy hair, and her two teen-age, twin daughters, Brenda and Bridget. The girls wore matching short shorts, T-shirts, hiking boots, and bored expressions.

I wiggled my thumb in the cup of ice Ruby had brought me. I tried to lock eyes with Jake, hoping that a smile would soothe hard feelings. No such luck. He looked everywhere but in my direction.

A jug of instant hand cleaner moved slowly around the table, its antiseptic scent mingling with heady wafts of body odor and grilled chicken. Sam and Ruby unfurled several sheets of paper towels and mopped sheens of sweat from their faces and arms. Fred followed suit.

Jake tapped a serving spoon against the rim of a bowl of cole slaw. Some chatter ceased. He tapped again, harder. All talk trailed off mid-sentence.

"Some of you like to start with prayer, so let's do it," he said.

The previous Saturday, he'd made the mistake of asking Fred to say the blessing. Five minutes into a rambling *Thank you, Lord, for this and that* and *bless this and that,* Jake had interrupted with a curt, "Amen. Now, let's eat."

Jake bowed his head. "Almighty God, we thank you for seeing us safely through this past week of our lives. We come from different places for different reasons. But this don't matter while we're here together building a house for Sam and Ruby. Bless this food and keep us safe to meet again next Saturday. Amen."

"In Jesus' name, Amen," Fred hastened to add.

Jake ignored the correction. If he was religious, he kept it to himself. I studied him as he ladled generous portions of food from the bowls that were passed his way. He wasn't a tall man, perhaps two inches more than my five feet eight inches. Age? My estimate was fifty to fifty-five. He was wiry and strong. One afternoon, I had watched him lift and stack forty-pound bags of concrete, never slowing or losing the rhythm he established. His head, shaved smooth, glistened with sweat. A firm jaw line hid in a bushy red beard. He made no effort to join the small talk at his end of the table.

"Cluck! Cluck! Chicken on the move." Neal pointed his fork across the table.

Sam held out a large aluminum pan. I speared one of the smaller breasts. Neal forked the largest breast in the pan and two bulbous chicken legs. He dropped all three pieces on a paper towel spread near a plate that overflowed with slaw, beans and two biscuits the size of saucers. I envied him his skinny gene.

As I concentrated on eating, my thoughts slipped back to the moment that, as Sam described it, words got stuck in the air between Jake and me. At the mid-morning break, he had gathered us in a circle and announced that construction was running behind, that we could catch up if we worked extra hours.

Before I caught myself, I blurted opposition. "It's too damned hot, Jake. We'll stop by three o'clock; otherwise, we'll be courting heat stroke."

Jake had folded his arms and stared at me for a full minute or more. Apparently, he wasn't used to taking supervision from a woman or something else was bugging him. He opened his mouth to speak, then clamped his teeth together and stalked off. We hadn't spoken since.

The confrontation was unintended. Although, technically, I was boss, it made sense for Jake to call the shots since he knew construction, and I didn't. I was annoyed with myself that I had come on so strong. The volunteers viewed me as second in command, although they didn't know the details. With the blessing of Dorothy Longview, director of the Creeks County Habitat for Humanity chapter, I was paying for the build and had hired Jake, with Dorothy's approval, as construction supervisor. Building a house for Sam and Ruby was something

I wanted to do, something that made me feel less guilty about inheriting millions and enjoying a cushy life.

"Heads up everybody." Jake stood and whistled through his teeth. Conversation stopped. He looked at his wristwatch. "Okay. It's back to work in five minutes. I need all of you guys to help Pete and me hammer roof trusses in place. Oh, before I forget, let's give our cooks a big hand for all the great food."

Gloria smiled and pushed a clump of damp, wispy hair off of her forehead. Brenda and Bridget ignored the applause and stared at the screens of their cell phones.

Ruby offered to clear my trash from the table, and I double-timed it toward Jake's retreating back. Before I reached him, he disappeared into the undergrowth, headed for the portable toilet. A few minutes later, I heard footsteps crunch through dry pine straw. As he emerged from a tangle of shrubs and tall weeds, I touched his arm. He jumped and wheeled toward me.

"Damn, Billie! Don't ever sneak up on me."

"Sorry, Jake. We need to talk."

"About what? You hold the purse strings. So we'll quit at three o'clock. But this is as good a time as any to tell you I won't be here next Saturday."

Surprise caught my breath. "No fair, Jake. I'm counting on you, and so are Sam and Ruby. Are you that upset about our squabble this morning?"

Jake shrugged his shoulders. "Hell, no. Squabbling has nothing to do with my decision. I've got urgent business elsewhere. But just so you know, I was pissed. Why didn't you challenge me in private? Don't worry about what you owe me. Give it to Sam and Ruby."

"How about a bonus, Jake? See this through, and I'll add a nice bonus. You do good work, something I've learned since I hired you." I hated to beg. On the other hand, I hated to see progress on the house grind to a halt.

Jake stared at me and tugged on his beard. "I think you mean well, Billie. But you live in another world, one far removed from mine. This thing I've got to do... It has nothing to do with money. It has everything to do with honor. After all these months of searching, I'm so close. I can't let anything stand in my way."

Before I could collect my thoughts, Jake wheeled and strode toward the house and the men who were waiting for him.

Chapter 2

After a trip to the john, I retreated to the shade of the big oak. My thumb had stopped throbbing but was tender to the touch. My T-shirt was sweat-glued to my body. My brain whirled around the bad news. This was Jake's last day on the job. He was the one who had pointed out that construction was behind. How could he walk off and leave things in limbo? Leave Sam and Ruby's dream on hold? I hadn't pegged Jake to be a quitter. And he seemed to care. Several times I'd watched him interact with Sam and Ruby, talking as much with his hands as his mouth, at ease with them in a way he wasn't with me. What the hell was so important, so urgent that he had to quit the build? *A matter of honor...so close*, he'd said. I shook my head.

I breathed deeply and refocused on the work at hand. Jake and the other men stood near the house, staring at a neat stack of trusses on the ground. Jake waved his hands over the lumber and then swept both hands toward the top edge of the house.

I watched Neal, Sam, and Fred lift a truss off the stack and walk it around to the front of the house out of sight. Jake and Pete tossed their ball caps into a patch of weeds and buckled on yellow hard hats. Jake climbed a ladder propped against the house and stepped onto the narrow cap of the sidewall nearest the trusses. Pete disappeared around the front of the house and resurfaced on top of the sidewall across from Jake. Their balancing act looked easier than it probably was.

As I admired their sun-browned legs and arms, Gloria walked up and cut off my view. The twins slouched a few feet away, busily thumb-punching buttons on their cell phones. Had I been that blasé as a teenager?

Gloria must have seen me studying the girls. She shook her head, cupped her mouth with a hand, and spoke in a whisper. "I'm hoping this build will teach the twins something about giving back. We'll see."

"Good luck." I hoped my smile came across as supportive.

"What are Jake and Pete doing?" Gloria pointed to the house and dabbed her brow with a dingy white handkerchief. "Looks like they could fall real easy."

"They're all set to nail the first roof truss in place. And don't worry. Monkeys don't fall out of trees."

Gloria missed the humor or didn't care.

"How'd they get that truss thing up there?" she asked.

"Pulled it up with ropes and then slid it along the tops of the side walls to where they're standing."

"Glad it's them and not me." She turned her attention my way. "What's left to do? Ruby's cleaning up the dinner mess."

"Help me pick up trash around the yard and house, then you and the girls can call it a day."

I gave each of them a medium-sized plastic bag and opened one for myself. We fanned out and worked our way toward the house, picking up coffee cups, empty water bottles, aluminum cans, crumpled napkins, nails, scrap lumber, metal straps, whatever was foreign to the red dirt. The trash barrel I'd provided was often ignored in the hurly-burly of construction.

I stooped and shooed a yellow jacket off the mouth of a drink can just as my cell phone vibrated. I bolted upright and fished my phone out of a jeans pocket.

"Hi, Billie. Do you have any druthers for dinner tonight?" Madge's words rode a Southern drawl.

Since February, Madge had been on my payroll as housekeeper and cook. A no-nonsense, energetic woman in her late fifties, she was becoming more than an employee. She wasn't surprised by anything I said or did, unlike Uncle Joe and his wife, Irene.

"Why do some country people call lunch 'dinner' and dinner 'supper'?" I asked.

Madge laughed. "Don't know, but I'm one of them. It took me years to make the switch and get the cow dung off my Sunday shoes. So what about *dinner*?"

"Something cool. We're melting out here. What's Carl up to?"

Carl was Madge's husband, on the payroll as my jack-of-all-trades and helmsman for outings on the lake, if I could get him to buckle down and learn the ropes. Unfortunately, he wasn't as enthusiastic about working for me as Madge was.

"Who knows what Grumpy is up to? He took his stiff knee out to the aft deck with one of the manuals that came with your houseboat. I love living on the water, but he misses terra firma, his big garden, and that darn lawn tractor."

We said goodbye. I tied a knot in my plastic bag, slung it over my shoulder, and joined Ruby who had waved to me from across the yard. We settled on a bench under a crepe myrtle near the back of the house. From our position, we had a good view of Jake and Pete silhouetted against a blue sky.

"This is big, Miz Billie." Ruby smiled and flashed perfectly aligned white teeth. "Sam and me gonna have a roof over our heads. A new roof. All the building troubles getting this far, well, now we can just bury 'um and move on."

I squeezed Ruby's calloused hand. Jake's unexpected departure would hit her hard.

"Look there." Ruby pointed to Gloria and the twins. "They mighty close to where Mr. Jake and Mr. Pete are working. Don't look safe to me."

I watched Jake and Pete gesture to each other from their perches on the sidewalls.

"Don't worry. If the girls are in any danger, Jake will shoo them off."

Ruby, who fretted over every detail of the house, nodded her head and clucked her tongue. Fretting was a good part of her sweat equity.

Jake turned around on the lip of the house and looked at the truss Pete and he had just nailed down at the back of the house. He removed his hard hat and tucked it between his feet. Sam tossed a bottle of water up to Jake who chug-a-lugged some of it before pouring the rest over his head. Jake couldn't talk without using his hands, so when he stood there, hands on hips, looking in our direction, I knew he was thinking.

At that moment, a sharp, faraway sound like a large frozen limb breaking off a tree in an ice storm ruffled the silence and echoed in my ears. I looked at Jake through an expanding cloud of pink. Pink what? I blinked and caught my breath. I watched in horror as Jake's body sagged and pitched forward off the lip of the house. Sam and Neal scrambled backwards and knocked Fred to the ground. Jake landed on the edge of the stack of trusses before he disappeared from sight.

My heart stampeded in my chest. I ran toward Jake. Behind me, Ruby screamed, "Lord God, no!"

I stopped near the twins. They were stapled to the ground, gaping at each other, wide-eyed. Pinpoints of pink and gray dotted their faces, arms, and T-shirts. Seconds later, as if responding to a starter gun, they screamed in unison and ran in erratic circles around Gloria, who had slumped to the ground.

"Get it off!" shouted one twin. Sobbing, she rubbed her arms and smeared a mix of pink and gray into a thin line.

The other twin stopped running, but her legs pumped furiously in place. She snatched her T-shirt over her head, wadded it, and scrubbed her face and arms. Seeing this, her sister struggled out of her T-shirt. Then, as if on cue, they ran to their mother, squatted beside her, and wiped her face with their soiled shirts. Their matching sports bras gleamed white against tanned skin.

I sucked in hot air but couldn't catch a deep breath. I turned to the men huddled a few feet from where Jake lay hidden behind the stack of trusses. They had turned their backs on him. I took several wobbly steps toward them. Neal, his face a ghostly white, left the huddle and stopped spread-eagle in front of me. He blocked my way with thin, outstretched arms. His body shook top to bottom.

"Jake's dead." His voice broke. "Gunshot. You don't want to look, Billie."

"You're sure? How can you be sure? Maybe there's a pulse."

"No way. His head…even his face…they're…"

"Move. I have to see for myself." I stepped closer to Neal. He kept his arms extended. Bits of pink and gray matter flecked his tanned, hairless chest. All that came to mind was *flesh and bone*. I pressed my fist to my mouth and gagged.

Behind me, Ruby wailed. "Sweet Jesus! What's happened to Mr. Jake?"

"Move, Neal. I mean it." My teeth chattered.

Neal stared at me for a few seconds and sighed. "Okay. But I'm right here."

I closed my eyes in a tight squint and inched forward. My crazy thought was that it might be easier to look at Jake through the blur of a squint. His body came into soft focus. Arms and legs were splayed. I squinted tighter and saw Jake's head. It wasn't all there. My breath caught and my eyes flew open. There was no blur to hide the horror. A sizable portion of Jake's brow was shattered, exposing pulpy, pinkish matter. What had been Jake's face was a mess of bloody tissue. The red beard seemed detached from his chin.

A wave of bile rose in my throat and ebbed. I leaned over as a second wave filled my mouth. I gagged and vomited. My knees buckled just as Neal's arm encircled my waist. He pulled me to his side. I wiped my mouth on my shirtsleeve and fought back another wave of nausea.

"It's okay. I've got you." He turned me away from the sight of Jake and steered me to where the others stood close together, enveloped in silence. Their eyes were wide, expressions dazed.

Fred kneeled. "We should pray." His pulpit-voice boomed in the eerie quiet. Sweat streamed down his face into dirty creases in his neck.

"No, no. Not now." Panic joined forces with shock. I grabbed Fred's wet, fat arm and pulled. "Get up. We can't stay here."

No one moved. They stared at me. I yanked again on the pudgy arm. "Dammit! We're in the open, people. You want your head blown off by some crazy? Come on." My bravado was false. All I wanted to do was curl up on the hard dirt and blubber.

A vision of spilled brains galvanized everyone. The twins, still crying, got on either side of their mother, grabbed her elbows, and propelled her in my wake. I led the way to the picnic tables.

"Where is Mr. Pete?" Sam asked. "I ain't seen him."

We exchanged confused looks. Feet shuffled. My heart kicked up its beat.

"Oh, Lord God. Not Mr. Pete, too." Ruby grabbed Sam's arm and rocked back and forth on her heels.

"One of us can circle back through the woods as cover and check for Pete on the other side of the house," I said.

"I only heard one shot," Neal said. "But I'll go."

"We need to pray first. Let's all get on our knees and pray for a man's soul." Fred stretched his arms to the sky and closed his eyes.

"Don't pray for me. And Jake damn sure won't know the difference."

The voice came from the woods behind us. We turned and watched Pete limp out of a stand of oaks and tall pines. He cradled a rifle in his arms.

Chapter 3

"Jake's dead, ain't he?" Pete stared at me. Sweat plastered thin hair to his scalp.

I nodded. Tears welled in my eyes, and I wiped them with a shirtsleeve. "We thought you..."

"No way," he interrupted. "I know a damn rifle shot. Nearly broke my neck jumping off the ladder. Got the rifle from my truck and hightailed it through the woods over to here. Well, not exactly hightailed it. Damn ankle slowed me down." He extended his foot and winced when he tried to rotate his ankle. "I called 911, but hung up after I told them what happened and gave directions. Needed both hands for my gun."

"You need to sit down, Mr. Pete." Ruby patted a picnic bench. Sam sat on the other end of the bench, elbows propped on his knees, head in hands. His bouncing right leg tapped his boot heel rhythmically against the ground.

"And you girls. You can't stand around in your bras. Ain't decent. Here. Put these across yo' shoulders." Ruby handed them black plastic bags. "Show poor Mr. Jake some respect."

"We need to pray for a man's soul," said Fred. He closed his eyes and pressed his hands palm to palm under a quivering chin.

"Anybody who wants to pray, go with Fred." I tried to keep irritation out of my voice. "Go over there under that pecan tree." I pointed in the general direction. "Please," I added, feeling guilty.

Sam and Ruby fell in beside Fred, and they walked away hand in hand.

I turned back to Pete. "I haven't stopped praying since I looked at Jake. Half of his skull is gone. It's awful. Could this be an accident? A stray shot maybe?"

"Wouldn't bet on it." He turned around and pointed toward the road. "See those two old cedars, one on each side of the driveway? I'm thinking the shooter had to be in the woods over there across the hay field. That's a distance of a football field plus some. He had to aim between those trees. And even if a deer was out there, maybe eating hay, the shooter's bullet would've been aimed more to the ground. Not high like the shot that hit Jake. And, duh, it's not even deer season. Nah, I don't think it was an accident."

Newly mown hay, baled in the shape of barrels, haphazardly dotted the field. Far across the beige landscape, a line of dark green pine trees bordered the field. The effect was pastoral, not sinister.

Gloria sobbed loudly and broke my train of thought. The twins patted her on the back and eased her into a rickety lawn chair.

Why wasn't someone depositing me in a lawn chair? Had shock so numbed me to Jake's ghastly death that I was on autopilot, fueled by disbelief?

"Ssshh!" Neal waved his hands and cocked his head toward the road. "Hear that?"

Two intermingled sirens pierced the air, one closer than the other. A black and white cruiser, blue lights flashing, slowed as it approached the driveway. I doubted that a small, hand-printed Habitat for Humanity sign near the road was visible. I ran full speed toward the car, stopped, put two fingers in my mouth, and whistled shrilly. It was a trick Uncle Joe had taught me, and I had used it periodically to embarrass my mother.

The moment galvanized everyone. Pete whistled with me. Neal ran to my side, punched his fists at the sky and shouted, "In here, in here!"

The twins abandoned modesty, stood on the picnic table and waved their black plastic bags. I looked toward the pecan tree and saw Sam and Fred break off praying and hustle to their feet. They pulled Ruby up and fast-walked to join us.

"Lordy." Ruby huffed and pressed a hand over her heart. "I never thought I'd be so glad to see the police." She hugged Sam's neck. He wrapped his arms around her, and they rocked side to side.

The cruiser turned in and parked parallel to the driveway. Its roof light bar cycled blue flashes. A short, stocky man in uniform climbed out of the car and hitched up his pants. He leaned into the front seat and came out with a Stetson and a clipboard. He spoke something into a radio attached to the shoulder of his shirt. Silently, we watched his every move, waited for some word or signal. He was about seventy-five feet from where we stood.

"Don't know him, but he's a deputy sheriff," Pete said.

The deputy stepped in our direction, away from his car. From his angle, I knew he couldn't see Jake.

"Listen up!" The deputy shouted at us through cupped hands. "The person who's in charge, get over here now. But walk around the edge of the lot. The rest of you stay put. Nobody leaves. This is a crime scene."

"Let's go," I said to Neal. We jogged along the edge of the woods.

As we cut right to cross the driveway, an ambulance silenced its siren and pulled in ahead of us. Racing around clay and gravel country roads had turned its white paint job a faded orange. Pulsing red and clear lights punched the air. We waited. Two EMTs piled out and looked around. One could have passed as a senior in high school. The other one wore a trim moustache under a receding hairline and appeared to be in charge. He said, "Who needs us, people? Time's a wasting."

"Jake is over there behind that pile of lumber. But you're too late," I said. A knot caught in my throat.

"We'll decide that," said the mustache.

The deputy followed the EMTs, and when they stopped, he stopped. He peered around them and took a wobbly step backward. I understood his recoil. Bile and phlegm rose in my throat. I swallowed hard.

The deputy turned on his heel and walked toward a second black and white cruiser as it rolled to a silent stop in the driveway. Its pulsing blue lights mingled with the lights of the other two vehicles in a crazy-quilt pattern.

A tall, lanky deputy with crew-cut blonde hair slid out of his cruiser. The two deputies talked, and our deputy pointed to the hay field. They talked some more. The second deputy climbed back in his cruiser and spun his tires on the gravel as he turned in the direction of the woods where Pete thought the shot had come from.

"You think the shooter left anything over there?" I asked.

"Wouldn't bet on it," Neal said.

The stocky deputy rejoined us. He jotted a few notes on his clipboard before looking at us.

"I'm deputy Owens. Curtis Owens. Who's in charge here?"

I raised my hand. "Billie Quinn. We're building a Habitat for Humanity house."

As the deputy wrote on the clipboard form, I blurted questions I didn't know I had. "Why isn't this place crawling with deputies? And where are the experts who can figure out how Jake died?"

Owens studied me for a moment, his expression impassive. "Big car wreck over at the lake takes priority. So you're stuck with me." He turned to face Neal. "And you?"

"Neal Mercer. I'm here every Saturday. The rest of the volunteers are over there." He pointed to the picnic tables.

"Who got shot? What happened?"

"Jake Wade," I said. "Construction supervisor. He was doing a great job. He kept to himself but seemed like a nice guy." I heard myself babbling. "As for what happened, he was standing on the top edge of the house when some idiot blew his head off." Memories of blood and brains and Jake's partially detached beard flooded me, and I gagged, as saliva spurted into my mouth.

Owens looked up from the clipboard. When I didn't throw up, he wrote more notes. "Can you add anything, Mercer?"

"High powered rifle," Neal said. "You can see it's a straight shot from over there to here—right through where the driveway cuts in to the lot. Jake was a sitting duck for a rifle with a scope. Somebody wanted him dead."

"Any idea why?"

"Absolutely none," I said. "We've been sweating, literally, over the house for the last three Saturdays. He was a worker. We're running behind schedule, but he thought we'd catch up today." I hesitated before continuing. "Jake did tell me this morning that this was his last day. When I asked why, he tensed up. Said it had to do with honor and being so close."

Owens stopped and looked up. "That's all he said?"

"Yes." Guilt stabbed me. I should have pressed Jake.

The deputy tapped his pen on the clipboard and studied me from behind dark sunglasses. "Okay. Let's move on. What about next of kin?"

Neal shrugged his shoulders. "Talk to Pete. They went for beers a couple of Saturday afternoons after we finished here."

"Dorothy Longview at the Habitat office has a file on him," I added. Although I'd hired Jake, I'd left the paperwork up to Dorothy, the local director.

The mustached EMT walked up and held out a thin, rectangular wallet. "The victim is obviously one hundred percent dead, but we left the electrodes in place to show we ran an EKG. I called the coroner."

"Check the wallet contents," Owens said. "You have the gloves on."

We watched the EMT open the wallet. He fished around and pulled out some folded bills. "Three twenties and a ten."

"Driver's license?"

"Florida. In the name of Jake Wade. Truck registration. Same name. No insurance card. That's it."

Owens opened a plastic zip-top bag and the EMT dropped the wallet into it. As the EMTs pulled out of the driveway, Owens labeled the plastic bag with a felt-tip marker.

"Where is the victim's vehicle?" Owens tucked the plastic bag into his waistband.

In unison, Neal and I pointed to the high-suspension Ford F150 that dominated all the vehicles around it. With not much overhang, my hybrid would fit in the pickup's bed. The next largest vehicle was Sam and Ruby's vintage Cadillac.

"Is it okay if I go back to the others and tell them what's going on?" Neal asked. "I don't know a damn other thing."

"Okay," Owens said, "but walk around the edge of the lot along the woods line. And tell them to stay put."

"Owens, you there? Harris here."

"Go ahead." Owens tucked his head and spoke into his shoulder radio.

"I've roped off the area the shooter might have used. It's the only opening in the pine stand along the hay field. Hard to tell though. Dirt under lots of pine needles is dry as a bone. There's one tire track out by the road, but I'd bet it's been there since the last good rain. There's definitely line of sight to the house. I'll wait here for forensics unless you need me there."

"No. Stay put. Ten four."

The deputy's sign-off surprised me. I thought the ten-code list had evaporated in an overhaul of national security.

Owens focused again on me. "And you...You go back over there where the others are. I'll take their statements after I check out the victim's vehicle."

Without asking permission, I detoured by the portable john where one hundred-plus degrees of heat and assorted ripe aromas walloped me. I breathed through my mouth. As I zipped my jeans and stepped out into sunlight, my cell phone vibrated.

"Billie, what the heck is going on out there?" Madge's words tumbled out at high decibel. I moved the phone away from my ear. "A friend of Carl's who's always glued to a police scanner called and said that somebody at your build was shot."

"Shot and killed. Jake Wade. You can't imagine the horror of it, Madge."

She gasped. "Jake? Who in thunderation would do such a thing?"

"I don't know. But I'd definitely like to express my sympathy to his next of kin. Can you imagine what a shock this will be for his family, wherever they are?"

Chapter 4

Deputy Owens wrote with a flourish on a form attached to the clipboard he balanced on one arm. He had recorded each of our statements in hurried handwriting. He pocketed the ballpoint pen and looked up.

"Okay. You can go," Owens said. "But keep handy. No leaving town. Oh, and you should tell the other volunteers to stay where they are. I'll get to them shortly." Without waiting for a response, he turned on his heel and strode back to the crime scene. Whether or not we were getting ahead of the evidence, I'd joined Pete and Neal in being convinced Jake had been murdered. What were the odds that a high-powered bullet shot from hundreds of yards would accidentally hit the small target of Jake's head? About as likely as I was to develop a sudden interest in managing my inheritance, a change of heart Uncle Joe prayed for.

Neal and I retraced our steps to join the other Habitat volunteers who were still huddled near the picnic tables, downcast and bedraggled. My throat ached and swallowing was difficult. I poured the last of a liter of water into paper cups and handed them around. That was it. No more water.

Pete held up his cup. "Rest in peace, Jake." He tipped his head back and drained the cup in one gulp. The rest of us followed suit.

"What about the house? Will we finish it?" Neal asked.

The looks on Sam and Ruby's faces gave me the answer, although doubts about logistics clouded my thoughts. I needed a fast replacement for Jake, someone who could take a quick look at where construction stood and move forward.

"You bet," I said. "It's something we can do for Sam and Ruby in Jake's memory. Can I count on you guys for next Saturday?"

"Yeah. I'm in," Pete said. "Hope my foot's better by then."

"I'll be here." Neal fingered a V for victory.

Fred shifted his weight and looked at something over my shoulder. Gloria and the twins studied their shoes and squirmed. Silence.

"Well, think about it," I said. "Meanwhile, the deputy cleared Neal and me to leave. He has questions for y'all, so stay put."

Pete waved a hand to get my attention. "Billie, did you tell him why I went for the rifle in my truck when I heard the shot and saw Jake falling off the house? Dammit, I didn't know who was next."

"No, but I'll brief him on the way out. You are legal with that gun, aren't you, Pete?"

"Yeah, but it's never a good idea to surprise the law."

I eased the Prius into my reserved parking space at Deep Water Marina and walked toward my houseboat. A blanket of heat rose from the dock. The sun blazed above the horizon and spilled fire across the lake. No breeze disturbed the water's glassy surface. Sweat and grime coated every inch of my body. I wondered if the tears I'd shed on the drive home had streaked my cheeks. I hadn't known Jake well, but the unexpected violence of his death pricked memories of my parents' deaths in a small plane crash. Here today, gone tomorrow—a cliché that still spoke to me.

I stepped from the dock onto the short gangplank that connected to the lip of the *Ebb and Flow*, my long-coveted, one-hundred-fifteen-foot Sumerset houseboat. So why, I wondered, stepping down onto the foredeck, was I having second thoughts about living full time on a floating home, a thoroughly modern and fully equipped boat, at that? Maybe moving onboard on April Fool's Day had been a jinx. Uncle Joe had sputtered into the phone when I'd asked him for six hundred thousand of my inheritance. He thought that much money plus some ought to go for a new house or condo in a trendy neighborhood.

"No way," I'd said. "I'm not the trendy type. Besides, there's a houseboat parked not too far from here that cost a million dollars plus. I'm being conservative."

Madge opened the door and a blast of air conditioning escaped. I stepped into a meat freezer masquerading as a living room.

"Thank the Lord you're here and safe," Madge said. "How awful about Jake. You said he was shot dead?"

Carl sat on the couch, hunched over a newspaper. The TV was on, the sound turned low. He didn't look up. This fit with other passive aggressive stuff he regularly sent my way. Madge had nervously confessed he wasn't sure about taking the job with me, that I should ignore him while he figured things out.

"Yeah, shot dead. By a sniper no less. It's weird." I scratched a stubborn itch in the middle of my sweaty back.

"Don't hold your breath the cops will ever solve this one." Carl kept his focus on the newspaper.

"Well, I hope you're wrong, Mr. Smarty Pants," Madge said. "And just imagine the horror when Jake's family hears the news." Madge touched my arm. "Honey, you look awful."

"That matches how I feel. We can talk more after I shower."

Twenty-five minutes later, I emerged from the bathroom in clean shorts, a T-shirt, and sandals. I sat at the bar and towel-dried my hair.

Madge sighed. "Damnation. I wish I had your hair, Billie. Shampoo, dry, and away you go." She ran fingers through short, thin strands of rust-colored hair.

"What about the shooting? You see it?" Carl sat on a stool at the far end of the bar, his stiff leg dangling.

Madge waved her hands at Carl. "Leave Billie be. She'll talk when she's ready. Men."

I sipped the dry martini Madge put in front of me and chewed on one of three large green olives stacked on each other at the bottom of the glass. A warm glow bathed my throat and chest and spread through my body. Carl nursed a Mexican beer, and Madge lifted a glass of Chardonnay.

"This is not a happy hour," I said. My throat tensed. "You can't imagine what a single bullet did to Jake's head. It blew away his face. Bits of brain and bone flew all around and hit some of the volunteers.

It was awful. I only looked once, but I'll never, ever forget the sight. No one deserves to die like that. And I feel so responsible. I hired Jake, for God's sake."

"Maybe we shouldn't dwell on what happened to Jake," Madge said. "None of us will sleep tonight."

"Speak for yourself, woman." Carl swigged beer.

"Good idea, Madge." I ate the last olive. "Let's talk about something else. Any news here?"

"Took a phone call while Madge was out shopping." Carl slid the spiral-bound message book across the bar top. I stopped it and studied the handwriting. "I can make out that Pam called, but the rest is lost in your perfect penmanship."

Madge laughed. "You got that. I've forbidden him to hand write his will."

"It's plain as day. She said she's bringing fresh shrimp on dry ice for boiling tomorrow night. We're to come up with the extras."

"Great." Pam Stevens was my best friend and had been since we roomed together at Agnes Scott College. She was 'best maid,' as we called it, at my wedding to Charlie and consoled me through the divorce—Charlie's call. I was best maid when she married Jeff and celebrated with her all the way through the divorce—her call. Jeff was an unredeemable philanderer.

"Shhhhh!" Madge waved her hands and pointed to the big screen TV. "I think they're talking about Jake."

I hurried over and turned up the volume.

A Habitat for Humanity building site in Creeks County was the location of a possible homicide this afternoon. The victim (identity withheld pending notification of next of kin) was killed instantly by rifle fire as he stood on the framework of the house. Sheriff Rodney Farr has asked the Georgia Bureau of Investigation for assistance in further identifying the victim, who had apparently been in town for only a few weeks prior to the shooting. According to Channel 2's sources, nothing in the victim's truck or motel room helps to identify next of kin, and the name he was using may be an alias. If you know anything about the victim, please contact the Creeks County Sheriff's Department."

A baldheaded, red-bearded Jake filled the TV screen. The image was distinctly out of focus. If I hadn't known him in person, I'm not sure I could have identified him by this photo. He looked older and more roughhewn than he had looked in life.

I turned the volume down. "I don't know what else the sheriff and GBI need to call it murder."

"Could have been a freak accident." Carl twisted the cap off a new beer. "If so, you can bet the fuzz will move on to regular business—burglaries, Saturday night shootings and stabbings, whatever. You can bet the victims want the crimes against them solved yesterday."

"Oh, stop it, you old grouch," Madge said. "That's more like Atlanta. With me, hope springs eternal. Jake's family will show up soon to claim him."

Carl shrugged. "Just trying to talk reality. Can't blame the sheriff if he puts his resources where he might have some success."

Carl avoided talking about his unwanted early retirement as an arson investigator for a national insurance company. He made no bones about a deep desire to be back on the job, primarily expressed by a subtle disdain for being employed by me. His disability was two pronged. Too many years of heavy smoking had led to early emphysema. And a stray bullet during an arson investigation had hit him in his right knee and left his leg stiff. Bouts of osteoarthritis pain plagued him, and he walked with a cane to help his balance.

We fell silent. I studied Madge's sturdy back as she stood at the kitchen counter, stirring something in an oversized bowl. Carl peeled the label off his beer bottle. The phone rang, startling us. I stretched to reach the phone at the end of the bar and pulled it to me.

"Hello? Hello?" I recognized Pete's voice.

"I'm here. What's up?" He had never called me at home.

The words spilled out and piled up. "Billie, I have Jake's secret box from his truck. In all the confusion this afternoon, I took it and hid it before the deputies got there. We drank too many beers one afternoon, and he showed me the box. Made me promise to hide it if anything happened to him. Not to let the police find it. Shit! I can't get involved. I haven't even looked inside. What I don't know can't get me in trouble with the police. You hired him. You need to take over. I'll bring the box to you first thing in the morning. I'd come right now, but my girlfriend says no."

Pete cut the connection without a goodbye. Madge and Carl cocked their heads at me.

"That was Pete," I said. They hadn't met him but knew he was a Habitat volunteer. "He's delivering something in the morning." I left it at that. Without warning, a crushing fatigue enveloped me. I wasn't sure I could chew my food.

Madge hustled dinner prep. She plopped a hefty Romaine lettuce, pepper, and tomato salad and a bowl of crackers on the table. I washed my hands in the bathroom. When I returned, they were seated at the breakfast table in front of soup bowls.

"Something cold and refreshing," said Madge. "Just like you requested this afternoon."

I took one look at bowls brimming with gazpacho, and my stomach lurched. I ran to the bathroom, hung my head over the toilet, and vomited martini juice and bits of green olives. My lunch was long gone, headed south. Ordinarily, I could wolf down two bowls of Madge's gazpacho. That time, its pinkish-red color and chunks of veggies reminded me too much of Jake's mutilated head.

Chapter 5

My alarm clock buzzed at six-thirty Sunday morning, rousing me from toss-and-turn sleep. My throat was parched, and I felt grumpy as hell. I realized that I'd been dreaming a special kind of dream—a lucid dream. You assume you're awake and thinking the content, whereas you're really asleep, and dream details play out realistically.

Pete and I starred in my lucid dream. I bawled him out for keeping a secret, not telling me right away he had plucked the mystery box from Jake's truck right after the shooting. He stammered and stuttered an apology. "I was scared shitless and di… didn't know what to do," he said.

"Well, how can I trust you anymore?" I shot back. Trust had taken on new importance after what I called Charlie's *great betrayal*. The tension between us had escalated as we explored options for having a baby once the fertility doctors declared my ovaries incapable of producing viable eggs. And without my uterus, which had been removed in my late twenties, implantation was out. Even so, I had been totally unprepared and deeply shocked by Charlie's great betrayal: he ditched me for the surrogate mother we had selected together.

I forced my thoughts away from the dream and the whole sorry episode with Charlie and selected denim shorts, a loose bra, and a faded, baggy T-shirt for my outfit. As I fastened the bra, I smiled, remembering the dozens of times I'd thrown it away only to rescue it within the hour. If I hadn't expected Pete and the mystery-box later in the morning, it would have been a no-bra morning. That was my definition of freedom.

While coffee dripped, I walked up to the marina and pulled an overstuffed Atlanta newspaper from my mailbox. A timid breeze stirred my hair and glanced off the lake. Blue-gray clouds played tag with the sun and shut off the oppressive heat that had dominated the previous week.

Before stepping onto my boat, I glanced toward Carl and Madge's houseboat, moored two slips away. No sign of activity. Sunday was their day off, and I basked in my hours of solitude. I provided the boat as part of their compensation. Although not nearly as large or amply furnished as my boat or the house they had sold, Madge said it more than met their needs.

I poured a mug of coffee, tucked the newspaper under my arm, and climbed the stairs to the party top. Once I was settled at a fiberglass table under the central canopy, my mood improved with each gentle slap of water against the boat. I closed my eyes and listened to mallards quack a series of alarms in the distance. Uncle Joe's disappointment in my decision to live on a houseboat still smarted. Try as I might to explain, he failed to understand how the lake and the lifestyle calmed me, kept the blues away.

I scanned the newspaper and stopped to read a short article on Jake's death. I learned that the name he was using, Jake Wade, was now considered an alias, ruling out identification of next of kin. My throat knotted. Interviews with Sheriff Farr and the GBI reinforced my gut feeling: "Suspicious death… foul play suspected."

I decided to call Uncle Joe and speed up Pete's arrival—like in the old days when I'd light a cigarette and, within two puffs, the waiter was there with my meal. God, was I thankful I'd kicked a nasty habit.

Aunt Irene answered, and we chatted about the heat wave for a few minutes before Uncle Joe came on the line. He asked how the Habitat house was progressing. I briefed him on Jake's murder.

"My God, Billie. Tell me you're not a magnet for trouble."

"I'm not a magnet for trouble." I sounded defensive to myself. "Life has troubles and, fortunately, joys. It's just trouble's time in the forefront, I guess."

"Well, what about this latest scheme of yours? Setting up a foundation to help women down on their luck smacks of trouble, young lady. Be sure you level with Pam. If she gets involved, it should be with eyes wide open."

I counted to ten. "It's not a scheme, it's a dream. And what's the point of having boo-coo millions if you can't help people? That's what I want to do from here on, Uncle Joe—help people, especially women, who didn't have the good fortune to be born into a cushy life."

"Your father and mother were patrons of the arts. Why don't you follow in their footsteps and help people appreciate the finer things in life?"

I answered with silence. After a minute, Uncle Joe sighed. "I forgot. To follow in your parents' footsteps is the last thing you'd do."

I didn't swallow the bait. Uncle Joe took seriously his role as proxy father, striving to live up to what he thought his deceased brother would expect in the way of protecting me. With my independent streak, I had a difficult time functioning as proxy child.

"Thanks for the packet of info on setting up a foundation. It came snail mail Friday," I said. "And let's not fuss, Uncle Joe. I love you."

"Well, I love you, too, Punkin. I just worry about you. Living on a houseboat and butting heads with the woes of the world. You know, you have the means to live life on a much higher plane."

We came at "higher planes" from different perspectives. So I tried for a soothing close by smacking a kiss and asking Uncle Joe to give Irene a hug for me.

Around eight-thirty, I spotted Pete's beat-up old truck as it pulled into the marina parking lot. The front bumper was loose, the tailgate wouldn't close, and a dark red paint job sported pink spots where rust had been sanded. I judged the motor to be in tiptop shape, considering a deep-throated roar that could turn heads. Pete slammed the door twice and headed up the dock in my direction. Under one skinny arm, he carried what had to be Jake's box.

I anchored the newspaper to the table with an upended chair and scooted down the ladder in time to open the door for Pete. He looked freshly showered. A small tattoo of a whale decorated the front of his right forearm three inches above the wrist. His brown hair, streaked with gray, was pulled into a neat ponytail.

"What's wrong?" I stood aside as Pete stomped into the living room. The clues to his mood were a frown that furrowed his forehead, shallow breathing, and flared nostrils.

"Shit! Pardon the French, Billie." He clamped Jake's box in his right armpit and waved his left arm in jerky motions over his head.

"Calm down, Pete, and tell me what's wrong." I took him by an elbow and steered him to a barstool.

"Some shit-ass prick just about killed me, that's what. I'm driving along listening to a country preacher going nuts about Genesis when out of nowhere a camouflage truck pulls up beside me. Smoked glass. Couldn't see the driver. But instead of passing, the prick starts easing over the line, forcing my tires off the pavement onto a sorry-ass gravel shoulder. I was fighting to control the truck and not roll over into a drainage ditch." Pete stopped, closed his eyes, and breathed deeply.

"Well, thank God you're here in one piece."

"Yeah, well, no thanks to my NASCAR talents. A car topped a hill ahead of us, and the shit-ass had to back off or join a head on crash. He passed me and took off. Must have revved up to at least eighty-five. Whoever the asshole was, I think he was trying to run me off the road."

"But why? Have you crossed some loony lately?" The Pete I knew from Habitat workdays was easygoing, so this was hard to imagine.

"Not that I know of, but, hey, it don't take much to rile folks who're looking for trouble."

From personal experience, I had to agree. "Did you get his tag number? You should report what happened."

"Couldn't read the number. Tag looked like somebody smeared it with mud. Besides, everything happened so damned fast." He sighed and ran fingers through a few strands of hair that weren't caught up in the ponytail. "Well, I can't waste any more time or energy on that SOB. But if I ever spot his truck—look out."

I offered Pete a mug of coffee and one of Madge's blueberry muffins and excused myself to make a fictitious, important phone call. For five minutes, I sat on my bed and watched some mallards cavort on the lake. In a kind of syncopated water ballet, they dunked their heads in the water and stuck their butts straight up in the air. Giving Pete some space and time did the trick. When I settled next to him at the bar, he was calm and focused.

He had placed a gray metal box on the bar top between us. It was what I called a cash box, the same kind I had used in grade school to keep track of lunch money the teacher had entrusted me with. The box's keyed lock was pushed inward, and an olive green, webbed belt was cinched around the box.

"My belt." Pete's mouth bulged with muffin. "I busted the lock for you."

"Have you looked inside?"

"No way. Like I told you, Billie, I don't want to know anything about Jake that the police would want to know. Mind you, my nose's been clean for years. But I sure enough got a checkered past to protect."

I didn't press Pete. His past was none of my business. Like the country song twanged, he was getting by the best way he knew how. I was okay with what I knew about him, except for the trust part. He worked hard at the Habitat site and got along with the other volunteers. Once, I thanked him for showing up regularly. "I don't have much," he said, "but I sure as hell got more than some folks."

"Okay, you don't have to look." I punched Pete on the arm, and he grinned. "But I'm curious. When Jake made you promise to rescue this box if something happened to him, did he seem to think he was in danger?"

Pete took another bite of muffin, chewed a few times, and added coffee to the mix. "Thinking back, I don't know. But that afternoon he was lower than a snake's belly. His face got longer with every beer. He talked about missing his wife but didn't say where she was."

Pete stopped for the last bite of muffin. I waited.

"Then Jake showed me a wallet picture of a real pretty girl. Said she was his daughter. I asked where she lived and I didn't expect what he came back with. 'She's dead, and it's killing me'. "With that, he paid for the beers and marched me out to his truck and showed me this box. That's all I know, Billie. I swear."

Had Pete fudged when he swore he hadn't looked at the box's contents? I decided to ignore my lucid dream and trust him. "I believe you, but if you don't want to know any more, you'd better vamoose. I'm definitely going to open this box."

Pete slid off the stool. I sent him on his way with coffee in a paper cup, another muffin, and the webbed belt.

Staring at Jake's box, I considered my options. Check the contents and keep what I found to myself, which would honor Jake's request of Pete. Check the contents before turning the box over to the sheriff. I decided not to decide at that moment. Instead, I called Carl. If he wasn't awake at nine-thirty, he should be.

"Can I come over with something that needs a trained investigator's eye?" I asked.

"Damn," said Carl. "I'm still in my underwear. It's not a pretty sight."

In the background, Madge laughed and said, "Amen."

"Five minutes. Ready or not." I said.

I used the time wisely. I dabbed a sponge with a little dish soap and washed the box, after which I buffed all sides with a dry dishtowel. Bye, bye Pete's fingerprints. I wasn't worried that I'd erased Jake's prints since the coroner would have captured them as part of his documentation.

Chapter 6

I stepped down onto the deck of Carl and Madge's houseboat. They—well, mostly Madge—had thanked me for forcing them to downsize from the large farmhouse they had bought on the spur of the moment shortly after Carl's forced retirement five years earlier. I smiled at the name painted on the hull: *Just Right*. Madge's choice for a name.

Carl met me at the door. Without his cane, he walked slower and stiffer than he would later in the day. Madge, dressed in a fuzzy robe, hair in curlers, sat at the breakfast table. She smiled and waved a Sudoku puzzle at me. Carl motioned me to the dining room table, where we sat side by side. I gently deposited the metal box on the glass tabletop.

"Okay. A cash box," he said. "Must be billions out there. What's special about this one?"

"It belonged to Jake Wade. Pete brought it to me this morning. After one beer too many and for unknown reasons, Jake asked Pete to rescue it if anything happened to him. So in all the confusion when Jake was shot, Pete snitched it from Jake's truck and hid it."

"Kind of convoluted, huh? Who's looked inside?"

"Nobody that I know of. Pete doesn't want to know the contents, and I wanted to open it with you. I might overlook something you think is important. You're the guy with investigative experience."

"Don't forget I was in insurance fraud," he said. "Tracking arsonists sounds sexier than it is. Most crooks stumble on their own stupidity."

"Don't let him hoodwink you, Billie." Madge spoke without lifting her eyes from the puzzle. "He was a cop at heart, just no uniform. And that's the good news and the bad news."

"And it's the cop in me that's warning you not to tamper with evidence." Carl's voice was edgy. "Stop right here, before you poke around in stuff Jake wanted kept secret. Deliver the box to the sheriff pronto in the morning. Get a life, Billie."

I laughed, sipped my coffee, and lifted the box's lid.

"Whoa. You're one hardheaded, nutty woman." Carl curled his fingers tightly, too tightly, I thought, around my wrist, as I released the lid in upright position. "Madge, honey, fetch a pair of latex gloves for Billie."

"Please," Madge coached.

"Pretty please," Carl said.

I took the gloves Madge held out and snapped them on. I rummaged around in the box and pulled out the largest item. Double-wrapped in a piece of plaid flannel was a four-by-six inch color portrait of a young woman who sat sideways on a white bench in front of a cloud-like backdrop. Her head, slightly tilted, was turned to the camera. She looked directly at me. Shiny, dark brown hair ended in a flip at her shoulders. A half- smile lit her face.

"Pete told me Jake showed him a wallet picture of a real pretty girl," I said. "Probably this one or a similar pose."

Carl grunted. "Daughter? Or maybe a trophy wife."

"That's so cynical, dear." Madge cinched her robe tighter and came over to look at the photo. "We should give poor, dead Jake the benefit of the doubt."

Charlie, my ex, popped into my thoughts. Well, maybe Ellen wasn't his trophy wife—more like his trophy uterus, taking the place of sterile me. I swallowed the lump in my throat and pushed the negative thoughts aside. Dwelling day and night for months on what had happened had gotten me nowhere.

"There's something Jake-like about the eyes—the shape and color. I think she's his daughter," I said.

"Maybe there's a date or a name on the back of the photo," Madge said.

"Too bad we can't say that about hundreds of snapshots we have in containers under the bed." Carl rolled his eyes.

"I'm only half responsible, you old grouch."

I ignored their testy exchange and slipped the photo out of the vertical tracks of a low-end, Walmart-quality frame. Nothing was written on the back of the picture, but in the bottom left hand corner was a dark blue circle around slightly blurred blue printing. It appeared to be a rubber stamp impression.

"Garmon Studio. Knoxville," I read aloud. "Nothing else."

Carl scraped his chair back and massaged his bad knee. "Better than nothing. With luck, the fuzz can put some flesh on the elusive Jake Wade."

Putting flesh on Jake's shattered head was not a visual I wanted to dwell on. "Better yet, Carl, this is a lead you can pursue."

Carl studied me for a few moments. "Not part of my job description," he said.

I thought, *Well, it is now.* Instead I bit my tongue. Carl was in the same league of hardheadedness as I was, so I tried a different approach. "You're correct, and I'm not going to rewrite your job description.

But I'm determined to get to the bottom of Jake's identity, to find his next of kin, and I can't do it without help."

"Oh, he'll help," Madge said. "It'll be a piece of cake for him to contact that Knoxville studio."

Carl glared at Madge but said nothing.

"What else is in that Pandora's box? I want in on it." Madge poured a cup of coffee and sat down at the table to my left.

I laid the box's contents in front of us: a business-size envelope sealed around some flat, hard items; a stack of traveler's checks held together by a sturdy rubber band; the title to Jake's truck; and a scruffy leather wallet.

"What's in the envelope?" Madge reached toward the envelope, and Carl caught her wrist.

"For God's sake, woman, don't touch anything. Billie's wearing the gloves. Let her take the heat with the GBI, if it comes to it."

I unsealed the envelope and dumped two plastic cards and two paper cards on the table. I inspected them one by one. "Florida and Alabama driver's licenses. Good forgeries, I'd say. A Social Security card. Real? Who knows? Georgia fishing license. Everything's in the name of Jake Wade. So the identity is consistent, even if false."

"What about the money?" Madge rubbed her hands together as I rolled the rubber band off the traveler's checks.

"Mostly one hundred dollar denominations. Couple of books of fifties. Must be several thousand dollars here. All in the name of Jake Wade." I restacked the checks and replaced the rubber band.

"Somebody was feeding Jake cash, or he had a bank account somewhere," Carl said.

"That leaves the wallet." I opened it and found a candid photograph of a fortyish woman holding hands with a young girl. They stood beside a palm tree. I held the photo up for Carl and Madge to inspect.

"I'd bet all these travelers checks that that's Jake's wife," Madge said. "And the young girl is the daughter. She's a younger version of the portrait we just looked at."

"Based on what?" Carl harrumphed. "Don't tell me. Woman's intuition."

"Exactly right. And to boot, I bet Jake took the picture. She's frowning like people do who don't want to pose for the camera."

"Interesting, but you can't use it in a court of law," Carl said.

"The palm tree suggests a Florida setting," I offered. "Fits with the Florida driver's license."

"Don't forget California. Or maybe they were on a Bermuda vacation. Anything else in the wallet?" Carl asked. Curiosity appeared to have overridden resistance.

I peered into the two sections for folding money. "No loot." Then I fingered the hidey pocket on the left side of the wallet. Nothing. In the right pocket, I found a five-by-eight- inch sheet of yellow paper, folded four times. I unfolded it to reveal a succinct message printed in red ink. I read it aloud: *You son-of-a-bitch! I want my $250,000 back now. No excuses. NOW!* The note was undated and unsigned.

"Now we're getting somewhere." Carl rubbed his hands together. "Get a plastic bag, Madge, and open it."

Madge complied and zipped the bag shut once I had dropped the note inside.

"You're thinking fingerprints," I said.

"Jake's for sure. Long shot for others. Every murder has a motive. Find the pissed person who wrote this note, and you may have the sniper who killed Jake. Could have stalked him to Creeks County or somewhere nearby."

"On the way over here, I wondered if I'd have to turn the box in to the sheriff," I said. "Now I know."

"Yep," Carl said. "But overnight, I'll have to borrow that photo you want checked out with Garmon Studio."

Madge and I exchanged quick glances with deadpan expressions. I returned the items we'd been discussing to the box, except for the studio photograph, which I left on the tabletop in front of Carl.

Madge looked at her watch and pushed back from the table. "Good grief. It's noon. Carl. We'd better get a move on if we're going to lunch before the movie. Anything we can get for you while we're out, Billie?"

I ran through a mental list. "No. But I forgot to tell you that Pam Stevens is coming tomorrow through Tuesday. She's bringing fresh shrimp for a boil tomorrow night."

Pam stayed busy in her job as director of the Atlanta Coalition for Justice, a nonprofit supported by a mix of taxpayer and private funding. I was courting her to head-up my "wild-eyed dream," as Uncle Joe called it, to develop a foundation to help women in need.

"Oh, good," said Madge. "I like Pam, although she's only been over that one time since you hired Carl and me."

"Another opinionated woman, if you ask me. There must have been something weird in the water where you two went to school."

"Right on." I clamped Jake's box under my arm and stepped through the door, looking forward to a quiet Sunday afternoon and night.

Chapter 7

I like to think I'm spontaneous, and, in some ways, I am. Don't ask me, however, to change my bedtime routine. Pam said this could be a problem if I ever succumbed to a torrid affair.

Ordinarily, I shower, don short pajamas, and prop up in bed to finish the routine: check the weather for the next day and browse in a book of trivia. Soon my head droops, and my eyelids slide to half-mast.

Sunday night, anxiety about Jake's box felled my routine. My brain whirled around which item or items caused him to enlist Pete's help to keep the box out of the law's hands. The demand note for $250,000 topped my list. Had Jake embezzled money and run away, only to be followed and killed by the embezzled victim?

I flattened my hand on top of Jake's box, a gray rectangle on the granite surface of the bar.

The metal had cooled under air conditioning but warmed quickly to my touch. Poor Jake. Alive and vital one second and dead the next second, all before there was time to shift from exhale to inhale. Only in unguarded moments like this did I dwell on the final, horrific minutes of my parents' lives. Was there even time, as their light plane nosedived to crash in a cow pasture, to say, "I love you"? Or did Paul struggle with the controls and curse as Nina screamed?

I shook off the disturbing memories and concentrated again on Jake's box. Aware that I might be flirting with some vague superstition, I decided that the box shouldn't spend the night alone and settled it on top of my chest-of-drawers.

Once in bed, I reverted to routine and scanned two pages of trivia I'd never remember. I turned off the bedside light, stuck a leg out on top of the sheet, and closed my eyes. Seconds later, my eyelids popped open. I turned the ceiling fan to medium speed, stretched out on my favored side, and repeated the Lord's Prayer, incorporating my revisions over the years, until sleep finally overtook words.

I awoke from a dream about water skiing on my head in churning waves behind a sleek speedboat. Awakening interrupted maniacal laugher of a strange man who sawed with a huge knife on the towrope to my skies. Turning to check the bedside clock, I discovered a crick in my neck. Two o'clock.

Not a good sign for going back to sleep, according to my slumber history. I was massaging taut muscles under my right ear when hair on my arms bristled.

Something wasn't right, starting with a barely perceptible shift in the boat's stance in the water, a perception Carl always insisted was bogus, considering the width of the hull. Still, I'd shown such eerie talent before. Had someone stepped onto the foredeck? I held my breath and listened in the darkness. Silence, broken in a few seconds by the muffled bellow of a bullfrog. Silence again.

I slid out of bed and crept the few steps to my bedroom door. I slept with it open to give my bedroom an expanded feeling. Holding my breath again, I turned an ear toward the front door. Nothing for a count of four, and then I heard the doorknob jiggle side to side. Damn! Somebody was trying to break in. My heart thumped in my chest.

I backed up until my butt touched the bed, and then I inched along the edge of the mattress to the bedside table. Gently, I opened the drawer and slid my hand back. My fingers curled around the butt of the .22 pistol that Charlie had given me when we were dating.

Fumbling for the box of cartridges I kept near the gun, I loaded six shells into the cylinder and pressed it in place, causing a click that sounded in the stillness like a bank vault closing. Had the prowler heard it also?

My thoughts tangled around what I needed to do to get away from danger, considering Charlie's long-ago warning. A .22 pistol loaded with shorts was great for target shooting but puny personal protection. What if the creep breaking in was six foot four and three hundred pounds? Even if I shot and hit him, he might keep coming. I couldn't take the chance. Not with no place to run. I tiptoed back to the doorway and looked up and down the dark hallway. What to do? Turn left and enter the living room where a burglar, or worse, was jimmying the door? No way. That left turn right and exit onto the aft deck.

At that moment, I thought of Jake's box. If the intruder made it to my bedroom, he'd see it for what it was, a cash box, and no doubt he'd take it. I eased the box off of the chest-of-drawers and shoved it under my bed behind a container of God knows what. Surely he was after something visible and valuable, like TVs and jewelry. Too bad for him he'd picked on me. My hand flew to the gold necklace I wore day and night. That and a few pierced earrings not worth insuring wouldn't be much of a haul. Damn, they didn't even dangle. I strangled an urge to laugh.

Hiding the box took no more than two minutes during which I sprang a cold sweat and registered a heartbeat at hummingbird speed. Ready or not, get the hell out of my bedroom.

I clutched the pistol in one hand, slid the other hand across the bedside table, and palmed my cell phone. I padded barefoot to the aft door and stepped onto a damp deck. I crouched and punched 9-1-1 into my phone. On the second ring, I whispered my dilemma and location to the calm answering voice.

"Hurry." The catch in my voice surprised me.

"Help's on the way, ma'am. Now I need for you to remain calm and stay on the phone."

"Can't. Not safe here." I slipped the still-on phone into the shallow pocket of my pajama top.

My breathing was ragged, and I fought off dizziness. Quickly, I nixed the idea of lowering myself down the swim ladder and clinging to it, as I'd be too easy to spot. And if I swam away from the boat, I'd have to give up the pistol. Besides, snakes and snapping turtles lurked in the dark water. I shuddered and gripped the gun tighter.

One option remained. Hide on the upper deck and take my chances. With my free hand, I clutched the railing of the spiral staircase and started up. Three steps later, my wet foot slipped and fire burned my shin as it scraped a rung. I bit my lip against the pain.

To right myself, I reached out with my other hand. The pistol slapped hard against the metal handrail. The cell phone popped out of my pajama pocket and clanged on the deck. Damn! Unless the prowler was deaf, he'd know I was on the loose.

When both feet gripped the upper deck, I crouch-ran to the center of the boat and hunched to the side of the stainless steel cooker where I could see in both directions. If the nutcase wanted me, not the TVs, he'd have to come up the fore or aft ladder.

I cocked my head to listen, but thuds of my heart against my ribs filled my ears. I inhaled and exhaled slowly to the count of ten. My heartbeats slowed, and I licked cracked, dry lips.

The boat shifted again in the water, as if someone had jumped on board. Had a second intruder joined the first one? A scraping noise floated up. I couldn't see squat. Clouds skittered across a puny thumbnail moon. I gripped the pistol with both hands and straightened my arms.

Chair legs scraped the lower deck, followed by a bang as a chair fell over. A muffled curse broke the silence. A flashlight beam wobbled up into darkness in a straight line with the fore ladder.

Damn! The idiot showed no fear. I gripped the pistol tighter and pointed it at the beam of light.

"That's far enough." I projected my voice in the lowest register possible. To my ears, I sounded like a scared schoolgirl. "I'm armed, and I'll shoot."

The flashlight beam waved back and forth.

"Hold on ma'am. I'm Deputy Sheriff Owens, answering your 911 call. Put the gun down and stand up." He swept the beam of light back and forth across the length of the deck and settled it on me.

"Show me some proof," I said.

"Aim the gun straight up, ma'am, and I will."

"Okay. Done. Now show me something I can trust."

The flashlight beam turned away from me and spotted a Stetson hat, beneath which a pudgy face was eerily lighted like a jack-o'-lantern.

"I'm coming up another step," he said. "Keep your cool, ma'am."

A torso came into the beam of light. A shiny badge sparkled on a pleated shirt.

I breathed deeply and scrunched my shoulders toward my ears to relieve tension. "Okay. But would you check the back deck before I come down—just in case." I felt like a wimp for suggesting it.

"Sure. You wait there, ma'am."

The deputy descended the ladder and returned me to inky darkness. I listened in vain for his footsteps; instead, I had to follow his progress by the glow that spilled from his flashlight, as he walked a pattern that took in both sides of the boat and the aft deck before he returned to his starting point.

"All clear, ma'am." He spoke in a loud voice from the bottom of the ladder. "It was a long shot, but I thought I could sneak up on the intruder. He probably saw me coming and slipped away after I passed by."

"Wait there, Deputy. I'm coming down the aft ladder. I'll meet you up front in a minute."

I engaged the safety on the pistol before clambering down the ladder. My cell phone wasn't in view. I detoured by my bedroom and slipped jeans and a denim shirt over my pajamas. Carefully, I slid the pistol to the back of my bedside table drawer. By the time I reached the living room, the deputy was knocking repeatedly on the jamb. I opened the door and he almost stumbled inside.

"I've been thinking you fell overboard, ma'am." His flushed cheeks suggested that adrenalin still flooded his body. "The door still being locked means you got lucky. The intruder was scared off before he could jimmy the lock."

I shivered at the good news. The deputy pushed his Stetson back slightly on his head, exposing a lock of sweaty hair. His face came into full focus. "I remember you from the Habitat site. You were first on the scene after Jake Wade was shot."

"Right, ma'am. But let's talk about what happened here to make you call 911. Shouldn't take long. Oh, I found this on the back deck." He reached into a back pocket and handed me my cell phone.

I sat at the bar and Owens stood facing me. He fished in a shirt pocket and removed a small notepad and ballpoint pen. He opened the pad and began scribbling on it. After several minutes, he launched a string of rapid-fire questions. What time did I hear the attempted break-in? (Around 2:00 a.m.) What did I do in response? (Called 911 and took refuge on the upper deck.) Had I had any recent trouble with houseboat neighbors—especially teenagers? (No.) Had I bought any high-end electronics lately and perhaps left telltale packaging in view in the trash? (No.) Did I keep a sizable amount of cash or valuable jewelry on board? (No and no.) Had I noticed strangers loitering in the marina? (No.)

Owens looked up from the notepad. "Can you think of any reason, ma'am, that a thief would have targeted you or your boat?"

"You covered everything. I'm at a loss."

"Well, wouldn't be the first time some loony or meth addict picked on a random target. They get desperate, you know. I'll file this report, Miz Quinn, but I wouldn't hold my breath that we'll ever find the perp."

Going through the reporting process with Owens had calmed my jitters but not erased them. It was one thing to think somebody with a loose screw had it in for me personally. It was quite another thing, and more comforting, to hear that I may have been in the wrong place at the wrong time.

Owens dusted the front door and jamb for fingerprints before he pulled his Stetson back in place and left. "Stay safe, ma'am." He saluted me with two fingers.

Silence descended as I made my way around the boat, locking all doors and windows. My hands trembled, signaling the return of jitters. I sat on the edge of the couch and fought back an urge to bite my fingernails, a habit formed and broken in childhood. I considered, and quickly abandoned, calling Carl and Madge. That would be selfish. Surely, I could make it to daylight, if I could feel safe.

I hurried to my bedroom and retrieved the pistol from the bedside table. I stood flatfooted, heart pounding, my finger trembling on the trigger guard. A mix of fear and anger surged through my body.

What if the creep had gotten in? Was there anything he could have stolen that would have devastated me? Not any of the TVs. Not my laptop since I kept it backed up. Not the Bose radio. I couldn't think of anything that I couldn't replace. Except for one thing. I knelt and ran my hand around under the bed until I connected with Jake's box. The metal was cool to my fingers, as I slid the box out and placed it on the bed. Jake had told Pete to keep it safe and out of the hands of the law. That was enough to tell me I would have been devastated had the box been stolen. Jake was in that box, and he deserved respect.

With the pistol in one hand and the box in the other, I returned to the couch, where I stretched out with my head facing the door. I turned the box on edge and nestled it between my hip and a cushion. I extended my right arm straight by my side, the pistol in a firm grip. Before drifting into light sleep, I mentally thanked Charlie for taking me practice shooting during our courtship. If the intruder returned, I was ready.

Chapter 8

The aroma of coffee, dripped on time-set, lured me into the kitchen Monday morning. My eyes and throat were scratchy, and I yawned repeatedly. I was stiff from tossing and turning on the couch between catnaps. Without the security of Deputy Owens's presence, every noise inside or outside the boat made my heart pound. Fight or flight had raged in my body.

I ate a peanut butter and banana sandwich, washed down with milk and coffee, and felt calmness return. Surely the loony who tried to break in was long gone, probably never to return now that he'd failed a simple robbery. I liked the deputy's theory, namely that I was a random target. For a few minutes, I let this thought deter me from briefing Carl and Madge. In the end, I decided not telling them would seriously damage the bond developing between us. Carl answered the phone.

"Thought you guys would want to know," I said. Details of the thwarted break-in spilled out in the lightest tone of voice I could muster. Carl never interrupted me, although I heard his breathing quicken. Several times, in the background, I heard Madge ask, "Who're you talking to? Is that Billie?"

Silence greeted the end of my monologue.

"Carl, are you there? I know you're not at a loss for words," I said.

He sighed. "You better hope that deputy has ESP. If you were a random target, the guy will move on to another house or office that looks like an easy mark. But just in case, I'll replace the door locks with something more burglar proof."

"What? What happened?" Madge must have moved close to Carl. Her voice sounded alarmed.

"Calm down, Madge. And don't pull on me. I'll tell you in a minute," Carl said.

"And tell her I won't be on the boat when she arrives this morning. I'm on the way to deliver Jake's box to the sheriff. You want to go along?" I asked.

"Hell no! And once you're shed of that box, you need to cool it with this obsession about Jake's identity." Carl cut the connection before I could respond.

I put Jake's box in a boat bag that I slung over my shoulder. After locking the door and double-checking it, I walked toward my car. When the bright red "open" sign in the front window of the marina store caught my eye, I detoured on impulse. I stepped from sticky humidity into a blast of air conditioning.

Flo Davenport, marina manager, greeted me with a three-finger touch to the brim of a pristine white ball cap that leaked rusty, gray hair around her ears. "Looky who's here," she said, as she broke a roll of coins into a cash register drawer.

"Hi, Flo. Heard anything from the grandkids lately?"

"Thank God for e-mail. Denver's a far piece from here. They're okay. New picture." She handed me a four-by-six photo propped against a box of hand-held air horns on a shelf behind the checkout counter.

"Nice. Looks like the little one grew half a foot since the last photo."

"At least." Flo returned the photo to its resting spot and turned to face me. "You're not big on small talk, Billie, so I'm gonna guess why you're here. Carl decided to get off his duff and learn how to drive the boat on big water. I'm ready to book lessons when he's ready."

I answered with a thumbs-down gesture. "Wrong. Balking on this is just one way he's sending me messages that he's not sure he likes his job."

Flo whistled softly. "Bet Madge is nervous. She's settled and happy as a pig in mud. So we're back to square one today. What's on your mind, Billie?"

"Oh, just curious." I knew she'd hear later in the day about the break-in hassle at my boat because the sheriff's men always kept her in the loop when there was trouble at the marina. She'd fume that I didn't tell her, but she wasn't one to hold grudges.

"In the last few days, have you noticed any strangers coming or going?"

Flo propped her fists on broad hips and cocked her head. "Sounds like more than curiosity."

"Just checking on our no solicitation policy." I mustered an innocent smile.

"You're not being straight with me, girlie, so I'm outta this conversation." She waved me off and began to rearrange twelve-packs of regular and diet cola.

"Well, keep a sharp eye out, will you, Flo?" I was half out the door when she called to me.

"Wait, Billie. Come to think of it, two pick-up trucks were around Sunday morning. One was an old truck with a loose bumper. The driver was a skinny guy with a ponytail, carrying some kind of box under his arm. When I asked his business, he said he was on his way to see you, that you were expecting him."

"Yeah. That was Pete," I said. "What about the second truck?"

"Another older model, except painted camouflage. Came in not too long after Pete parked his truck. Couldn't see the driver, but after one slow pass through the lot, he pulled on out. I see scads of this kind of truck pretty often during hunting season."

"Thanks. Probably nothing to worry about." I smiled, although my scalp tingled. I remembered how agitated Pete had been Sunday morning when he arrived with Jake's box. A camouflage truck had goosed him off the road onto gravel and caused him to nearly lose control. So, could this have been the same truck? Was he followed? I couldn't spot any logic in the thought. Still, coincidence seemed a stretch.

Pulling out of marina parking, I opened all the car windows halfway, cracked the sunroof several inches, and turned the air conditioning on full blast. Even so, I was awash in a light sweat before the car's interior cooled enough to close up. I phoned the Creeks County sheriff's department and explained that I was on the way to deliver some personal effects of Jake Wade to the sheriff.

First, though, I detoured by Pronto Prints. I found a free machine, snapped my hands into disposable plastic gloves, and made three copies of everything in Jake's box that would copy. A longhaired young man at the machine next to me stared at the gloves and snickered.

"Germs. Can't be too careful." I crinkled my nose, and he laughed.

I separated the copies and placed each set in a letter-size manila envelope. I thought that the third set should go to Jake's next of kin, if a next finally showed.

Once cleared at the front desk for access to the sheriff's hideaway, I followed a uniformed woman across a small area crowded with several unoccupied government-issue metal desks and chairs. I surmised these were homes away from home for deputies in the field. A single telephone rang somewhere to my left and was answered on the fourth ring. My escort rapped on a closed door decorated with a screwed-on wooden plaque that read *Sheriff Rodney Farr.*

"Come in." The voice behind the command was more baritone than bass.

I hitched the boat bag higher on my shoulder and stepped across the threshold. Sheriff Farr kept his seat and motioned me to a straight-back chair positioned in front of his desk. The office's ambiance was one of *no loitering permitted.*

I guessed Farr to be in his late forties. He had escaped the dreaded bald spot on top of his head, but brownish-gray hair had retreated from his forehead. Thin lips and sky blue eyes dominated a deeply tanned face. He filled out his uniform—what I could see—without bulging anywhere. He fixed a neutral expression on me.

"Ms. Quinn. I understand from your telephone call that the items you're delivering belonged to Jake Wade. How did you get them?"

"From a Habitat for Humanity volunteer who agreed to keep a lock box for Jake." Technically, Pete had swiped the box from Jake's truck after the sniper had killed Jake. Sometimes, little white lies pop out of my mouth unbidden. I kept my expression neutral to match Farr's deadpan.

Without comment, he eyed the boat bag.

I removed Jake's box and placed it on the desk in front of us.

"And why didn't this volunteer bring the box directly to me?"

"I'm not sure. Maybe some kind of loyalty to Jake."

After a moment of hesitation, Farr changed direction. "You've inspected the contents?"

"Yes, but I wore gloves."

Something unreadable flickered in Farr's eyes. He made a note on a legal pad.

"Look, this wasn't out of morbid curiosity. I hired Jake for the Habitat job. I feel responsible."

"Did the volunteer inspect the contents?"

"He said he didn't, and I believe him." I sat up straighter, ready to catch any curve ball Farr tossed.

"Uh, huh." Farr pushed the notepad and pen toward me. "I need his name, address, and telephone number."

I wrote "Pete Witcher" on the pad. "I don't have any other info. You could check with Dorothy Longview at the Habitat for Humanity office." Surely another lie bump would erupt in my mouth. I knew Pete's cell phone number.

"When you see Witcher again, Ms. Quinn, tell him we're looking for him, just in case he's a hard man to find." Farr pushed his chair back, stood, and hitched up his pants.

I stood and faced the sheriff with only a little looking up required. He was shorter than I had anticipated.

Farr tugged his chin with a thumb and forefinger. "You did the right thing, bringing this evidence to my attention. Now, you need to do a smart thing. Don't let your feelings for Jake Wade lead you to do anything that would jeopardize or compromise our investigation."

Creepy crawlies marched across my scalp. Nice, smooth way to warn me to butt out.

Farr opened the office door and waited. I walked past him and turned around. "What if no next of kin is found? What happens to Jake's body? And what about his truck and other personal belongings?"

"If the body is unclaimed, the coroner can either bury it or cremate it. His call."

"What if I offered to give Jake a decent burial?"

"Talk to the coroner, Ms. Quinn."

"And his truck and personal belongings? What happens to them?"

A frown erased Farr's neutral expression. He studied my face before answering.

"Well, the truck's impounded until claimed by a next of kin. There was a vintage pistol in the glove box. Definitely untraceable. The items we found in Wade's motel don't qualify as top secret." Farr held up his left hand and counted fingers as he talked. "There was a duffel bag, a few clothes, sneakers, a book of Sudoku puzzles, and two fishing rods. These items are bagged and stored in the evidence room. The man traveled light and under an assumed name. There's not much to go on, unless the GBI comes up with something later in the week."

"You'll find a threatening note in the box from someone who said Jake owed him $250,000. Find out who wrote it and you might find the killer."

"Is the note signed?"

"No."

"Then that's no help right now, Ms. Quinn. First we have to identify the victim. It also means that you can't say the writer of the note was a *he*."

A slight smirk in Farr's voice failed to register on his face. He stepped past me into the outer office and motioned to a woman rising from a nearby desk. She hadn't been there on my arrival. Walking toward us, she smoothed her skirt and tugged an askew blouse into place over her ample bosom. Up close, I saw gray at the roots of her blonde hair. Like the sheriff, she was short on smiles.

"Eunice, please see that Ms. Quinn finds the front door."

I hadn't taken five steps when Farr spoke to my back. "By the way, Ms. Quinn, I know about the attempted break-in at your houseboat last night.

Should I consider this a random criminal act, or is there something in your life that brought this on?"

Over my shoulder, I said, "It's your question to answer, Sheriff."

Coroner Albert Riggs was a welcome contrast to the controlled demeanor of Sheriff Farr.

"Come in, my dear." Riggs smiled and held open the door to his office, which was tucked into a cubbyhole in the rear of Forrester's Funeral Home. When he took off his coroner's hat, he donned the hat that led grieving families through selection of a casket or urn to the last amen of a service. Riggs's body reminded me of the Pillsbury Doughboy. A round, pink face showed no sign of a five o'clock shadow. Wispy gray hair hung over his forehead, pointing the way to small glasses perched on the end of his nose. He sat down in a swivel chair behind his desk. Gratefully, I eased into a padded chair designed for humans.

"Yes, it's very sad about Mr. Wade," he said. "Such a violent way to go. The post-mortem photo for the file is not one next of kin should see. No face to speak of."

"About next of kin, Mr. Riggs—"

"Call me Albert, my dear. Life is too short for formalities."

I paused to assess *my dear*. Intuition told me he meant no affront, that he was still stuck in the mid-twentieth century. I decided to accept his invitation to address him by his given name.

"What happens, Albert, if Jake Wade's true identity remains a mystery? There would be no next of kin to claim the body. What do you do in such a case?"

"Procedure, my dear. After several days to a week or more, if he remains unidentified, I will dispose of the body by either burial or cremation. In Mr. Wade's, Jake's case, I would opt for cremation, saving, of course, some DNA. I think even six feet under, the violation of his body might continue to haunt me."

"And what about the ashes?"

"I'm required to keep them indefinitely." He waved a pudgy arm around the room. "I have ashes around here going on six years. I never give up hope that a loved one will turn up."

I glanced around the office. Numerous cardboard boxes, vases, and simple urns took on new significance.

"What if I asked for custody of Jake's ashes?" I shifted forward and held my breath.

Albert looked from me to a spot on his desk. He removed his glasses and polished them with the wide end of his tie.

"I can release the ashes to anyone I believe will be responsible and respectful. I believe, my dear, at least on first impression, that you might qualify on both counts."

"Great." I breathed deeply.

"Of course, I reserve the right to change my mind, my dear. You know—in the event I find out something untoward about you." He propped the polished glasses on his nose, looked at me over the rims, and smiled. "At any rate, you would have to sign a release saying you would deliver the ashes to any kin that showed up—even twenty years down the road."

"Certainly."

I exited the funeral home by a rear door and walked to my car through a soup of humid hot air that morphed into furnace heat when I slipped behind the wheel. Five minutes into the drive home, I surprised myself by veering off onto a feeder road and heading for a place that had been lurking in my imagination—the site from which a sniper had murdered Jake. A glance at the dashboard clock told me I had the leeway before the arrival of Pam."

Chapter 9

Standing in the middle of a small clearing in scrub pines, sweat beading on my forehead, I exhaled a feeling of letdown. What had I expected? To stoop and uncover in the needles underfoot a calling card left by Jake's killer? The sheriff and GBI had thoroughly combed the area. The only sign of their presence was a piece of yellow tape hanging limply from a thorny weed off to the side.

I turned in place until I looked directly across the hay field toward the Habitat site. Over the golden oval-shapes of baled hay, I saw the house, looking forlorn in its incomplete state, with no human activity in sight. An image of Jake pitching off the lip of a sidewall, falling in death, faded mercifully when I squeezed my eyes shut.

What could motivate one human being to kill a fellow being in cold blood? Whatever the motive, and I couldn't think of one that would move me to murder, did the killer then struggle with the method of dispatch? Did he sit around the kitchen table debating knife, gun, poison, choking, hit and run, whatever? And what did settling on death by sniper fire say about the killer's psychology, state of mind? Detached and clinical? Prone to faint at the sight of blood? Coward came to mind.

A bead of sweat rolled down my forehead and caught in an eyebrow. I wiped my face with the bottom of my T-shirt and sighed. Try as I might, I couldn't put myself in the head of Jake's killer.

I headed for the road and stepped out of the mottled light of the pine thicket into full sunlight. As I jumped across a narrow ditch that ran parallel to the road, a red, jacked-up pickup rolled to a stop behind my car. A slim man in overalls and a straw hat slid from behind the wheel and waited for me between the vehicles.

"Howdy." He pushed the hat back on his head.

"Hi." I blushed under the heat-flush of my face. "Something tells me you own these woods."

"You got that right, lady. Sidney Polk is the name. Saw you from my house." He pointed to a white, frame house down the road.

"I'm Billie Quinn." I held out my hand, and he grasped it with a calloused hand. "I guess I've trespassed on your property. Please, forgive me."

"You got trespass right, lady. Maybe you could tell me why." One bushy gray eyebrow rose on his forehead.

"I'm responsible for the Habitat house that's going up over there across the hay field. The man I hired to supervise the work was the one killed by a sniper that fired from your woods."

"Don't say." He looked at me expectantly.

"Like I said, Mr. Polk. I apologize for giving in to morbid curiosity."

"You didn't find anything to satisfy that itch, did you now, lady? The sheriff and GBI crawled over every inch of that little opening where the shooter hid. The most they found was a tire track caught in dried mud, and that was out by the road. Made one of them molds you see on TV. Smoothest tire track you ever saw. Couldn't have been the tires that were every day on the truck the killer drove. He couldn't of trusted them far as I can fling a pig."

The hair on my neck stood up. "Truck? How did they know it was a truck?"

He shrugged. "My grandson, Aaron's the name, saw a truck down here the day of the shooting. He's only a kid and don't talk at that, but the sheriff seemed to believe him."

I was curious to know more about Aaron's sighting, but Mr. Polk had turned his back on me and walked to his vehicle. I was also running late to get back to the boat. He opened the driver's door and turned back to me.

"Just my opinion, lady, but maybe you shouldn't be messing around out here in the woods with a crazy shooter on the loose."

"I hear you." A shiver ran down my spine.

I padded barefoot into the living room, aware of shower steam trapped under my fresh clothes. The doorbell ding-donged again. I expected Pam, so I opened the door with a flourish, ready to grab my best friend in a bear hug. We hadn't seen each other since April, when she had come over to help me christen the *Ebb and Flow.* Too long.

"Whoa! This isn't my usual frosty reception. But I like it."

"Hank! Dammit, don't you know how to wait for an invitation?"

All six feet two inches of Hank Knotts filled the doorframe, showing off sun-bronzed skin in all the places I cared to see. He grinned and ran his fingers through a full head of hair the color of Florida beach sand. How could he look like that and also have multi-millions from the sale of his software company?

"Talked to Madge yesterday afternoon. She told me a friend was coming to visit and that the first festivity would be a shrimp boil. Nothing goes better with shrimp than Mexican beer." He pushed a six-pack toward me. I backed up as he entered.

"That was no invitation," I said. But from experience I knew Hank would not be deterred. I put the six-pack on the bottom shelf of the fridge.

"Madge also told me about Jack. I'm sorry, Billie."

"Jake. And you're sorry with a smile."

Hank shrugged. "Smiling at you. You look great straight out of the shower. Bet you smell good, too."

He stepped toward me. I held my hands out to keep him at bay. "Forget it. And why don't you amuse yourself with TV or something?"

"Good idea. Surely, I can find some reruns of tennis or golf." He helped himself to a beer, twisted the cap off, and settled on the couch.

I gave him the remote after setting the sound level.

He grinned. "You're the only woman I'll let play with my controls."

Carl and Madge arrived next. For reasons beyond me, Madge doted on Hank. She poured a glass of Chardonnay and sat close to him on the couch. Carl was lukewarm toward Hank and joined me at the round table on the aft deck. We rolled up the plastic drop curtains and sat in silence. Carl lacked chitchat talent, and it wasn't my long suit either, although you couldn't have Nina for a mother and not learn the tricks. A sinking sun turned the lake's surface into shards of glass. After another day in the mid-nineties, the mid-eighties were welcome.

"She's here," Madge shouted.

I stepped back into air conditioning as Pam came through the door. Madge hugged her across a large wrapped package that Pam held with both arms.

"Hi, Madge. You look great. Here's the shrimp." Pam handed over the package.

"Do I get a hug, too? I hope." Hank grinned and held out his arms.

"Stand aside. I'm next," I said.

Pam grinned her elfish grin. I gripped her in a bear hug, and we rocked side to side for a few seconds.

"Thanks for calling me about Jake," she whispered in my ear. "I'm so sorry."

I responded with a squeeze. She was my sister in every way except for DNA. We'd clicked from the moment we'd flipped a coin to see who would claim the prime bed in our dorm room at Agnes Scott College. Not that a red-hot pimple or two hadn't popped on the face of our friendship as it grew. Nina had adored Pam. They had often shopped together and, once home, modeled the clothes they'd bought, oooing and ahhing over some and giggling over others. On the other hand, I hated shopping for clothes, a conclusion Nina arrived at when I was fourteen. My mother loved me, but she did not adore me. And although I loved my mother,

her standards for me were so high that adoration was impossible. Was I still jealous? Nina and Paul had been gone nearly two years.

Carl hobbled forward and stuck his hand out.

"Now?" Hank asked, as he shook Carl's hand.

Pam studied him for a minute. "Oh, what the hell. You must be Hank. Billie's told me about you."

"Uh, oh." He bent and enveloped her in a loose, gentle embrace. "See? I'm not the lecher Billie thinks I am."

We gathered around the large table on the party deck and gorged on boiled shrimp, boiled ears of corn, garden salad, saltines, and copious amounts of beer. Madge dumped the debris of our feast into a plastic bag, closed it with a tight knot, and dropped the bag down the ladder onto the deck below. The sun sank into the water, and the light of a full moon wiggled across the lake.

"Damn! They're here." Carl slapped his cheek.

"Who?" Pam looked around.

"Carl is the canary in the mosquito-mine," I said. "We'd better get inside before they smell new blood."

Carl navigated his stiff leg down the ladder. Madge shoved containers around in the fridge and made room for leftover food, after which she took Carl by the elbow and they left. Carb-induced sleepiness tugged on my eyelids, but, before succumbing, I wanted to talk with Pam. I needed to tell her more about Jake, and I wanted her first reaction to my offer that she quit her job and move to Gainesville to head up the foundation I was envisioning.

"Nothing like shrimp and beer to give a guy a full head of steam." Hank patted his six-pack abs. "Who wants to walk by moonlight over to my boat for a night cap?"

"I've seen your houseboat," I said. *Get out of here* was what I wanted to say.

"Is it far?" Pam asked.

"Under five minutes. Let's go." Hank swept an arm toward the door.

"Pam!" I heard the aggravation in my voice.

"Oh, I won't be long, Billie. I'm not sleepy yet, and it's a beautiful night. Come with us."

I shook my head and watched Pam and Hank disappear into darkness. Their voices faded, leaving me surrounded by disbelief. Whatever she was doing and thinking, it qualified as another pimple on the face of our friendship.

Chapter 10

I didn't wait up for Pam to return from the visit to Hank's boat. No way was I going to reward her behavior with a show of curiosity. Instead, I holed up in my bedroom and flicked the TV from channel to channel, looking for something to distract me. Finally, I settled on *The Late Show*, but even that receded in my consciousness, replaced by low grade fuming. I didn't hear Pam come in, but when she tapped on my door, I answered by turning up the TV volume.

Tuesday morning, I slipped out before Pam stirred and indulged in a no-no breakfast at a Waffle House. Afterwards, I washed and vacuumed my car before returning to the marina. The goal was to tame the unbecoming woe-is-me attitude that had lingered overnight. By the time I parked my car and ploughed toward the boat through the heat waves that rose from the dock, I was back in control.

"Hey! Up here!" Pam waved from the party deck. I waved back.

Her suntanned skin contrasted with a light green two-piece bathing suit. Years ago, we had sworn off bikinis. At that moment, she looked like she could break the vow and get away with it. Me, I'd never take the chance. She disappeared from view and met me in the living room. Air conditioning enveloped my body and the coconut scent in Pam's suntan lotion filled my nostrils.

"Madge went shopping." Her voice was chipper. "Carl headed to marine supplies to buy something—a screw or a bolt or who knows. I made sandwiches. Let's eat outside before it gets any hotter."

We settled on the aft deck in a patch of shade. I nibbled at the edges of a chicken salad sandwich and licked the salt off several baked chips.

"Why so quiet?" Pam asked. "Thinking about Jake, maybe?"

"That and other things." I turned my chair to face her directly. "You're a fig," I said

Pam's eyebrows shot up, and the smile faded.

"And you're a walnut," she said.

"Marshmallow."

"Rock."

"Soft avocado." I made a face.

"Raw potato."

"Cream puff."

"Peanut brittle." Pam raised her hands. "But whoa right here. What are you pissed about, Billie?"

We had invented this stupid game of verbal sparring in college and played it whenever thorny issues needed airing. The one bent out of shape started the name-calling. And the names invariably spoke to qualities that distinguished us physically, mentally, and emotionally. Bottom line: Most people found Pam easier to digest than me.

"Don't play innocent. You know what the hell's bothering me." I stirred my tea, removed the spoon, and flicked a few drops of liquid her way.

Pam threw a chip at me. "I knew you were pissed last night when you refused to open your door when I tapped. I'd have been back earlier if Hank hadn't showed me every inch of his boat, all the time yakking about you, by the way. Time just got away."

"Did he show you any of his other inches?"

She threw another chip at me. "No! And if he had, why would you care? How many times have you complained to me that Hank won't take no for an answer? You're so damned conflicted about men; I thought I could flush out your real feelings for Hank. And looky, looky, you're green-eyed jealous."

I sighed. "I'm not jealous of Hank, you idiot. I'm jealous that you have the gift of drawing people to you. You waltzed in, and, a few hours later, he tangoed you off-stage. Something about me keeps people at a distance."

"Hogwash. Uncle Joe and Irene, me, Madge, Carl, and now Hank, we're all part of your fan club. And Charlie, think of Charlie. He loved you to pieces."

"Charlie." I heard the wistfulness in my voice. I closed my eyes and he was there. Tall and lean, with sparkling blond hair all over—head, chest, arms, legs. "Charlie left me. That's not love in my book."

"Okay, so he morphed into a turd." She patted my hand. "But, dammit, you have to open up a little, so the guys who are interested aren't scared off."

"I know. And I'm sorry I took my frustration out on you. You can have Hank."

Pam laughed. "How generous of you, but no thanks. He's obviously sniffing your trail full time. He was a perfect gentleman with me."

We left it there and retired to air-conditioning. After Pam showered and changed into shorts and a T-shirt, we sat cross-legged on my king-size bed, facing each other. Between us, I dumped the information Uncle Joe had rounded up on starting a non-profit foundation from scratch. While Pam reviewed a formidable document, I rambled on about the nubbin of my idea.

"That's enough for now." Pam pressed her hands to her ears. "In a nutshell, you want to give megabucks away to women in need, and Uncle Joe thinks it's a flaky idea?"

"He can be won over. Especially if you agree to head up the foundation. He wishes I had your financial savvy."

Pam tapped her fingers on her thigh and looked at something beyond me. "Okay. I'll think about it. But remember, I like the job I have now. Best of all, I'm vested."

I smiled. "My middle name is benefits."

By mid-afternoon, the predicted ninety-six degree heat spike pushed the air-conditioning to a steady hum. Pam had retired to her bedroom to check e-mail and take a nap. Madge rhythmically chopped red and yellow peppers and dropped the pieces on a platter of Romaine lettuce. Carl pored over a schema of the boat's innards. I parked at the bar and worked a Sudoku puzzle. When my cell phone trilled, I jumped before answering.

"Billie, Pete here. Hate to bother you, but I need help with Jake's girlfriend. Well, don't guess she's really a girlfriend. Jake ain't been in town that long. But he struck up with her and saw her most every day. Laverne's her name. She's taking this real hard and rambling on about things I didn't know about Jake. I'm thinking a woman could maybe help her."

"You mean right now, Pete?"

"Yeah. She's a waitress here where I'm calling from. The Lakeside Bar and Grill. You know it?"

"I was there once," I said. The rustic structure was popular with the lake crowd that gravitated to personal watercraft and fishing by every imaginable method. "Stay put, Pete. I'm on the way."

Madge wiped her hands on her apron. "Will you be back for happy hour? Pam will want to know."

"I hope so. But start without me if I run late."

Thirty minutes later, I eased the Prius into a graveled parking space. The lunch crowd had disappeared and the dinner crowd was still on the lake. I stepped into subdued lighting and a faint cloud of tobacco smoke. Mournful country music played in the background. I only caught the gist of the story: a woman had Texas two-stepped her way out of her two-timing lover's life.

"Over here."

I turned toward the voice. Pete waved. He sat hunched over a table in the bar area, across from a woman whose platinum hair shone in the gloom. As I sat down, I noticed that her fire engine red lipstick matched her glued-on nails. Her low-cut blouse hugged full breasts.

"I'm Laverne." She looked at me with glistening eyes and gripped my outstretched hand. "Jake talked about you. Said you were paying for that Habitat house. That's swell of you. Jake said he was glad he could help."

"You must be shocked," I said. "I'm sorry. Jake seems to have been special to you."

She nodded and dabbed her eyes with a cocktail napkin. Pete raised his hand and a short, stocky bartender waddled over and set three bottles of beer on the table.

"Most of the guys who come in here... Well, they're weekend Romeos. They don't care if their girlfriends see them laugh and flirt with me and the other gals who wait tables. And some of them, when the booze kicks in, they don't like their flirting turned down." She pulled a piece of wet napkin from under her beer bottle. "Jake wasn't like that. Used to sit at a table all alone, unless Pete here was with him. He'd drink three or four beers and eat a steak sandwich. Sometimes he'd read in a sporting magazine. Never laughed and didn't flirt neither. That's why I took a shine to him."

She didn't indicate that the shine included sex, but I suspected it did. I was happy for Jake that he had found even a transient antidote for some of his loneliness. Whatever had weighed on him seemed never to lift.

I squeezed her hand. "Jake needed a friend, Laverne. You can be proud he chose you."

"Maybe." She blew her nose, tilted her head, and guzzled beer. "Haven't dumped on anybody like this for a long time. I'm feeling a little better. Not so tore up. Pete said you're working on finding Jake's family."

"Didn't think you'd care," Pete said quickly.

"It's okay, Pete." I turned to Laverne. "Do you know anything that could help me?"

"Maybe. One night Jake showed me a picture of a real pretty girl. Said she was his daughter. Then he choked up real bad. Told me she was murdered and that the son-of-a-bitch got off scot-free. He banged his fist down on the table so hard that he knocked peanuts out of a dish."

"Can you describe the girl?" I asked.

Laverne sloshed a sip of beer around in her mouth. "Hard to see things clear in this dim light. But I remember she was smiling. Looked to be about twenty. Dark hair cut middling. I remember the look on Jake's face. He got all teary-eyed."

My heartbeat quickened. *That's it.* Laverne had described the photo I found in Jake's box. A murdered daughter. A suspect Jake thought had walked. A father on the move. All this had to be connected. The daughter was the key or a large part of the key to Jake's mystery. I wondered how the grief and anguish he experienced at losing a child compared to the grief I experienced in not being able to conceive a child.

I nudged myself back to the moment. "Did Jake ever call his daughter by name?"

"Not with me," Pete said. "It was so quick that time he showed me that photo."

"Humm…" Laverne closed her eyes and tapped a forefinger on her chin. "He did use her name, but only once. I don't think I remember. Wait!" Her expression brightened. "August...Augusta... Something a little different. But don't hold me to it. I'm just not sure."

"That's okay. Can you think of anything else about Jake that would help me find his family? Did he tell you where he came from? Or talk about his work? Did you ever go to his motel room? Maybe you saw something there."

Laverne took the questions in stride, especially the motel reference.

She shook her head. "Sorry. Jake just fell in with me out of nowhere it seemed. I'd ask him stuff, but he wouldn't talk anything personal. He did talk about working with Habitat. He liked that."

"Well, you've been really helpful."

We exchanged cell numbers, plugging them into our phones on the spot. "Please, call me if you remember anything else," I said.

"Sure. And you'll let me know if you find his family?"

I stood to say goodbye. When I tried to pay for the beers, Laverne waved me off.

"The beer is on the house," she said. "There's not a shit load of benefits working here, but there's a few."

Chapter 11

As I pulled out of the parking lot, I called Carl's cell phone via Bluetooth. When he answered, I summarized my conversation with Laverne, saving the kicker for last.

"Jake told Laverne that his daughter was murdered and that her killer walked away a free man."

"Whoa! Tough for a parent. And lots of fathers and daughters have a special bond. Could explain why Jake was traveling around under the radar."

"You mean he could have been tracking the killer? And the killer got to him first?"

Carl grunted. "That's possible, Billie, but you need to keep your thinking out of a box. There's another possibility."

I accelerated around a pickup truck and veered back into my lane, just in time to avoid a crash head-on with a Volkswagen bug. I deserved the irate driver's long blast of a car horn. Once again, I swore off of driving while talking on the phone, but, first, I needed to finish my conversation with Carl.

"I give up," I said. "What's another option?"

"Thought you'd never ask. Remember the hand-printed note in Jake's box? There's a pissed some-body out there who says Jake owed him or her $250,000. Hell, some guys and an occasional gal will kill for twenty-five bucks."

"You're right." I relaxed my death grip on the steering wheel. "But the note isn't signed. We're sty-mied until we find out Jake's real identity."

Carl's silence frayed my patience. "Knock, knock, anybody there?"

"Google," Carl said.

"If that's supposed to be funny, it's not. I need some real help here."

"You were supposed to answer 'Google who?'"

I bit my lip before complying.

"Google any site that can run Jake Wade, Jacob Wade, hell, turn it around, Wade Jacobs, through an identity and locator filter." Carl paused for a deep breath. "Pam can help me with the easy and free stuff, like White Pages and Switchboard. I've already asked a buddy who worked suspected arsons with me to run the names through the sites that require pay-ment or membership. These are the gigantic data-bases that are used by high-end PIs, government, and big businesses. Hell, we were always skip-tracing fire bugs who torched homes and businesses and even churches for personal reasons or just for the fun of it."

I had listened to Carl with a growing sense of excitement that translated into a renewed white-knuckled grip on the steering wheel.

"You mean it might be that easy? Plug the name Jake Wade or some variation of it into one of these search sites and, duh, we find out if he's who he claimed to be and maybe where he's from, where his family lives?"

"Well, that's the jackpot," Carl said. "We could find out that Jake Wade, Jacob Wade, Wade Jacobs, that all of these names are aliases."

"Carl, you really think he could have just switched first and last names to confuse easy identification? I'd almost be disappointed."

"If he had a first and last name that were easily interchangeable, why wouldn't he keep it simple? Creativity not necessary, thank you. Take your names: Passing yourself off as Quinn Billie wouldn't work."

"Very funny." I shifted to "B" to engage motor drag, and the Prius rolled to a stop at a red light. "Before I wreck myself talking on the phone, I have one more gigantic question."

"Shoot."

"Why are you suddenly so willing to help me with the Jake mystery? Up to now, you've been the resident curmudgeon every time I venture near the subject."

Carl's sigh was heavy in my ear. "For starters, I can see how stubborn you are. You won't give up until his family knows how he died and until his ashes are delivered to them. Correct?"

"That's my goal."

"Okay, then I'm game to help you meet your goal, if you'll promise to drop the matter there and let the law handle finding his killer."

"I promise." At the moment, I believed myself.

"Good. Take it from me, Billie; in my thirty-plus years on the job, I've seen how low humans can sink. People set fires knowing a spouse, children, pets will die. You don't want to mess with the person who blew Jake Wade's head off."

I shifted into drive and crept toward the next light a block away. "I'm in commuter traffic and at least another thirty minutes from home. When you and Pam begin the easy Google searches, throw *August* and *Augusta Wade* into the search. Laverne thought Jake referred to his daughter by one of these names."

Carl and I hung up, and I concentrated on driving. We'd both left Madge out of the computer assignment. She was a proud technophobe. When pressed to get with the twenty-first century, she always repeated her mantra: "God made smoke signals, face to-face gab, and telephones. If they're good enough for God, they're good enough for me."

My thoughts slipped back to the Saturday that Jake was shot. We had clashed. "Words in the air," Sam had called it. Although I wasn't sure I could quote Jake, I remembered the gist of what he said: The thing he had to do, it had to do with honor. He couldn't let anything stand in his way. He'd also jabbed me personally when he said that I couldn't understand, that I lived in another world.

A blazing sun ball hung inches above the horizon, waiting patiently to drop out of sight. I stepped onto the boat and let myself into the living room. Carl and Pam sat at separate ends of the bar, hovered over laptops. Each held up a hand in greeting but remained focused. Madge sat at the breakfast room table, pencil in hand, crossword puzzle at the ready.

"Martini?" Madge asked.

"Not tonight." I poured a glass of Shiraz and plopped on the couch.

To dampen my curiosity about what Carl and Pam had learned from Googling variations of Jake Wade's name, I focused on TV, sound muted. Weather forecast banners flowed across the bottom of the screen. A chance of rain later in the week. I switched to Channel 2 Atlanta. The screen filled with a close-up of the wrinkled face of an elderly white woman who had wandered away from a nursing home. *Poor Jake,*

I thought. *He'll never grow old physically, but already he's old, stale news. And not even an obituary to leave to the genealogists.*

"I give up." Pam put her laptop to sleep and turned on the barstool to face me. Her lipstick was long gone, and her hair was rumpled; otherwise, she looked fresh in soft denim Capri pants and a pale yellow scoop neck shirt.

"Ditto." Carl scribbled something on a notepad. He turned to me, rubbed his bad knee, and stretched his arms toward the ceiling.

"Well?" I looked from one to the other, as I sat down in a chair I'd pulled away from the dining table and positioned to face the bar.

"We split up the searches based on stuff in Jake's box and other info we've uncovered," Carl said. "Made more sense. You go first, Pam."

Pam referred to notes she'd made on a legal pad. "I pushed *August Wade* and *Augusta Wade* through the White Pages, Peoplefinders, and Switchboard. Nothing, unless you count an Augusta Wade, age 86, in Vermont or an August Wade, age 55, in Tucson. I Googled the same names in Georgia obituaries. Zilch, but then the daughter could have been murdered in another state. I tried to verify the Social Security number Jake used, but I hit a wall."

"No problem," Carl said. "My buddy has access to the Social Security Death Index. If Jake didn't want to be found, my bet is the SS number he used belonged to a dead person. We'll know as soon as Joel gets back to me."

Pam placed her notes on the bar and yawned. "Sorry, but that's all I came up with."

"Thanks for trying, Pam." I smiled, wanting to ease the weariness that rode her slumped shoulders. "Unfortunately, if we're not using real names, we can't unearth real information."

"Yeah," Carl said. "That might explain some of my results." With a nod, he thanked Madge for the fresh beer she thrust at him.

Behind Pam and Carl, Madge worked with salad fixings: chopped Romaine lettuce, grape tomatoes, a yellow pepper, and English cucumber. Grilled meat would be added later. Pam heard my stomach rumble and grinned as she offered a bowl of roasted pecans she'd just tapped. I took a handful of nuts and motioned her to remove temptation.

Carl looked up from the notes he'd been reviewing, and then set the pad aside. "Searched on *Jake Wade, Jacob Wade, and Wade Jacobs*, using the databases Pam used. Got five hits, but I could easily rule out four of them. Based on age, they were either too young or too old. Made a phone call to rule out the fifth hit, a Jake Wade in Kentucky. His age was about right." Carl paused.

"Well, don't keep us in suspenders. What did you find out?" Madge walked around the bar and sat down at the dining table.

"I found out what shitty luck some people have," Carl said. "The Kentucky Jake is in a wheelchair, paralyzed from the neck down. I talked to his nighttime caretaker."

"Oh, how terrible." Madge touched a hand to her heart.

"No other leads?" I asked.

"Nope. But then I didn't expect much from the databases we used. It looks more and more like Jake Wade was a damn good alias."

I didn't like the dead end sound of that. "If that's the case, is it possible to trace forged documents?"

Carl sounded a raspberry. "Hell, if I'd cough up the money tonight, I'd have a dozen forged licenses, even a passport, in a couple of days. The Web is teeming with jerks that specialize in fake documents. The likelihood of finding the vendor Jake used is about zero. Forgers on the Internet are like snakes. They slither in and out of Web sites before you can get there with a cyber hoe."

We lapsed into silence that lasted for several minutes. Madge sighed, pushed out of her chair, and returned to dinner preparation. Carl stared at the floor.

Pam cleared her voice. "Carl, didn't you call somebody in Knoxville before we started Googling?"

"Yeah, I called Garmon Studio in Knoxville. Thought they might be willing to check the name *Wade* in their records. That got me a hoo-hah. They didn't begin computerizing their records until the first of last year, and they're only halfway through the alphabet. The W paper records are in their basement buried under the boxes containing K through V records. I made the mistake of saying I wasn't sure of the name. Can't say that I blame them for balking."

"So we bombed on every front," I said. "But, Carl, won't the sheriff and GBI hit the same wall?"

"Depends. We'll know more when I hear from Joel's searches of the major databases. He'll get back to me early tomorrow."

Pam slipped off the barstool and stretched on tiptoe. "Why do I feel so depressed?"

"Because you have good sense and aren't fixated on this Jake Wade business like Billie is," Madge said.

When Pam looked at me, I smiled. "It doesn't help that you took annual leave to come over for some relaxation and, instead, had to glue yourself to a computer."

Pam made a face. "Anything for a friend. Fair warning, however. My volunteer instinct has stalled."

"So let's change the subject and not ruin a good dinner." Madge banged a serving spoon on a bowl of rice pilaf. She lifted the lid of a large, counter-top grill and released aromas of garlic, lemon, and salmon filets. We served ourselves and gathered around the dining room table. I opened a bottle of Pinot Noir and filled wine glasses.

"Ooops! In all the hullabaloo, I forgot." Madge suspended a fork full of salmon at her mouth. "Habitat called. Dorothy, what's her name?"

"Longview," I said.

"Uh, huh. She said to tell you that the building site is cleaned up. She'll know by the end of the week whether she can scrounge up a new construction supervisor for you. But she didn't sound too hopeful, Billie. Two other homes are under construction in the tri-county area."

Good news for Habitat and Dorothy. Bad news for Sam, Ruby, and me. I put it on my mental checklist to fish the Sunday paper out of recycling and read the classifieds under "Work Wanted." That was the way I had found Jake.

Chapter 12

Wednesday morning, my anxiety level zoomed when Carl called with Joel's findings: the SS number belonged to a dead person and no megadatabase version of *Jake Wade* or *Wade Jacobs* was worth pursuing. Carl's conclusion: We, the sheriff, and the GBI were definitely dealing with an alias.

I was so down that Pam insisted we close her visit with one of our favorite activities, a back roads ride-around that always included an interesting destination unfamiliar to us.

She sat next to me at the bar and swiveled my stool so that I faced her. "I know just the place we can aim the Prius GPS for. It's been on my ride-around list for eons. We'll have fun. Just like old times. And, for sure, you need diversion."

I didn't want to go. Spending the day in bed with the covers pulled over my head was more in tune with my feelings. I was never going to find Jake's family. They, perhaps a wife, perhaps children other than the murdered daughter—they would never learn what had happened to him. His ashes would join all the other unclaimed ashes in the coroner's office. Whether it was rational thinking or not, Jake was killed on the Habitat site on my watch, and I couldn't let him join the unknowns of the world.

"Come on, Billie. You need a change of pace." Pam patted my knee. "And so do I."

A note of wistfulness in Pam's voice nudged me away from morbid self-absorption. If we didn't do something different, I'd drag Pam into the pit with me. It wouldn't be fair.

"Okay, what's this adventure you've had on your wish list?" After a sigh, I managed a smile.

"How long would it take to drive to Elberton?"

That destination surprised me, as Elberton is a small town east of Athens. Its primary claim to fame is being "The Granite Capital of the World." "If we hustle and traffic is in our favor, two hours. Your sights aren't set on the Granite Museum, are they? Been there, done that."

"Nope." Pam's smile was triumphant. "The Georgia Guidestones are a few miles north of Elberton, on the way to Hartwell. Some of that famous granite went into a gigantic, mysterious monument that has spawned ongoing controversy."

"You're kidding. I'm embarrassed that I've never heard of these stones."

Pam laughed. "Don't be. My hobby is scouring the Net for kooky, bizarre places to track down."

"Why are the Guidestones so controversial?"

"For starters, the monument attracts fans of rational thinking, as well as certain cults. And some defenders of conservative religions want to demolish it because they're convinced Satan created it."

I was hooked. Pam's ride-around ideas were always superior to mine. We agreed to go in two cars and leave her car in Athens so that she'd have a direct route back to her condo in Atlanta when our excursion was over. Before we left, she printed out the Wikipedia entry for the Guidestones to provide more background.

In Athens, Pam parked her car near the main entrance on the backside of the mall and strapped herself into the Prius's passenger seat. The blast of hot air that came in with her taxed the air conditioning for several minutes. I drove the speed limit, while she poured over the Wikipedia notes and read some of the interesting details to me.

In the spring of 1979, a mysterious man with money, using the name R.C. Christian, commissioned a prominent Elberton granite company to build the monument and to forever hold secret the names of the men behind its conception. The structure's message, consisting of ten guidelines or principles written in eight languages, was unveiled in early 1980. Several astronomical features were built into the stones, including a hole in the center column through which the North Star is always visible. When I asked Pam to read aloud the ten guidelines, she folded the notes and stuck them in her purse.

"No way. We'll read the guidelines together while we're standing at the monument."

We finished the drive to Elberton in easy silence. I cruised several streets in the small downtown, looking for a local eatery. We were running late for lunch, and our stomachs grumbled.

Pam pointed to a man and two women who exited a car on a narrow street. "Let's follow them. They look like hungry natives."

I parallel parked without taking any fenders or bumpers, and we followed our quarry into McIntosh Coffee Shoppe and Antiques, tucked into a historic building that boasted wide-plank wooden floors, original brick walls, and exposed ducts and pipes in the ceiling. Ten people in line to order and a fifteen-minute wait to have our order delivered to the table assured us that we were in an eatery highly valued by the locals. Our chicken salad and fruit plates sealed that analysis. Before we left, we took in the many antiques and vintage furniture pieces.

About eight miles north of Elberton, just off Highway 77, I slowed when the foreign-looking Georgia Guidestones soared skyward from a hilltop. The sharp angles of four massive, nineteen-feet-high slabs of granite, arranged in a circle around a smaller center slab, stood in sharp contrast to surrounding pastureland.

"Wow!" Pam held her hands up. "Beam me up, Scottie."

I turned off the highway onto Guidestones Road, drove a short distance to the monument and parked close by.

We found the slab with the ten guidelines inscribed in English. I stood still and craned to read from the top down, while a cloak of humidity wrapped my body. When I'd finished reading, I rubbed my neck and waited for Pam's reaction.

"You have a sweat mustache," she said.

"So do you."

We laughed and pulled the bottoms of our tank tops up to wipe our faces.

"Well, what's your first thought?" Pam asked.

I glanced at the slab message. "I don't see a guideline I would delete, but one is already out of date. With a world population in the billions there's no way to maintain humanity under 500,000,000."

"Yeah, I saw that too." Pam hesitated. "Am I being too critical, or do these guidelines smack of New Age?"

"Maybe that explains the anger of the nut cases who're planting graffiti protests all over these slabs. In a few more years, every word in every language may be defaced."

"Yeah. People ain't got no couth," Pam said.

"Which guideline strikes a chord with you?" I asked.

"Hummm." Pam studied the inscribed messages. "Based on the experiences of a working gal in the nonprofit world, I can relate to number seven: *Avoid petty laws and useless officials.* What's your pick?"

"Easy. Number nine: *Balance personal rights with social duties.*"

Pam grinned. "That fits. You've got the money to live apart from us low-lifes, and we can't get rid of you."

"Thanks for that analysis, Dr. Freud, but don't send me a bill."

Pam pinched her tank top and pulled it away from her body. "Whew! I'm melting in this humidity. Let's go."

"In a minute. I've just focused on the guideline Jake Wade would have picked, based on what little I know about him."

"Okay, I'll bite. Which one?"

"Number five: *Protect people and nations with fair laws and just courts.* From what Laverne, his waitress friend, told me, Jake was convinced the man who murdered his daughter escaped a just court."

Pam sighed. "So ends my valiant attempt to distract you from all things Jake Wade. Let's go before I suffer heat stroke."

"Sorry." I shrugged and followed her to the car.

On the drive back to Athens, I bombarded her with every detail of Jake's death, my encounters with the sheriff and coroner, Carl's reluctance to help me until recently, and my frustration with multiple failures to crack Jake's alias.

"I keep fixating on how I'd feel if you or Uncle Joe or anyone I loved walked off and never returned. I can't imagine how I'd live the rest of my life not knowing what happened to you. Would the grief ever end? I'd like to spare Jake's family that fate."

Pam listened patiently to my monologue. At the mall, before we said goodbye and she drove off, headed for Atlanta and home, she gave me her feedback. "You've always been one to fight for the underdog, Billie, but maybe this fight won't end with a win.

And if it doesn't, you need to give yourself credit for an all-out effort."

Thursday and Friday rekindled my anxiety. I spent far too much time hounding the newspaper and TV news shows, hoping for word that Jake's real name had been discovered, only to be disappointed. Adding to my angst were several hours spent on the telephone, an activity that registers at the bottom of my fun list. Several requests for a call back from Sheriff Farr died in possession of his secretary, Eunice. Sam called, and in his usual forthright manner, pinned me to the wall.

"What about our house, Miz Billie? What with Mr. Jake dead—God bless his soul—how we gonna finish things? And what about Saturday? We'll be there, but maybe everybody else is too scared."

I could almost hear Ruby breathing down Sam's neck. "Keep your hopes up, Sam. I'll meet you at the house, and we'll see who comes back to volunteer. I don't want to put pressure on anyone."

"Okay then. Ruby and me, we're praying everything works out."

To Sam's credit, he did not pepper me with additional calls. I can't say the same for Dorothy Longview. We talked five or six times. First, she thought she'd found a replacement construction supervisor, but, no, he'd backed out in favor of a permanent job with benefits. She had word out in two adjacent counties so far, without any responses. She was also checking the papers daily for leads via "work wanted" ads. No luck. Did I want to back out of sponsoring the house to completion? If so, she'd take over and simply mothball the project until the stars lined up for a renewal of construction.

"No. We have to keep going," I pleaded. "Let's see what volunteer commitment surfaces Saturday and keep our fingers crossed that the Sunday paper will deliver another Jake or that someone responds to your offers."

Chapter 13

Saturday morning dawned with gray clouds skittering across the sky. A breeze ruffled the lake's surface, setting up a gentle slap against the boat. I fought the temptation to roll over for another thirty minutes of snooze time, and, instead, stuck my legs into jeans and arms into a denim shirt. Sitting on the edge of the bed, I pulled on hard-toe work boots.

I drove by rote to the Habitat site, the scary automatic driving that makes you wonder aloud, "Damn, how'd I get here?" I parked next to Sam and Ruby's old Caddy. They waved from the picnic table and walked toward me. We met on a patch of bare earth in front of the skeleton of their house.

"Morning, Miz Billie. Looks pretty sad, don't it?" Sam shook his head.

I agreed with a sigh. The walls were up, but no doors or windows. Two lonely roof trusses jutted skyward. Without bright sunlight, unpainted lumber had traded a golden glow for a gray patina. Since the previous Saturday, wind had blown trash from the road into the yard. Several pages from a newspaper clung to the foundation of the front porch. I looked away from the stack of roof trusses behind which Jake's body had sprawled grotesquely.

"Will it ever get finished?" Ruby's soft voice broke my reverie.

"Of course." I smiled, attempting more confidence than I possessed.

"But nobody's here but us this morning," she said. "Who's gonna do the work?"

"Don't fret, Ruby. Here comes some more help." Sam pointed toward the road.

Pete pulled his truck into the parking area. The front bumper had had a stroke, its right side drooping. The slam of a truck door broke the morning stillness. Neal trailed behind on his motorcycle and gunned the motor before cutting the ignition. They walked in lock step to join us.

"Are we it?" Pete asked.

"What about Jake's replacement?" Neal asked.

"Can't nobody replace Mr. Jake." Ruby crossed her heart.

"Habitat put the word out, and I'm looking on my own," I said. "Keep your fingers crossed."

"What about this morning? Maybe we ought to go home and wait till you call us back," Pete said.

Frowns furrowed Sam and Ruby's faces. Ruby reached for Sam's hand.

"Come on, guys. Let's stay positive." I rubbed my hands together. "And first things first. We need to show Jake some respect, so we won't have to tiptoe around a horrible memory when we're back at work here."

We circled the plot of dirt where Jake's life had ended. I said a silent *thank you* to Dorothy's cleaning crew. No obvious blood met the eye. Dark spots flecked several of the neatly stacked roof trusses. I chose to see the flecks as defects in the wood. A light dusting of a white powder, probably lime, topped the clay soil.

"He's with the good Lord now," Sam said.

"Amen." Ruby steepled her hands under her chin.

My own goodbye, I said privately. *Rest easy, Jake. If it's humanly possible to find someone who loves you, I'll do it.*

Neal closed his eyes and shifted his weight foot to foot. Pete lowered himself to a cowboy squat and pressed two fingers into the lime-coated soil.

"Okay, that's all for today." I swallowed the lump in my throat. "But keep Saturdays free, if you can. I'll call when we can get back to work."

We stood around in silence, reluctant to leave. Neal was the first to mumble goodbye. As he turned to leave, we looked in unison towards the sound of gravel crunching in the driveway.

"Who's that coming?" Ruby asked. "Never seen that car."

An older model black SUV rolled to a stop beside my car. Front and back doors opened simultaneously. A tall, lanky man slid from behind the wheel, and a shorter, older man exited the passenger side. A young woman, red hair tied in a ponytail, stepped down from the back seat. She turned and stretched across the seat to get something. A baby.

"I don't recognize the SUV," I said, "but we know the tall guy."

"Damn right!" Pete snapped his fingers. "He was the second deputy here last Saturday. You know… the one who went to check on where the shooter probably hid." He pointed to the woods across the hay field.

We walked over to the car. The young man stepped forward and thrust his hand in my direction. I was grateful he applied only light pressure since my hand was lost in his large grip.

"Morning, everybody. I'm DW. DW Harris. I wasn't sure anybody would be here."

He shook hands all around and then turned to me. "I saw last week you could use more help with the house. I was telling Bernie about it and…" He nodded toward the older man. "Bernie, here, he's my father-in-law. He suggested we volunteer as a family, and we all agreed. Dawn's my wife. And that's Tim she's holding."

"I've got a bum back," Bernie said. "But I like to cook and can help with lighter chores. Painting, maybe."

Too much sun had leathered Bernie's skin and furrowed his forehead. A gray stubble, aged several days, speckled his cheeks. He looked like hundreds of other men I'd seen around the lake, working, fishing, and hanging out.

"And I can help Bernie when Tim will let me." Dawn smiled and blushed for no apparent reason. She picked up one of Tim's hands and waved it.

"Great. Volunteers are always welcome," I said. "What about you, DW? You have a house building specialty?"

"I worked a couple of summers for a man who developed spec houses and office buildings. Moved from job to job and call myself a fair carpenter. Also discovered a talent for close measuring. Someday, I'll build a house for Dawn and me."

Sam and Ruby stared at DW with open mouths.

"Interesting," I said. "What would you do next on this house?"

DW pushed a ball cap back on his head and studied the house. "Well, that's pretty easy. The roof needs decking when the rest of the trusses are in. After that, doors, windows, siding, then all the inside stuff. That's when things slow down."

I waited, thinking Pete might challenge DW, but he didn't. I checked Neal's expression. Neutral and attentive. Sam appeared transfixed, as if Jesus had dropped out of the sky.

His assessment matched what Dorothy had told me would be the case. "Would you consider supervising the completion of this house? What about Saturdays? Are you available?"

DW looked at Dawn. She shrugged her shoulders.

"I'm working Saturday nights for the next month or so." He hesitated. "Yeah, I'll supervise things. Habitat's a good cause. And Sheriff Farr likes his deputies to get involved in the community. I've been looking around for a project."

"Then it's settled. I'll contact Dorothy Longview at Habitat, and you'll hear from her. She's the local director." DW and I shook hands.

We agreed to meet the next Saturday. Pete and Neal exchanged high fives with DW and left. Ruby and Sam hung back.

"Bless you, Mr. DW. You're surely sent from heaven." Ruby displayed a face-splitting smile. "Come on Sam, let's go kick up our heels." They drove out with the Caddy tailpipe hanging low and spitting white smoke.

DW and I exchanged phone numbers. I also explained that I was footing the bill for the house and told him how to place materials orders on the house account at Lowe's.

"How do I pay for food?" Bernie asked.

"Bring the bills on Saturday, and I'll write you a check on the spot."

With essentials wrapped up, we said goodbye. Dawn handed a fussy Tim to Bernie, who parked the baby on his hip. DW and Dawn locked hands and followed Bernie toward the SUV. I struggled not to scratch an itch of curiosity but lost the battle.

"DW, wait!" I ran after him.

DW stopped and motioned for Dawn to go on. He walked back to meet me. He removed his ball cap and ran fingers through sweaty, blonde hair. "Something wrong?"

I looked up and into blue eyes. He was at least six feet two inches tall. "Can you tell me anything about Jake Wade's case? Any luck finding next of kin?"

DW studied me with an unreadable expression and hooked his thumbs over his belt. "Sheriff Farr told all us deputies you're bulldogging this case, Ms. Quinn. That's why I won't tell him just yet I'll be helping with the house. As for the Wade case, you can read all about it in Sunday's paper."

"Any chance you'd preview it for me?" I ventured a small smile.

DW laughed. "You're a bulldog all right. Don't guess it'll hurt to tell you that the sheriff and GBI are at a dead end. *Jake Wade* is an alias for sure. We recovered the bullet that killed Wade, but that won't help until we can find the rifle that fired it. No shell casings were found where the sniper hid, so no help there. And no witnesses have come forward. We'd have a better chance to crack this case if Jake Wade had lived in Creeks County. He just appeared out of nowhere a couple of weeks ago."

"So, now the law will just twiddle its thumbs, waiting for something to break? Is this a fair statement?"

DW shrugged. "Yeah, that's pretty much where things stand. We get these mystery murder victims now and then. Just have to move on to cases we have a chance to solve. Shootings, stabbings, hit-and-runs, domestic violence... Families crawl all over us wanting answers."

So, Carl's earlier assessment had been on the mark. "Well, I don't have to give up," I said. "Surely, there's something we've all overlooked. The Jake I knew might have used an alias and moved around, but, in my opinion, he was no itinerant. Somewhere, a family is waiting to hear from him."

DW shrugged. "Suit yourself, Ms. Quinn."

"Call me Billie." My words trailed him to his car.

Chapter 14

The rain threat that boiled in dark clouds at sundown Saturday erupted during the night with thunder, lightning, and a rocking horse ride in bed. By the time I finished my second cup of coffee Sunday morning, the boat swayed gently, signaling the worst of the storm was over. A hazy glow from the security lights reflected in puddles on the dock. I donned a poncho and jogged to my mailbox for the newspaper.

Armed with a fresh cup of coffee and a bagel loaded with cream cheese, I spread the paper on the bar and extracted the junk sections that, for me, included the sports section. The murder of Jake had never made the front page of the Atlanta paper, and I was losing hope of any update when I found an article on page twelve entitled *Murder Victim Still Unidentified.* The first paragraph summarized the article:

"Still unknown is the identity of a man killed by sniper fire last week on a Habitat for Humanity building site in Creeks County. The victim is listed in the records of the sheriff of Creeks County, the coroner, and the Georgia Bureau of Investigation as *Jake Wade*, now determined to be an alias. The victim's fingerprints are not on file, and nothing in his personal belongings is helpful to establish identity. Drivers' licenses and Social Security cards are forgeries, according to the GBI. A DNA sample has been submitted for analysis and comparison with state and national databases. According to Sheriff Rodney Farr, a massive backlog in DNA laboratories is expected to delay processing of the victim's sample for several months."

I chewed the bagel, letting the cream cheese coat my tongue. A big swig of coffee melted the cheese. I understood why Jake's autopsy photo didn't accompany the article. His face was blown away. But why didn't the sheriff or GBI elect to print the photo of the young woman believed to be Jake's daughter? Could withholding this info establish later on the credibility of anyone who might come forward claiming knowledge of Jake's identity?

As the last act of reading the paper, I scanned the "Work Wanted" classified ads. No one came close to matching DW's construction background, confirming my decision to hire him to finish Sam and Ruby's house.

I spent the rest of the morning under the party deck canopy, lounging and/ dozing to the muffled sounds of quacking mallards and faraway motorboats. When the heat and humidity became uncomfortable, I ate a sandwich lunch at the downstairs bar before checking e-mail. Pam advised she had inched closer to declining my offer to head up a project that would help women who are down on their luck. "But," she closed, "I'm capable of chucking good sense where you're concerned." Uncle Joe wanted to know if I'd like to join him and Irene in September for a special Saturday night soiree at the High Museum. I replied, "Maybe. Back to you later." I almost erased a message from DW Harris before I recognized his e-mail address. He wanted me to know that his father-in-law, Bernie, had terminal prostate cancer, but wouldn't talk about it. It was, in fact, Bernie who pushed for the family to get involved with the Habitat build. He wanted to give something back while he had time. "But Bernie's okay to cook for volunteers. Dawn and I will keep a close watch on him." I replied how sorry I was to learn of Bernie's diagnosis and thanked DW for giving me a heads up.

By four o'clock, sunshine and a light breeze ruled the outer world. I stretched out on the couch and read the current issue of *Houseboat News*. I earmarked an article on mildew, the scourge of living on the water, for Madge to read.

I dozed and awoke to tapping on the front door. My watch said five o'clock. I released the dead bolt and let Madge in. My mouth was lined in kiwi fuzz.

"Hank's providing pizza, so we don't have to cook tonight. Hallelujah." She plunked two bottles on the bar. "And here's some Chianti to wash it down with."

"Funny, I don't remember inviting Hank." I let an edge tinge my voice.

"Well, I didn't invite him either," Madge said. "You know Hank. He just appears, and we're all too nice to tell him to beat it. Not that I'd want to, mind you. You have to admit, he is a hoot."

"Who's a hoot?" Hank asked, as he pushed through the door. "I admit it's one of my goals, but I keep falling short."

Hank's man-of-the moment attire included trendily rumpled khaki cargo shorts, a short sleeve navy polo shirt with one khaki stripe running horizontally across his chest, and boat shoes with no socks. His blond hair gathered in subtle spikes. He handed me a jar of olives.

"Note the stuffing in those olives—pimento and a sliver of nut. Imported. All martinis crave them." Hank smacked his lips. "Pizza will be delivered at seven. Save the Chianti for then."

I put the olives on the bar, and, in spite of myself, I smiled. Hank did look good, and I thought nostalgically of the rapport we'd shared on a few dates, before I learned of his playboy past.

Hank raised one eyebrow in surprise. "You wouldn't be mellowing toward me, would you, Billie?"

I felt myself blush and turned quickly toward Madge.

"Where's Carl?" I asked. "I thought he'd be on your heels."

"Oh, he'll drag in soon. He's just getting over a migraine that hit last night after dinner."

"Sorry to hear that." Actually, I was relieved that Carl wasn't boycotting me, which he had done a couple of times in the past. I suspected I was the first woman he'd ever worked for and that acceptance wasn't easy.

Madge and Hank concocted a round of new, improved martinis and delivered them to the fore deck, where we settled around a round table and several bowls of microwave popcorn.

"Did you see the article about Jake in today's paper?" I asked.

They both nodded yes.

"It's a shame." Madge clucked her tongue. "Somebody somewhere is looking for him. What a shock when they learn what happened."

"Family can't find Jake if they don't know what name he's been using. And if they live out of range of the Atlanta paper, they won't know he's dead," I said.

"You're right. Bummer." Madge fished an olive out of her martini.

"So you leave it to the sheriff and GBI to get to the bottom of things." A blast of air conditioning came out the door with Carl. He surveyed us from behind darkly tinted sunglasses. A deep furrow split his forehead.

"If you're saying I should back off, I can't."

"I know that feeling," Hank said. His smile was mock angelic.

I ignored him.

Carl eased into a chair and nudged it closer to the table. He pulled the tab on a sweating can of ginger ale he'd brought with him.

"Sorry about the migraine, Carl." It was my peace offering.

"Yeah, sure," he said.

"Oh, cheer up everybody." Madge started to pass the popcorn bowl around the table and then held on to it. "Never mind the popcorn. Here comes the pizza man."

Hank paid for the pizzas and, I noticed, slipped the roly-poly deliverer a big tip. I opened a bottle of Chianti and we gathered around the dining room table to demolish veggie and pepperoni supreme pizzas. Except for Carl. He sat quietly, eating yogurt and drinking water. His mood seemed to infect the rest of us. We ate silently except for several short-lived attempts by Madge and Hank to discuss movies and local politics.

Madge and I cleared the table. Hank turned his chair toward the TV and clicked to CNN. He lowered the volume immediately when he noticed Carl wince. Why did I let my irritation override Hank's good qualities? I knew what Pam would say. I was running scared, afraid to get too close.

At that moment, I decided that I'd shoo them off and go to bed early unless... I stood behind my chair and looked around the table. "I want to talk about Jake some more."

Madge groaned. "Don't you want to sleep tonight, honey?"

Hank studied me. "Okay, but I have to admit, I haven't followed all the details of his case."

"What's to talk about, Billie?" Carl removed the sunglasses and rubbed his eyes. His color was better, less pasty.

"The jackpot questions, of course. Since the man who came to town and worked for me wasn't Jake Wade, who the hell was he? He had money, and he wasn't uneducated. I'd say the sniper who killed him knew who he was. And is the sniper still around or long gone?"

Carl sighed. "Those are the same questions the sheriff and GBI are hassling. Don't go poking around in their business. You'll just gum up the works."

"And what if they come up empty-handed and give up? This seems to be the path they're on."

"Then that would be the end of it." Carl crushed the yogurt container and laid it on top of Madge's plate. "Jake would end up DOA and unidentified. A lot depends on whether the cops can think outside the box or will even try."

"That's it!" I said. My heartbeat quickened.

"What's it?" Carl looked surprised.

"Yeah, what's it?" Madge turned her palms up and shook her head.

Hank lowered his chair to all four legs.

"We're all thinking in circles," I said. "We're coloring inside the lines. There has to be something critical that we've missed. Everybody stay put. I'll be right back."

I rummaged in the office desk and found a deck of blank three-by-five cards. From another drawer I grabbed black and red permanent markers. For the next ten minutes, I produced clue cards. Everything I knew about Jake went on an index card, a separate card for each bit of information. When finished I had two stacks of cards—one with clues written in black and one with clues written in red.

I returned to the table and interrupted a heated discussion of the pros and cons of living year-round on a houseboat. Everyone was talking at the same time, but Hank had the edge on volume. "Don't try it through a bad winter. Mothball the boat and head for Key West."

I slapped the two stacks of cards on the table and laid a single card, blank side up, between the stacks. Conversation ceased.

"What's with the cards?" Carl asked.

"This stack, written in black, is what seems to be dead-end info about Jake," I said. "And this other stack, written in red, may stimulate out of the box thinking."

"What's the single card between the stacks?" Hank asked. He reached for it, and I let him turn it over.

The turned over card revealed *JAKE WADE* printed in block letters. "Think of poor Jake as a puzzle, a jigsaw puzzle, ready to reveal his secrets if we can fit pieces of info together."

Carl took a bathroom break. Madge refreshed our choice of beverage, and we regrouped. I turned over each clue in the black deck, and, after discussion, we either left the card in the black deck or underlined it in red and moved it to the red deck.

"Okay, let's review." I spread the retained black clue cards face-up on the table. "We've declared this info to be of no help in identifying Jake. "Fingerprints."

"Yeah," Carl said. "They're not in any database."

"Truck's a blank," I said. "Registered to Jake's alias. Probably paid for in cash. Ditto for the Social Security card, traveler's checks, and forged drivers licenses."

Carl turned over the last card to reveal belongings found in Jake's motel room: clothes, shoes, fishing rods, Sudoku puzzle book.

"A man after my own heart." Hank raised his wine glass. "He liked to travel light."

"So much for the clunker clues. Now, on to the red meat." Madge rubbed her hands together. Cooking imagery came easily to her.

I turned the red clue cards face-up on the table and read them off: formal photograph of a young woman Laverne identified as Jake's murdered daughter (perhaps named August or Augusta) with *Garmon Studio Knoxville* stamped on the back; a candid photo of a middle-aged woman and young girl standing in front of a palm tree (perhaps Jake's wife and their daughter). The note accusing Jake of stealing $250,000.

"That note isn't signed. Why leave it in the red pile?" Madge asked.

"Easy," Carl said. "If, big if, Jake is identified, somebody will know who demanded payback. And, bingo, the law will have a living, breathing suspect."

"Right." I clapped my hands and stood. "Okay, time to get off your duffs and think outside the box. Come on. Up and at 'um."

"Women and their games," Hank said, as he stood.

Carl mumbled but let Madge coax him out of his chair.

I shuffled positions of the cards, changing orientation of the writing. The upside down cards looked like gibberish.

"Is this like reading tea leaves?" Madge asked. "I don't see any pattern."

"Same here," Carl said.

"That's the point. Let's walk around the table and get new perspectives. Look at the clue cards from every angle. Open up to intuition." I nudged Hank forward with a jab to his lower back.

"Hummm...higher," he said.

"Grow up," I mumbled.

After three turns around the table, Carl broke ranks and collapsed in a chair. "Hell! Hocus pocus won't work. We just don't have anything solid to work with. The man we call Jake is a joke on us."

Madge moved behind Carl and massaged his shoulders. "I hate to say it, Billie, but Carl makes sense. You're all worked up. Can't you just back off and catch your breath, at least for a while?"

As I sighed, my shoulders slumped. Hank came to my side and slipped an arm around my waist. For once he wasn't flippant, and I didn't move away.

"If I'm ever in deep doo-doo, I want you on my side," Hank said. "Your problem, no your strength, Billie, is that you don't know when to quit."

Tears stung my eyes.

Chapter 15

After my mini-breakdown when the clue cards failed to produce any new avenues for identifying Jake Wade, Madge offered to spend the night with me. So did a grinning Hank. Carl just stared at me, as I dabbed my eyes and blew my nose. I protested I was just tired and needed a good night's sleep. I shooed them out and locked the door but not before a blast of hot air sneaked in.

After a long, lukewarm shower, I donned clean pajamas and crawled into bed. As my head touched the pillow, my eyelids popped open. My brain felt swollen, and it pulsed with memories designed to keep me awake.

I closed my eyes, told my scalp to relax. No good. There they were, in living color on the back of my eyelids. My parents. Tall Paul, with his Irish good looks, easy smile, and ready laugh. In an uppity boy's school, he learned tricks of dress and poise that he honed for the rest of his life. His hugs highlighted my childhood. Nina, tall and pencil-slim, with dark hair and blemish-free olive skin. I heard "elegant" so often, I thought for a while it was her middle name. Often, her hugs were delivered with suggestions for improvement in my dress, speech, or behavior. Later, when she had the least power to "Ninimize" me, she fired suggestions and opinions broadside, all subtlety gone.

What did I have against sororities? Her sorority had teamed her with the elite girls of the Southeast. What was wrong with golf and bridge as lifelong pursuits? They opened quick doors to the people you wanted to associate with. Charlie was a nice young man. But marry him? I loved my mother, but I refused to compete with her.

I was grown and divorced by the time I drew a parallel between my parents and Ronald and Nancy Reagan. Each couple shared love and devotion that left little room for a child.

Stop thinking, I ordered. Gingerly, I massaged my temples. The worms wiggled on. I turned on the bedside light, plumped pillows behind my back, and called Pam. After eight rings, she picked up.

"What?" Her voice was croaky.

"It's me. I can't sleep."

"Neither can I—now. For God's sake, Billie, it's one o'clock."

"I know. I'm sorry."

"It's about Jake, isn't it? You can't turn off the horrible details."

I picked a loose thread in the bedspread. "Well, for sure, Jake's in the front of my brain, but something I never told you is eating away the back of my brain tonight."

Silence. "Okay, I'll bite. Since we're each other's personal dumpsters, I can't imagine what you've been hiding."

I cleared my throat. "My parents left for a long cruise when I was about eleven. I hung around the kitchen until Lilly was absorbed in cooking dinner. Then I sneaked off and searched every nook and cranny of their bedroom, sitting room, and Paul's desk."

"Looking for what? Money?"

"No, silly. At eleven, money was too abstract. I was desperate to find my birth certificate. I was convinced that I'd find 'unknown' or 'adopted' on the lines for father's name and mother's name."

"Did you find the certificate and, I hope, have your fantasies dashed?"

"Nope. I cried all the way through dinner. Turned down banana pudding. Nothing Lilly said or did consoled me."

"Oh, Billie. You ninny." Pam sighed. "Of course you're Paul and Nina's daughter. When you're not so damned uptight, you have your father's sparkle, and—look in the mirror—you have your Mom's blue eyes, olive skin, and dark hair."

"I know."

"You know?" Pam sputtered. "Then why the hell did you put me through this middle-of-the-night tale of woe?"

"You know everything else about me. Remember when we drank ourselves loopy on cheap red wine and promised *no secrets ever?*"

Pam laughed. "Yep. At the beach the summer we graduated from Scott. It's been a bumpy road since then, hasn't it?"

It was my turn to sigh. "I'll say. Your divorce, my divorce. Your breast cancer scare, my HIV scare. No babies for either of us…"

"Enough already." Pam sounded a raspberry. "Any more and we'll never sleep again. Back up and tell me how you learned you weren't a bastard or adopted."

I laughed. The raspberry always worked. "Lilly. She was frightened and told Uncle Joe about my crying jag. He came to the house and confronted me. He opened the spigot and out poured all my fears and anxieties."

"Wow! How shocked was he?"

"I remember his face turned white. And he nearly broke my ribs in a hug. Then, without a word, he stormed out of the house. I cried louder. Lilly patted my back and kept saying, 'Hush now, child.

Everything's gonna be all right.' And it was. Uncle Joe was back in an hour with my birth certificate. He made me promise never to tell Paul and Nina what I suspected."

"Did you keep that promise?"

"To the bitter end. They crashed their plane and died without ever knowing their child believed she was adopted."

Pam's silence hung between us. "Billie…" More silence.

"I know. I know. I need to make peace with my parents. You and Uncle Joe sing off the same page. I'm working on it."

"Good." Pam yawned. "It's been fun, old pal. Ripped out of sleep and dumped on. But, hey, what are friends for? Shut-eye is calling now."

"Thanks for putting up with me," I said, as Pam clicked off.

I turned off the lamp, adjusted my pillow, and closed my eyes. No way. My eyelids opened wide. I stared at the lazy rotation of the ceiling fan. The mystery of Jake was gnawing on the front end of my brain.

Chapter 16

Sometime after three o'clock, I turned loose of the memories of Lilly and my parents and slept fitfully. I awoke Monday morning to sounds of Madge puttering in the kitchen. Parchment paper lined my mouth and throat, and I was tired in mind and body. I slipped on flip-flops and trudged to the kitchen.

Madge looked at me and did a double take. "Lordy! The cat's been out dragging stuff home again."

I poured coffee without comment.

"Okay, I can see you don't want to talk, but how about listening?"

I groaned.

Madge laughed. "Something tells me you'll want to listen to a message on the answering machine. From Laverne, I think she said. Must have come in while we were shuffling clue cards outside yesterday."

"I didn't check messages last night." I groaned again. "This could be important."

I pushed the play button and listened with my forehead pressed against the bar top. *Billie, it's Laverne. Thought I'd better tell you, I'm not sure about Jake's daughter's name. I told you August or Augusta, but the more I think about it, that's not right. I'm remembering he said his birthday was in August and his daughter was named for a calendar month, but I'm not sure which month. I hope this helps. I hear the sheriff and GBI gave up on identifying him. I sure hope you'll keep on the trail.*"

Madge held up three fingers. "I come up with April, May, and June."

A spurt of adrenaline energized me. "Ditto. Now I'll need to search those names with *Jacob* and *Jacobs and Wade*." I was surprised by how desperate I was to uncover new information, anything that would give me another shot at identifying Jake.

I settled at the breakfast table with my laptop and began a new Internet search. Madge fortified me with fresh blueberry muffins and dripped a fresh pot of coffee before she left to run errands. I scoured the White Pages, Peoplefinder, Switchboard, and multiple links from each site. By the time Carl showed up for lunch, I had exhausted the search with disappointing results. I briefed him on Laverne's call and then shared my findings over chicken salad sandwiches and iced tea that Madge had left in the refrigerator.

"I got several hits on May and June Jacobs. Ditto with May and June Wade, all of them ruled out either by age or with telephone calls. There's an April Jacobs in Mississippi, but her age is iffy, and the listed telephone number is kaput."

"Hummm." Carl tapped his chin with a finger. "I smell a dead end."

"Maybe. But the more I think about it, the daughter was young and probably still dependent on Jake. She might not have left much of an Internet trail. I even tried the social networking sites."

"Maybe she was killed before Facebook and Twitter or used a nickname." Carl checked his wristwatch. "I'm going topside and give the stainless steel grill a cleaning. You need to buy a cover for it, or give the birds a lesson in poop control."

I waved him off and settled on the aft deck to scan the newspaper. No news of Jake. The media had moved on. A fly buzzed my head, and a bead of sweat trickled out of my hairline and down my cheek. I wiped my face on a sleeve.

I caught myself jiggling my left leg ninety to nothing. Lack of sleep and failure to unearth anything substantive regarding Jake Wade's identity had jangled my nerves. To distract myself, I decided to drive to Athens to take care of errands that pre-dated Jake's death and to commit to a birthday present for Uncle Joe. For the umpteenth time, I faulted myself for not switching my business to Gainesville, but I'd been living in Athens when I bought the boat and felt more comfortable there.

I opened the hybrid's sunroof and all windows and within two miles had blown the worst of the heat out. I closed up, turned on air conditioning, and cruised with satellite radio.

Once in the Athens area, I navigated to my bank and dropped some financial papers on top of stuff in my safe deposit box, relieved that I didn't have to rummage around and see or touch my wedding ring. Next stop was the ABC package store, where I stocked up on gin, vodka, and wine. The last stop was at Barnes and Noble to shop for Uncle Joe. In recent years, a book had become my traditional birthday gift for a man who had everything.

I explored the center aisle and new books displayed by category on separate tables. Some were best sellers, hardback and paperback. Others fell in the category of esoteric or downright kooky. I flipped through a book entitled *My Mother is My House Cat: How to Recognize Your Parents in Other Life Forms.* Way too kooky.

I settled at a table in the coffee shop with a latte and an oversized history of Athens and The University of Georgia. UGA was Uncle Joe's alma mater, documented by an entire wall in his den filled with certificates, history books, and memorabilia. I flipped through pages of old photographs: Broad Street as a rutted dirt road; the football stadium when players wore leather helmets; an angry crowd at the Arch protesting desegregation; the Varsity in its heyday, jam-packed with students in cars, and car-hops delivering the famous hot dogs and French fries. More recent photos captured students in all manner of dress and undress roaming downtown on Saturday nights, in and out of bars that featured the latest, live music.

Chipmunk-style, I packed cheesecake into one cheek and tongued a bit out to mingle with each sip of coffee. I was in this vulnerable state, prone to choking, when my brain clamped around parallel thoughts. Athens—home of The University of Georgia. Knoxville—home of The University of Tennessee. Athens—crawling with thousands of students the age of Jake's daughter. Knoxville—ditto. Could this explain what a pretty young woman, Jake's daughter, was doing in Knoxville? Did she pursue an education there and, in the process, sit for a photograph at Garmon Studio?

A surge of elation mixed with hopefulness flooded my thoughts. Hurriedly, I paid for the book and goosed the hybrid back to the marina, courting a speeding ticket all the way. After a bathroom break, I poured a glass of tea and Googled a telephone number for the University of Tennessee registrar's office. I punched the number into my cell phone and held my breath for six rings. A woman with a polite voice and efficient manner listened patiently to my request: Was a young woman by any of these names ever enrolled in the university—April, May, or June Jacobs, or April, May, or June Wade.

Silence. "Is this a joke of some kind?"

I hadn't thought about how the request might register with a stranger. "Absolutely not. The person I'm looking for probably has one or the other of the surnames Jacobs or Wade and, for the given name, a calendar month."

"Oh." She rolled the syllable out to great length. "Hold, please, while I check with my supervisor."

The hold dragged on. Canned music played in my ear. I shuffled through a stack of mail Madge or Carl had fetched from the marina box. I extracted the junk mail and tossed each piece over the bar, ringing the trash can three of four tries. Only two pieces of first class mail: a bank statement and a hefty envelope from Uncle Joe—no doubt more financial data to lull me to sleep.

"Hello?" The tone of voice sounded hopeful that I had abandoned the call.

"Yes. I'm still here."

"Our records show that an April Wade was enrolled from freshman year through junior year. She did not return for her senior year, which would have been two years ago. The other names are not in our database."

My heartbeat quickened. I sat up straighter. I had the same feeling once when I pulled back on a bowstring and zinged an arrow to the center of a bull's-eye.

"Great," I said. "And her parents' names and addresses would be much appreciated."

"I'm sorry. The University's privacy code prohibits sharing any additional information." The flat delivery sounded as if she had read from a prompt sheet.

"You're sure?" I pushed my luck.

"I checked with my supervisor. I'm sure."

The bureaucratic response wasn't her fault, so I closed with a civil response.

I muttered *privacy shmivacy* and called Carl. When I reviewed my epiphany at Barnes and Noble, he didn't gasp or otherwise reward me for what I knew was a real breakthrough.

"The daughter's name is April Wade. She was a student at the University of Tennessee, but that's all the school will reveal. I found no trace of her on the Internet, so I'm inclined to hire a private detective in Knoxville. Can you credential someone?"

Carl sighed. "I can, but will I?"

A flush heated my face. "Look, I'm asking nicely. Why don't you just cooperate in like manner?"

He ignored me and said, "How did you get the daughter's name?"

"Tell you later, but nothing illegal, if that's what you're worried about. Come on, Carl. Time's a wasting."

"I'm thinking."

"And I'm counting. One…two…three…"

"Okay, okay. I'll do it, but it's against my better judgment."

As if on cue, we simultaneously broke the connection.

Chapter 17

Tuesday morning, when my mouth was full of banana and cereal, Carl called with news he delivered in a brusque voice.

"Stay put for a telephone call from J. Sugsby, a Knoxville detective. A friend of mine recommended him, and the Better Business Bureau never heard of him. A good sign he's clean."

To pass the time and do something constructive, I settled at the bar and yawned my way through a mound of additional information Uncle Joe had sent on the ins and outs of establishing a private foundation to help women in need. His scribbles in the margins of several documents included numerous heavy underlines and exclamation points. He still wasn't sold on the proposed venture.

A musical trill broke my train of thought. I unfolded my cell phone and pressed it to my ear. "Hello. Billie Quinn speaking."

"Johnny Sugsby here. Private investigator. You called?" His voice was bass, hoarse, and all business.

With his heavy breathing as background, I laid out the information I needed. When I finished, there was silence and a rhythmic tap-tap of a pencil or pen against, I guessed, his desktop.

"Okay, let's see if I got this straight from talking to you and the guy who called me—Carl." He cleared some gravel out of his throat. "You want to know all I can find out about the subject, April Wade, who went to UT, maybe freshman through junior years. Maybe sometime in the past four years. You want to know where she lived in Knoxville, in addition to a home address, and the names of her parents. Got it so far?"

"You're on the mark. Go on."

"You'll fax me a photograph of the subject for checking out with Garmon Studio, a local business. Is the young woman in the photo identified as April Wade in Garmon's records? If so, who paid the bill? And you want to know if local records or newspaper obituaries show her as a murder victim—either in Knoxville or elsewhere. Anything more?"

"You got it." Johnny Sugsby's listening skills impressed me, and I hoped his investigative skills matched them.

"I charge one fifty an hour, four hours minimum." He delivered this news in a monotone, making me think this might be an overcharge.

"Fair enough." I wasn't in the mood to nitpick. "I'll overnight you a cashier's check as a retainer. And if you can answer all the questions in forty-eight hours or less, there's a five hundred dollar bonus."

He coughed up some gravel. "I got other cases, lady. But ain't nothing like a bet to spice up life a little." He cut off without a goodbye.

I was in the middle of dressing for the second trip to Athens in two days. The thought made me grimace. When the phone rang, I considered not answering until I saw the call was from Pam.

"Hi. What's up?" I buttoned my jeans and reached for an electric blue T-shirt.

"Guess what?" Papers rustled in the background. "Your dream of helping women who've fallen on bad times— I'd really like to help, Billie, but, according to the mountain of info Joe sent me, you can't directly transfer significant dollars from your personal assets to an individual, at least not as a private foundation. I had to plow through a lot of legal mumbo-jumbo to find that choice tidbit."

"I know. Uncle Joe says a 403(b) organization would have to be the go-between. That means a board of directors and other trappings I want to avoid."

"That's my take." Pam's voice relaxed. "Sorry to unhorse your Robin Hood dream, Billie."

"I'm not giving up. There has to be a way."

"Good luck," Pam said. "In the meantime, I'm sticking with my day job."

I left Madge a note taped to the fridge: "Off to Athens on errands. Back for H hour." One of the errands had been percolating since the day I'd visited the sniper's hideout. In a paper sack I packed a peanut butter sandwich and a banana to eat on the road.

At the bank, I held the door open for a white-haired woman using a walker. Her humped back announced osteoporosis. I said a silent prayer of thanks for scans that always showed my bones were strong. I decided not to smile at the teller, just in case my teeth were encased in the brown residue of peanut butter. I took the cashier's check to the post office and mailed it overnight to Detective Sugsby.

That task out of the way, I focused on the mission at the top of my list. I turned off Alps road onto the Atlanta highway and headed west. Short of reaching the mall, I entered the parking lot of Academy Sports and Outdoors, impressed, as always, with the enormity of the building. Cool air enveloped me as I pushed through the front door and walked several hundred feet to the rear of the store, where all manner of guns, rifles, and accessories were sold.

I hung back as a balding salesman explained what made for the price difference between two shotguns lying side by side on the counter. The prospective buyer, a young, squat guy wearing shorts, grungy sneakers, and a loose gray T-shirt, hefted one of the guns, turned sideways, and pressed the butt to his shoulder.

"Nice feel, huh?" The salesman propped his elbows on the counter and leaned forward.

"Yeah." The young man shook his head and handed the gun to the salesman. "But I can't buy today."

And maybe not for many days, I thought.

The salesman shrugged. "Sure. Come back when you're ready." He turned and placed the shotguns on their roosts on a wall behind him.

With his back to me, I saw a bald spot on top of his head and suntanned crinkles on his neck. He turned around to find me bellied up to the counter.

"You here to buy a gun?" He cocked his head. A slight smile tugged at his lips.

"No, and I'll step aside if a live customer shows up. If you're willing, I'm here to pick your brain about murder. Murder by sniper fire to be specific."

He pressed his hands, palms down, on the counter and spread sausage fingers. "You a cop?"

"No. I knew the victim, Jake Wade. He worked for me, and I'm trying to locate his family."

"Was this the shooting in Creeks County, at the Habitat site? I read about that."

"That's it. Will you help me?"

"Damn right." He stuck his hand out, and I shook it. "I'm a hunter. Been around guns all my life. Just don't believe in using them against people, unless, of course, it's war. I'm Bob."

"Billie Quinn. I've got some questions that will surely reveal my ignorance about how Jake Wade was killed."

"Okay, shoot." Bob laughed. "No pun intended."

I set the scene, describing how Jake had been standing on the house's top plate and how the shot had come from a pine grove across a hay field, a distance the length of a football field and a half.

"Given what I've told you, how do you think the sniper pulled this off?" I asked.

"Hummm." Bob tugged on his chin. "You said there was no sign of a tree stand. To me this means he either shot from the ground or maybe stretched out on the bed of a pickup. Either way, he probably used a bipod to keep a steady aim from that distance."

"What's a bipod?" I tried not to envision a critter with two toes.

Bob reached under the counter and came up with a two-legged gizmo with a notch at the top. He removed a rifle from display on the wall and placed the rifle's stock in the notch.

"Bingo. Takes most of the shake out of sighting a rifle. Another trick is to exhale a deep breath and while the lungs are empty sight and pull the trigger."

"Does this mean the shooter was trained as a sniper? Maybe in the military?"

"Anything's possible." Bob took the rifle out of the cradle and laid it lengthwise on the counter. "But on a good day, it's a shot I could make, Billie. Got antlers and witnesses to prove it. Difference is, I'm a sharpshooter, not a sniper."

"Would that hold true for the guys you hunt with?"

Bob's expression clouded. "Well, I guess that did sound like bragging. Sure, a couple of my buddies could make a long distance kill, and so could a lot of guys in this neck of the woods. We practice a lot off season."

"I'm disappointed but not surprised. I was hoping the pool of suspects would be limited to one or two well-known local marksmen."

"Well, you can rule out any guys who're afflicted with Parkinson's." Bob laughed.

"Very funny," I said.

"Hey, Bob." A slender black man wearing a burgundy polo shirt emblazoned with the Academy's logo appeared at the counter to my right. He turned to me. "Sorry to interrupt, ma'am."

"Hi, Jamal." Bob slapped hands with his colleague.

"That special shipment you been looking for. It's here, man."

Bob waved acknowledgement as Jamal walked away.

"Where were we?" Bob asked.

"I was about to ask you a really burning question."

"Fire away. Oops! No pun intended."

"How could the sniper be sure he killed Jake since Jake fell off the house and landed behind a stack of lumber?"

"That one's easy. Probably the same way I know if I've killed a deer that bolts after being shot."

He motioned for me to follow him to an adjoining display counter, where be plucked camouflage-painted binoculars off a shelf and gingerly set them on the counter.

"A seasoned hunter is never far from a good pair of field glasses. Sometimes, I pull the trigger, and a deer drops like a rock. Other times, the deer leaps out of sight and drops a little ways away. Of course, you have to walk up on the deer to know if it's as dead as it looked through the glasses."

I stared at the binoculars before lifting them to my eyes and turning around to face the open expanse of the store. I focused on a distant mannequin clad in slacks, T-shirt, and wide-brimmed sunhat. A portion of the hat filled my field of vision. The nub on the canvas was clear, as were the jagged edges of a small chip in the mannequin's face. I turned around and set the binoculars on the counter.

"Wow! Even if the sniper couldn't see Jake's body, he'd have a pretty good idea he'd succeeded by the way all of us reacted. It was horrible."

"Yeah. But how do you know exactly what the shooter could see from that far away unless you run a test yourself?" Bob pushed the binoculars toward me.

"You're right." I extracted my credit card from my wallet, and Bob rang up the sale.

He returned my card on top of his business card.

"Any more questions, call me. Helps pass the time during the week. Most of my sales are on the weekend."

"Thanks." I turned to leave but stopped when Bob spoke.

"Don't forget, Billie, the shooter got there and left in a vehicle. Bet my paycheck it was a truck. You could narrow the search if you follow that trail."

Goosebumps rose on the back of my neck, remembering what the farmer had said when I was at the sniper's site. His grandson had spotted a truck that drove up and down the road before the kid lost interest in it. And the marina manager had told me of a truck that drove slowly into the parking area on the afternoon of the night someone tried to break into my boat. Both were described as being painted in camouflage patterns.

Happy hour that evening was actually grouch hour, so I kept to myself what I'd learned at the sporting goods store. Madge and Carl were in the midst of one of their infrequent spats. Carl's modus operandi was to park on the couch, TV remote in hand, headphones glued to his ears.

Madge's and my responses were predictable; we'd practiced them during previous spats. I watched as she leaned toward Carl, lifted an earphone and shouted into his ear. "We can't hear the TV, you lunk head. That's not very considerate. Unplug the damned things."

Following the script, Carl said, "Billie, is it okay if I listen to TV in private? You and Madge can look at the kitchen TV."

I came back with my standard line: "Fine." I ignored Madge's scowl.

On numerous occasions, Pam and Uncle Joe had chided me for tolerating what they called Carl's "insubordination." Admittedly, sometimes I lost patience with his passive aggressive style; however, in a strange way, his questioning of my motives and actions tended to center me.

The only thing that enlivened the dinner hour was Hank's unannounced arrival. He whizzed in on a cloud of great-smelling aftershave lotion, refused food, and poured a glass of wine. He pulled a chair to the table beside me and looked around at each of us.

"God, this is a glum scene. You must have already talked about it," he said.

"It what?" I asked.

"The little article on page four of today's paper."

"I hope somebody who really needs it won the mega jackpot," Madge said.

"Somebody we know got busted for meth production," Carl said.

"Nope and nope."

I held my hands up. "We give up."

"Jake was cremated today."

Cremated jumped out of Hank's mouth and lodged in my throat. Jake—reduced to crumbly, gray matter, his DNA up the crematory chimney. I excused myself without finishing my perfectly grilled London broil. I stretched out on my bed and listened to muffled conversation. After some thirty minutes, I heard the fore door open and close. I waited a few more minutes before I tiptoed down the hall far enough to see that the kitchen and living room were empty.

"It's up to you, Johnny Sugsby," I whispered. "Give me Jake's real name and identify someone somewhere that I can deliver his ashes to. Is that too much to ask?"

Chapter 18

As Johnny Sugsby and I had agreed to in our initial telephone contact, he vibrated my cell phone on Thursday in hour forty-six of his forty-eight-hour window to earn an extra five hundred dollars. Madge was out shopping. Carl and I settled at the bar and listened to Sugsby's report on conference call mode.

"An April Wade was enrolled in the University of Tennessee freshmen through junior years. She failed to return for senior year. If the university was advised of her death, my source was unwilling to verify. Her permanent residence was listed as Daytona Beach, Florida, the address of her parents, Tony and Sylvia Wade."

Zing! There it was, the answer I'd coveted. Relayed in a rough voice by someone who had no inkling what this meant to me. My heartbeat quickened, as I saluted Carl with a V for victory. Silently, I mouthed the new name—Tony Wade, Tony Wade, Tony Wade. Carl smiled, in spite of himself, I suspected.

"Great work, Sugsby," I said. "What else do you have?"

"I'm getting to that. I took the name April Wade and the photo you faxed me to Garmon Studio. The receptionist, a single mother of two, was minding the store and wasn't going to help at first. But she turned cooperative on receipt of a fifty-dollar token of your affection, Ms. Quinn." He hesitated, as if expecting me to laugh.

"Go on." I spoke in a flat tone, hoping to discourage any further sit-down comedy.

"To wit, I compared a negative in Gaston's file with the photo, and they're a perfect match. This established that the young woman in the photo and the young woman who attended UT are one and same April Wade. However, I found no evidence that this young woman was murdered in Knoxville." He cleared the gravel in his throat. "That's about it. I'll fax a written report with a few more details when you pay the final bill."

"Hold on just a second, please." I put the call on mute. My heart was thumping. "You satisfied, Carl?"

He shrugged. "It's not me who's busted butt to get satisfaction. You got what you wanted—Jake's real name and, to boot, the names of his wife and daughter. Be happy."

I stuck my tongue out at Carl and took the call off mute. "Good work, Mr. Sugsby."

"Sugsby Detective Agency's motto is *We Deliver the Goods Accurately and Discreetly.*"

"Oh, I do have one more question," I said.

"Sure. What?"

"How did you know the receptionist was a single mother of two?"

"Easy. I asked about a photo on her desk, and she dumped. You know, to establish some rapport. All part of the job."

"Uh huh," I said, wondering if the word "rapport" was taught in detective school. "Fax the bill and check your overnight mail for payment."

"Bingo!" I cradled the phone, slid off of the bar stool, and did an end zone dance. "Jake Wade is *Tony Wade*. I wonder why he chose *Jake* as an alias? Not that I care."

Carl shook his head. "I have to hand it to you, Billie. You may have outfoxed the law."

The last statement jolted me. "I have to share this with the sheriff, don't I?"

"What do you think?"

"I think Sylvia Wade deserves to receive her husband's ashes from someone other than Sheriff Farr's rep."

Carl stood and stuck his hands deep in his pants pockets. "Proof again that you don't really care what

I think." He stomped out, at least as readily as his stiff leg would let him stomp.

Carl's pique was difficult to decipher. He had committed himself to helping me identify Jake Wade; yet, in our moment of triumph, he exuded no elation. I was disappointed but not deterred. I grabbed my purse and car keys and headed for the coroner's office.

Parking spaces in front of the funeral home were scarce, indicating that visiting hours were on for someone with an abundance of family and friends. I opened the back door and almost slammed a short woman stuffed into a black pants suit. When I announced my business, she escorted me to Albert Riggs's office. He looked up from a pile of deskwork and motioned me to sit down in the same cushioned chair I'd sat in on my first visit.

"I must finish something," he said. "So hold your horses, please, my dear."

He focused on a sheaf of papers in a file folder, scanning pages and turning them over in a stack to the side of the folder. Occasionally, he stopped and scribbled notes on a yellow legal pad.

I used the time to scope out the office. I counted the small vase-shaped and chest-shaped containers on several bookshelves and on a card table nestled into a corner of the cluttered office. Eight. One probably held Jake's, uh, Tony's cremains. I couldn't imagine the vital man I'd known crammed into such a small space.

Riggs tapped the papers into a neat rectangle, leaning sideways to speak. "Ready with the notes, Missy."

I expected the lady in black. Instead, an angular, gray-haired woman walked in with her pelvis thrust forward. She looked to be in her late sixties. Taking the folder, she smiled at Riggs and ignored me. The door clicked shut behind her.

"I've been expecting you, Billie. You must have seen the notice that your friend Jake was cremated."

"I did. And I'm wondering if it's too early to ask for custody of his remains."

Riggs studied me over half-glasses. "I'm inclined to wait longer. If or when next of kin appear, and this does happen, I can often answer questions they have about the death. And," he added in a conspiratorial tone, "there is personal satisfaction in releasing remains to a loved one."

A surge of anxiety gripped me. I wanted to be the one to reunite Tony Wade with his widow. What tack could I use short of confessing that I'd learned Jake's true identity? I searched through jumbled thoughts, trying to order them in a winning sequence.

"Alfred…" My mind went blank.

He tilted his head and waited. A wisp of gray hair curled on his balding head.

"Alfred, I'm having trouble sleeping. I hired Jake Wade for what should have been a safe job—working on a Habitat house. Now he's dead and cremated to boot. I feel responsible. And, if you'll forgive me, Alfred, I can honor Jake's ashes better than you can with your limited space." I glanced around the cluttered office and held my breath.

Riggs lowered his head. A frown creased his forehead. He leaned back in a rickety old wooden chair that snapped, crackled, and popped. He closed his eyes for a good two minutes before he returned the chair to upright. He opened his eyes, rubbed them, and focused again on me.

"You don't think much of my office do you?"

Damn! I had come across as too critical.

"I don't think I expressed myself too well." I forced a smile. "You're doing a great job, taking care of all these remains. It's just that I owe Jake a special resting place with me for however long it takes to find a loved one. It's the least I can do."

Riggs sighed. "You're right, you know. This office is a mess. But I can't forget the stories sealed in every container in here. See that one on the second book shelf near the elephant sculpture?"

I nodded.

"That, my dear, is an unidentified white male, a teenager. His body—a little flesh but mostly bones—was found in the trunk of a wrecked car in a vehicle graveyard. He'd been in that trunk a long time. A forensic artist used his skull to model what he might have looked like, but no one recognized the image. Nice looking youngster. He's kept me company for seven years. I call him Thomas."

That's that. I resigned myself to walking out empty-handed. I pushed my chair back and was halfway standing when Alfred motioned for me to sit down again. He opened his center desk drawer, removed a single sheet of paper, and shoved it and a pen across the desk.

"Fill this out. Every line. Sign it. Then you can take Jake home with you."

While I filled in the form's blanks, Riggs walked to the card table, removed a gray, plastic container, and returned with it to his desk. I handed him the form.

"Good enough," he said, without reviewing anything I'd written. He walked me to his office door and handed the container to me.

The weight of Tony Wade's cremains didn't surprise me. My thoughts flashed back to the rainy afternoon I'd come home with two ceramic urns containing the remains of my parents. I had set the urns on kitchen workspace and opened them. I'd studied the plastic bags nestled in each urn and cried tears I hadn't cried at their memorial service. Ten soggy tissues later, I'd fished in the plastic bags and came out with Paul in my right hand and Nina in my left. The heft of their ashes surprised me. I'd pulled the remains of my parents to my chest and sobbed.

Alfred cocked his head at me. "Are you okay, Billie?"

I swallowed hard and nodded. "I'm okay. Thanks for entrusting me with—Ton—uh, Jake. I'll take good care of him."

I'd almost said Tony, but Albert showed no reaction. A guilt pang stabbed me. I'd convinced the coroner to relinquish ashes he thought belonged to a man using the alias Jake Wade. What would he think of me when he learned that I'd withheld information he needed in his job? I might have spilled the truth to him but feared the info would leak back to the sheriff. After all, Albert was the one who'd told me to beware of sharing information. I know a rationalization when I concoct one, but I left it at that and hurried to my car.

Chapter 19

Friday morning, I crossed my fingers, wondering if Carl would come to work with Madge since he had stomped out on me the previous afternoon. Usually, but not always, his moods blew over rapidly, and we'd return to semi-civility with no acknowledgement on his part that anything had ever been amiss.

At eight o'clock on the dot, Madge pushed through the door and closed it behind her. Damp hair clung to her head like a skullcap, suggesting she'd recently showered or had stuck her head under a faucet somewhere. I saw Carl, behind her, stop short of the door and stare at his feet or the decking or both.

"Morning." Madge smiled broadly. "Did you remember to pull the sheets off your bed?"

"Yep. What's up with Carl?"

"Well, if I may use a colorful word, he's working through being pissed at you. I told him to grow up and quit trying to control you."

I watched Carl take a step toward the door and stop again. "I have to tell you, Madge, I wonder if Carl will ever feel comfortable with me. And if he can't, the three of us will never make a team. Frankly, Uncle Joe wonders why I put up with his attitude."

Madge's face crumpled, and she slumped against the bar. "Oh, Billie, you've been so patient with Carl. Please, don't give up yet. He won't let me tell you, but there is a good reason he acts like a shit ass with you."

I was surprised, but before I could press Madge for more information, the doorknob turned, and Carl stepped into the living room. He looked from Madge to me and back to Madge. "If this is girl talk, I guess you don't need me."

"Oh, give it a rest, honey." Madge tipped her head back and rolled her eyes. "Anything you need, Billie, before I put the sheets in the washing machine and head out on errands?"

"No, thanks. But keep your cell phone on, in case I think of something."

"Will do." She shot me a pleading look before heading down the hall toward my bedroom.

"And the plan for me?" Carl asked. "I'm not good at twiddling my thumbs."

"First, I'll call the Daytona Beach number I got from long distance information and verify it still belongs to Sylvia Wade. You'll listen with me. Four ears are better than two."

Carl hoisted himself onto a barstool and swiveled toward me. "This should be good."

I punched in the telephone number and activated speakerphone. On the fifth ring, a feminine voice answered.

"Sylvia Wade?" I asked.

"Yes. Who is this?" The voice was soft and slightly husky.

I disconnected quickly and set the phone in its charger. I wasn't at all sure of how to proceed.

Carl's laugh was abrupt and rough. "Now what?"

"Now I have a next of kin to deliver the ashes to."

"Let's see. You'll ring the doorbell, Sylvia will answer, and you'll hold out the ashes and say, 'This is your husband, Tony'."

"Very funny. Don't be sarcastic."

"Then we're back to now what?"

"I'm thinking."

"While you're doing that, I'll shop for the pantry." Madge walked past me and slung her purse onto a shoulder. "The sheets are washing. See you later."

"You sure you don't need me?" Carl used a plaintive voice.

"Stick it out, Carl." The door clicked shut behind her.

Carl settled on the couch, turned on TV, and donned the earphones. I decided to walk my way to more clarity about how to approach Sylvia. I paced the hallway from the kitchen to the aft deck. Back and forth, back and forth. On the sixth trip, I stepped out on the deck and breathed morning stillness. I looked past other houseboats to dimpled lake water that spilled over the horizon. At a distance, two personal watercrafts zigged and zagged around each other like hummingbirds guarding their territory. Back in the living room, I sat on the ottoman beside Carl's outstretched legs. I motioned for him to remove the earphones.

"What?" Carl dropped the earphones around his neck but continued to watch TV.

"How's this for a plan, Mr. Grumpy." I waited for him to look at me. "I'll call Sylvia's number and ask to speak to Jake—uh, Tony. Whatever she says, I'll build on until a clearer picture emerges of their relationship and her knowledge of what her husband has been up to. I won't tell her he's dead on this phone call. Just thank her and hang up."

Carl slid his legs off the ottoman and rubbed his bad knee. "Worth a try, if you're determined to get in over your head. And I see no evidence to the contrary."

We took our regular places at the bar, and I punched in Sylvia's number after selecting speaker-phone mode. After four rings, a woman said hello, the same woman I had hung up on within the hour. Her voice was soft, almost indistinct. I pressed the phone closer to my ear.

"Good afternoon. I'm trying to reach Tony Wade. I hope this is the correct number."

Silence. A long silence. No sound of breathing. No sign of life on her end.

"Who is this? What do you want with Tony? I'm his wife." The voice remained gentle, but a tone of suspicion was detectable.

"My name is Billie Quinn. I'm a friend of Tony's."

More silence during which I heard the unmistakable sound of ice cubes sloshing around in liquid. Then I heard her swallow. Was she drinking a Coke or tea or something stronger? Something stronger could explain the indistinct voice.

"Tony isn't here. Hasn't been for nearly a year. And I haven't heard from him in three months. Have you seen him? Is he all right?" I thought of the box of ashes and crossed my fingers. I'd have to stretch the truth, even lie, unless I just blurted the facts.

"I met him in North Georgia, where I live."

"I've been so worried, Betty."

"Billie," I corrected. "I'm sorry, Sylvia. The last time I saw Tony, he was living in a motel, not that I visited him there," I hastened to add. "But he's not there anymore."

She swirled ice cubes in my ear, thinking and assessing, I assumed. I waited.

"How did you know how to find me? Did Tony tell you about me?"

My mind slipped back to the dog-eared snapshot of the woman with long, black hair standing with a slightly bow-legged young girl. A palm tree behind them divided the picture in half, a little of the trunk growing out of each of their heads. I had always assumed that the husband and father had snapped the picture.

I closed my eyes before taking the plunge. "I found you through your daughter, April. University of Tennessee records identified you and Tony as her parents."

Carl's eyes widened, and he waved a hand at me to signal slow down or stop.

Sylvia gasped. "My daughter is dead. Murdered. What right have you to invade her privacy, our grief?" Her words were now slurred.

"Forgive me," I said. "I imagine your memories of April are still very painful. However, what I want to return to you, among other things, is a portrait of April and a photo of you and April. They were dear to Tony."

"Wait... Something's not right." Her voice was stronger, not so gentle. "Now you're talking about my husband in the past tense. And what are the other things you want to return?"

I hesitated. Carl shrugged his shoulders. So much for my plan not to reveal all on this first phone call. It was now or never. "His personal belongings. I'd like to fly to Daytona Beach as soon as possible. I have something you deserve to receive from someone who knew Tony and admired him."

"Oh, my God! He's dead, isn't he?" Sylvia sobbed the way she spoke—softly.

I waited for her to regain composure. A cramp grabbed my left foot; I slid off the bar stool and stood flatfooted. The cramp tightened. I raised and lowered both heels several times. The cramp subsided. Carl looked on with a half-smile.

"Sylvia…" I waited.

"Yes, I'm here, Billie. It's just such a shock. How did Tony die? I need to get him home for a proper burial." She blew her nose and hiccupped.

"I'd like to fly there on Monday, visit with you, give you all the details. Is this okay with you?"

"Yes, yes. I'll be waiting."

"And, Sylvia, I'll be bringing Tony home for a proper burial. He was cremated."

In the middle of another gasp from Sylvia, I cut the connection. My heart pounded.

"Coward," Carl said.

Chapter 20

Something buzzed from across the room. A bee? Why would a bee be in my bedroom? I opened one eye and squinted at the clock on the chest of drawers. Damn! The buzz was my second, backup alarm. I groaned and stretched to turn on the bedside light.

I was running late, so a decent breakfast was no option. I dressed in my usual Habitat work clothes, grabbed a banana, and, on impulse, slipped the binoculars I'd bought at Academy into a small boat bag loaded with my sun hat and sunscreen. I eased the Prius through the usual Saturday morning lake traffic, a good portion of which seemed to have detoured by the Golden Pantry that I pulled up to.

The line in front of me at the register included a young woman dressed in shorts that exposed her navel and barely covered her crotch, a middle-aged man in shorts to his knees and a T-shirt emblazoned with a NASCAR scene, and a male teenager moving to music that was piped into his brain via ear buds. I paid for two bags of ice, dumped them into coolers in my trunk, and nestled eighteen bottles of water in the frosty beds.

I challenged the speed limit all the way to the building site. Turning into the gravel driveway, I was chagrined to see that everyone had arrived before me. I parked in a tight space between DW's SUV and Pete's old pickup. Off by itself near the picnic tables was a new, jacked-up Ford truck with a small flat- bed trailer attached. Bernie was nearby, fiddling with a large grill that must have been on the trailer. After setting the coolers on the ground within sight of Bernie, I buckled my hammer holster around my waist and headed for the loose circle of people waving to me.

"Well, thank the Lord," Ruby said. "Sam and me was getting worried."

"Sorry I'm late." My cheeks felt hot.

"Too much fun last night?" Pete twirled an imaginary moustache.

"Yeah, I bet it was boot-scooting kind of fun." Neal drawled the words.

DW laughed. "Okay, let's cut the lady some slack." He adjusted a worn leather tool belt that hung loosely on his slim hips.

Bernie joined us, and DW formed a tighter circle before reviewing an action plan for the morning:

the men would work together to attach and stabilize the roof trusses; I would review the house plans with Ruby, reminding her of room layout, so that she could think about furniture and double-check decisions she and Sam had made regarding paint colors. Bernie and Dawn would prepare lunch, and Ruby would help if she and I finished early with the plans.

"Okay, gang, let's do it." DW started high-fives around the circle. "We'll take a morning break around ten o'clock. Bernie, you whistle us up."

"What about a prayer?" Sam asked.

Technically, he was correct. Habitat for Humanity recommended beginning the workday with prayer; however, I'd been lax in meeting the standard because Jake had refused to cooperate. Not in a nasty way. He'd simply walked off after he outlined the day's work, leaving Sam and Ruby to pray on their own.

"Sure, Sam. Go ahead," I said.

No ball caps came off, but we lowered our heads. Bernie stood next to me. Out of the corner of my eye, I saw him glance at his wristwatch.

"Lord God," Sam said. "Thank You for helping me and Ruby get a new house. Thanks for the good folk here this morning, helping with our dream. Keep all of us safe in our work today. And thanks, Lord, for the life of Mr. Jake, who's in Your keeping now. In Jesus' name, amen."

As Bernie turned to walk back to the cooking area, I asked if he'd noticed the coolers of water I'd left near the grill. He answered with a grunt.

"I'll find a shady spot for our meeting," Ruby said.

"Great. I'll join you in a minute, after I check out something."

To satisfy my curiosity, I walked to the house, stood to the side out of the way, and observed the procedure for installing the trusses. My doubts that only four men could handle the task were dispelled quickly. Sam and Neal worked with separate ropes. I watched them knot a rope around each end of a truss, and then toss the loose ends of the ropes to DW and Pete who stood, perfectly balanced, on wall plates opposite each other. Hand over hand, DW and Pete hoisted the truss and lowered it to lie flat on top of the walls. Still in synch, they dragged the truss into place next to the last truss that had been attached and stabilized. One at a time, the trusses would be installed, from the back to the front of the house.

I looked around and spotted Ruby sitting on a picnic bench under the big oak. On the walk to join her, I unbuttoned my work shirt and flapped it to fan my torso.

"Whew! Ain't it so," Ruby said. "Where's a breeze when we need it?" We sat side by side, the house plan spread on our knees. She confirmed previous decisions that I had documented in scribbles on the edge of the plan. Vinyl floors everywhere except for carpet in the bedrooms. No change in paint colors she and Sam had chosen: goldenrod walls in the kitchen and bathroom and light green walls in the living room and bedrooms.

"Did I ever tell you, Ruby," I said, "that the doors are extra-wide? If you or Sam ever become disabled, you can still get around in a wheelchair."

She smiled. "Lord willing, we won't need a wheelchair." She studied the plans again for a few minutes and then looked up. "And tell me again how big the house is, Miz Billie."

"Eleven hundred square feet." It sounded meager to me, but I smiled.

"Eleven hundred square feet." Ruby repeated the magic number with a wide smile.

A shrill whistle caught us by surprise. We looked up and saw Bernie waving us toward the picnic tables. I watched DW and Pete climb down from the lip of the house. Four more trusses jutted skyward, like the orderly ribs of an upturned boat hull.

"Look how good Mr. DW and Pete work together. It's gonna be a roof sure enough." Ruby clapped her hands.

I smiled at her childlike amazement. "Yep. A roof that won't leak like the one you and Sam are living under now. That's a promise."

I rolled the house plan into a cylinder and secured it with a rubber band. Ruby volunteered to put it in my car on her way to the porta-potty. I made a beeline for the picnic tables. Bernie and Dawn had set several thermoses of coffee and a box of mixed-flavor donuts in the center of the longest table. Choosing a cinnamon donut, I stood a little to the side and sipped on coffee strong enough to cauterize a stomach ulcer. I waited for DW and Dawn, holding Tim, to sit down at the table and then quickly slipped into place across from them. My goal was to learn more about them, as I'd noticed that neither was big on small talk.

"You guys been married long?" I looked from DW to Dawn.

"Six months the first of August." Dawn smiled and revealed white, slightly irregular teeth. She held her ring finger out for me to admire a modest diamond.

Tim squirmed and gurgled. Dawn bounced him on her knee. He looked to me—no real judge of a baby's age—to be at least nine months old. This was another example of the conception to marriage gap that set Uncle Joe and Irene to tsk-tsking.

"Did you have a fun honeymoon?" I addressed the question to DW who seemed distracted.

"Not then." Dawn jumped in with the answer. "But in the spring, I won a contest, a ten day Caribbean cruise that left out of Miami. DW took some extra time off. We just got back two weeks ago. My sister kept Tim, bless her."

DW's smile was tight. "It was great," he said. "But I'll probably have to work extra shifts for five years. Sheriff Farr will bend some, and that's good for morale. But, in the end, he makes sure the department isn't shortchanged." DW looked at his wristwatch and glanced around the table. Everyone was still eating.

Neal waved his fork in the air and muttered, "Damn fly! Go get your own donut." Laughter rolled around the table.

"I'm curious, DW, How did you get involved in law enforcement?"

"Ask me another time." He stood and hitched his jeans and tool belt higher on his hips. "Time to go back to work, folks. Be sure to drink lots of water. We'll be working in Hades soon, unless the sun decides to set in the next thirty minutes."

After DW saw that everyone was in motion, he turned back to me. "Did you and Ruby finish reviewing the plans?"

"Yep. I think I'll use my slack time before lunch to check on something over there where the sniper fired from." I pointed across the hay field.

I wasn't prepared for DW's reaction. Rather than looking where I pointed, he locked eyes with me and glared. "What the hell for? We didn't find any evidence, and neither did the GBI. One measly tire track was so smooth we figured the shooter put worn-out tires on whatever he was driving just to throw us off."

I flared at DW's tone of voice. "Not that it's any of your business, I'm interested in seeing what the sniper could see from there if he used binoculars."

Sam and Ruby had gone to check on the inside of their house, but Pete, Neal, and Bernie stood together staring at us.

DW hesitated. Tim whimpered, and Dawn rocked him faster on her knee. "And what exactly do you think the sniper saw that would interest you?" His tone was softer.

"Maybe I'll share that info with you if my binocular experiment proves anything. Call me on my cell phone if you need me."

"You're the boss. Let's go, guys." DW marched toward the house with Pete and Neal in tow.

Bernie cleared his throat. "Not sure what you're looking for, but I'd be glad to go with you. Dawn can handle what little bit of cleanup there is from the break. I would have to get back in time to cook, though."

"Thanks but no thanks." Bernie looked so uncomfortable that I smiled and patted him on the shoulder. "Chalk it up to the way I shop for clothes. When a sales clerk offers to help me, I say, *No thanks. I'll know it when I see it.*"

Chapter 21

I smothered the urge to stomp on the accelerator and spin out of the driveway. Instead, I pulled onto the dirt road slowly. In case DW was watching, he wouldn't have the satisfaction of knowing that he had pushed my anger button. I was puzzled. Why had he overreacted when I said that I wanted to take time out from work to visit the sniper's lair? Was he pissed that I wasn't satisfied with official findings? Or was it a need to control, a character flaw I hadn't spotted until that moment?

I followed the dirt road that ran parallel to the hay field and pulled onto the shoulder of the road, not far from where I had parked on my first visit to the sniper's hiding place. After popping the trunk lid, I fished in the storage net for the binoculars. They hung like a stone around my neck. I closed the trunk, jumped a narrow ditch, and stopped at the edge of a stand of pine trees. I glanced quickly at the farmhouse down the road. Mr. Polk's red pickup was in the carport, but there was no sign of activity around the house. Good. With luck, I wouldn't have to contend with him again and apologize the second time for trespassing.

Thirty or forty feet into the orderly rows of half-grown pine trees, I emerged into a small clearing, the sniper's lair, a spooky time capsule. Nothing had changed since my first visit, except that the crime scene tape had blown into a prickly bush. Pine needles crunched underfoot, and sunlight filtered through the canopy, depositing ragged patches of gold throughout the opening. Goose bumps paraded on my sweaty arms.

I turned and looked across the flat, parched hay field. The Habitat site was clearly visible, although it reminded me of inspecting an ant farm. Even without the binoculars, DW's lime green T-shirt was visible where he balanced on the lip of the house. What I needed to establish, however, was what the sniper could see after he shot Tony, assuming that he'd wanted some assurance his target was dead.

After stretching full-length on the ground, I balanced on my elbows and pressed the binoculars to my eyes. Broken pine needles pricked my bare skin. My field of vision filled with an enlarged picture of the Habitat site. Slowly, I swept the binoculars along the bottom half of the scene, taking in the driveway entrance, the lower half of the house, and the parking area. I hadn't expected to see so much detail. Sam and Ruby's Caddy, Pete's truck, and Neal's motorcycle came into sharp focus. Pete was parked approximately where Tony Wade's truck had been parked. My heart rate spiked.

I scrambled to my feet and again swept the binoculars over the Habitat scene. I lowered the glasses on the neck strap and brushed pine needle residue off my arms and the front of my jeans. There was no doubt that the sniper, using binoculars, could have assumed, from our squeamish physical reactions, that Tony was probably dead. A new thought centered on the likelihood that the killer saw Pete rummage in Tony's truck and come out with an object that he then stashed in his truck. Could the object have been identified at long distance as the cash box Pete later delivered to me? Possibly, but nothing to bet on.

I heard pine straw crunch behind me and wheeled to the sound. Mr. Polk held up his hands in defensive mode. He was a carbon copy of himself on my first visit—faded overalls, straw hat, and low-cut boots.

"Whoa, lady! Don't panic." He pushed the battered straw hat back on his head, leaving bushy gray eyebrows cocked over eyes opened wide.

"Sorry, Mr. Polk. You scared me," I said. "Looks like you caught me trespassing again." I wanted to ask him if he did anything other than watch 24/7 for people to pull off the road and step onto his property.

"Yeah. You got that right. But what brought you back, lady? Like I told you that other time, the sheriff and GBI picked this place clean. Didn't find nothing important, neither." His tone was wary but non-threatening.

Embarrassed, I reverted to what I'd told him on the first visit. "It's not much of an excuse, but I feel really guilty about a man I employed being killed in front of me. And he was shot from this spot."

"Yeah, that's what you said before, but that don't explain what you're doing here, right now, today." He emphasized the last few words by punching a forefinger into an open palm.

I held up the binoculars. "I wanted to see what the sniper could see that day."

Mr. Polk scratched his chin. "Just being nosey, then? Trying to find out something the law won't tell you?"

The silence between us grew, as I pondered how to answer the questions. The simplest course would be to agree with his conclusions, yet a voice in the back of my head nudged me in another direction. "Actually, I've been investigating and now know the true identity of the man who was murdered. He used an alias. I think his family deserves to know what happened to him. Frankly, I think the sheriff and GBI have washed their hands of the whole mystery."

The quizzical expression on Mr. Polk's face instantly morphed into a hardened mask. His eyebrows bunched in a straight, gray line over squinted eyes. I thought I'd lost any sympathy he might have developed for me.

"I hear you, lady. My daughter disappeared two years ago. Left behind that grandson I mentioned before. You know, Aaron. The law played around a few months at finding her, then come and stood flat-footed in the kitchen. Told me and the wife that our daughter just walked off of her own free will. Her own free will, my butt. Something bad happened to her, mark my words, and we still don't know. She wouldn't leave Aaron. He's smart but what the teachers call challenged. The boy needed his mama. Still needs her."

Mr. Polk's emotional eruption wound down as quickly as it started. He took his hat off and rubbed a hand through a mop of damp hair that matched his eyebrows.

"You and your wife are raising Aaron?" I asked.

"Yeah, till the daughter comes home." He studied my face for a few seconds. "You really think you can outfox the law, maybe find the killer before they do?"

"Locating his family came first," I said. "But, you're right, I do have an itch to find his killer. Do you know anything that could help me?"

Polk hooked his thumbs in the side pockets of his overalls and studied me. I kept my gaze locked with his until I could no longer ignore a ticklish sensation on my forearm. Looking down, I saw a black tick inching north. I brushed the icky thing off and stepped backward.

Polk smiled. "Better check your skin good tonight, missy. You might find you took home some of that tick's family."

"Thanks. I will." I returned his smile. "Have you thought of anything that might help me, Mr. Polk? I'd really appreciate whatever you can share."

"Maybe. Just learned something yesterday messing around with the grandson. Haven't reported it to the sheriff and might wait awhile, seeing as how he moved like molasses in looking for my daughter. Course it might not make a hill of beans difference to you."

I smothered any outward display of the excitement my heart rate was registering. "Try me," I said.

He stepped closer and lowered his voice. "Well, the day after the killing, the sheriff came himself to talk to me. But I wasn't home for the shooting. Just the missus, who didn't see anything, didn't even hear the shot. She's getting pretty deaf. It was the grandson that seemed to know something. He played outside that day. When the sheriff came, Aaron tugged on his hand and scooted out to the front porch and pointed up the road to right here where we are. Then he yelled *bang, bang* and scooted back to the living room and the pile of toy cars and trucks he plays with all the time."

"What else did Aaron say?" I asked.

Polk shook his head. "Nothing. One of Aaron's challenges—that's what the teachers call them—is that he don't talk much. Understands lots but don't talk. It was what he did. He took a little police car and a two-toned truck out of the pile and raced back to the front porch. He squatted with them and started up again, pointing this way and yelling *bang, bang.*" Polk was into the story and talking with his hands. "Only the more the sheriff worked with the grandson, the more confused things got." Polk stopped to catch his breath.

"How so?" I decided that to keep Polk talking, I'd have to show patience with the details.

"Well, every time the sheriff pushed the police car up and down on the porch floor and said *bang, bang,* Aaron would nod his head off and point this way. But when the sheriff did the same with the little two-tone truck, Aaron would shake his head no. So, finally, the sheriff asked me to take the truck back to the toy pile. I got to the porch door and Aaron's right there, pulling the truck out of my hand and yelling *bang, bang.* Almost crying he was. Every time we tried to get rid of the little truck, he made a fuss." Polk stopped and shrugged his shoulders.

"That is a strange reaction," I said. "What did you and the sheriff make of it?"

"Well, a sheriff's cruiser did come here to check out where the shot came from." Polk swept his hand around to take in the clearing we stood in. "I don't know what the sheriff made of the grandson's shenanigans. He didn't say. But after the sheriff left and I thought about things, I had my suspicions."

A blanket of humidity had settled on us. I wiped my forehead with a shirtsleeve, as a trickle of sweat rolled down my back. Polk extracted a faded bandana from his back pocket and wiped his neck. No air stirred in the clearing.

"Well, you know Aaron better than the sheriff. What did you think?" I asked.

Polk scratched his thigh. His fingernails were unusually long and moved noisily against overall denim.

"I think Aaron spotted a truck on the road that day, about the same time he heard the shot. But the truck didn't look like anything in his pile of toy trucks when the sheriff was here. So he substituted with a two-tone truck. He was trying to tell us this when he wouldn't let the sheriff roll the truck and say *bang, bang*, but he could roll the truck and say *bang, bang*."

"Well…" I hesitated, trying to keep doubt out of my voice.

"I know, but now I got proof." Polk paused and looked at me.

I wanted to reward him with a total body show of excitement, but my energy was melting in my private sweat lodge. I screwed my face into what I hoped passed for curiosity.

"Proof. That's great. What is it?" I asked.

"Yesterday morning, the missus tackled the big housecleaning she does every month. I was reading the paper in the living room, and Aaron was lying on the floor, coloring. She was poking under and behind every stick of furniture with one of them false feather dusters. You got one of them, missy? They work great."

"A bright blue one," I said. "What happened next?"

"Well, the missus brushed that duster under the big stuffed chair and out came one of the grandson's toy trucks. You should have seen the look on his face. He jumped straight up off the floor and grabbed the truck. Held it up high, and said *bang, bang* over and over. Nearly drove me crazy. Even went to the pile of toys and pulled out the police cruiser. He raced both of them together on the floor—the found truck and the cruiser—yelling *bang, bang* at the top of his lungs."

My body oozed sweat, and my ears rang. I wondered later if I knew what was coming, but all I remember is staring at the triumphant look on Polk's face. "I take it the found truck was somehow special," I said.

"Yer darn' toot'n. The only one he has in that big collection of toy vehicles. Painted camouflage it is. Spiffy looking. That's why Aaron picked the two-tone truck when the sheriff was here. Closest he could get since the camouflage truck was missing."

I sank to my knees to avoid a swoon, or worse, a faint. Polk's words set me in front of a slot machine, watching the spinning wheels stop one by one until three cherries filled the window. Jackpot. The man that had tried breaking into my boat was no doubt in the camouflage truck Flo had seen cruising the marina that day. And he was after Tony's box. He had stood here in the clearing, after he shot Tony, and watched Pete take the box from Tony's truck. He must have shadowed Pete for hours but hadn't seen a chance to steal the box until Pete delivered it to me. If the killer didn't know what was in the box, he obviously thought it contained something that could incriminate him. But what? Was it the note demanding $250,000 from Tony?

"You okay, missy?" Polk took a step toward me and held out his hand.

"Just a little woozy in this heat." I took his sweaty hand and pulled upright. "What you just told me, Mr. Polk, is very important. I'm convinced the man who killed my Habitat supervisor was in that camouflage truck. You need to tell the sheriff right away."

What I didn't share was the unexpected suspicion that the driver of the sheriff's cruiser and the driver of the camouflage truck could have been working together.

Polk stood straighter, and his chest swelled with pride. "I know it's important news. But, like I said, the sheriff took his sweet time looking for my daughter. I ain't in any hurry to do him a favor."

I brushed pine straw off my knees. The dizziness had subsided, although I feared a return if I didn't get out of the oppressive heat of the sniper's lair.

"You sure you're okay?" Polk asked. "You look mighty pale."

"I'm fine." I smiled to reassure him.

And now I'm super-focused to boot. Carl would have known instantly that Polk's news had catapulted me to a new goal: find Tony Wade's killer or killers.

Chapter 22

I left Mr. Polk at the sniper's lair and drove back to the build, only to discover everyone had left early. Had DW quit before the usual three o'clock, still in a funk about our angry exchange, or had he deemed the heat so oppressive that he put health concerns ahead of progress on the house? The site was almost eerie in the humidity and silence. I shielded my eyes against the sun and checked the roof trusses. It looked to me as if they could easily be finished in the next work session.

I was relieved that I didn't have to face DW. I was still unnerved by Polk's discovery, through his grandson, that a camouflage truck was seen leaving the vicinity of the sniper's lair about the time of the murder. To me, it followed that the same camouflage truck had been cruising the marina, perhaps to frighten me or to establish some of my habits and patterns. Either way, a target was tattooed on my back.

Easing onto the dirt road, I turned the air conditioning to high and drove slowly while dialing Pete's cell phone. He answered on the third ring.

After the usual back and forth hellos, I jumped to the bottom line. "Why did DW close shop early today?"

"The heat got to Sam real bad. He was better after we stretched him out on the ground for ten minutes and put cold rags on his head. Guess it helped that Ruby fanned him ninety miles to nothing." Pete chuckled. "DW said no need to take chances. We'll easy finish the roof trusses next week."

"Do you think DW stayed peeved with me?" I needed to know but hated to sound too interested, too wimpy.

"Nah. He never even looked up the road for your car. Maybe he's the kind of guy that blows quick and cools quick."

I thanked Pete, turned onto the paved road, and headed for the marina, thankful that air conditioning had shriveled my sweat glands.

As I stepped onto the dock, the door to the marina office opened. Flo stuck her head out and waved to me.

"Saw you parking," she said. "Got something to show you, if you have a minute."

I stepped into the cool of the office and shut the door. Flo reached behind the counter and came out with a digital camera. She turned it on, and several musical tones sounded. After pressing a few buttons, she turned the small screen to me.

"Looky what I captured for you Friday afternoon just about dark. I decided to sit on it until today. Didn't see any need to send you off worried to the Habitat build."

I took the camera and studied the image on the small screen. Part of the side and back end of a camouflage truck were clearly visible but at a distance. Also, the lighting at dusk muted the truck's colors. Obviously, Flo had not had her camera at the ready.

"Well, this is proof we're not making things up," I said. "But without a tag number, I'm stymied."

"Would you believe no tag this time? The time before, remember, he'd smeared mud all over the number."

"Yeah. I'd have to sit up here 24/7 to get a whack at him." I heard the discouragement in my voice.

"Maybe all's not lost." Flo plopped in her director's chair and motioned for me to sit on the low stool nearby. "A friend of mine who sells used trucks over in Gainesville at the Truck Mart came by and took a look at this photo. Hope I'm not butting into your business."

"For God's sake, no. What did he say?"

"He verified what I thought. Mostly you see these trucks during hunting season. Some are spray-painted camouflage by the owners; others have a more professional paint job. And lots of the guys who own them are always buying and selling, mostly by word of mouth. Jeff said Truck Mart hadn't had one to sell in over a year."

My spirits sagged again. "Sorry, but that doesn't sound too encouraging that our mystery truck can be identified. Thanks anyway for trying."

"Don't give up yet," she said. "My friend has contacts all over North Georgia. He's gonna check around and keep an eye out."

I thanked Flo for her help and had one foot out the door when she spoke again. "Oh, I hope everything's okay with Carl and Madge. They left this morning wheeling small suitcases behind them."

"All's well, although Carl grumbled and tried to stay home. Madge's sister in Alabama decided at the last minute to have a birthday party. They'll be back tomorrow late afternoon."

I trudged on to my boat. By the time I unlocked the door and stepped into the living room, a light perspiration had coated my skin. The dog days of summer were living up to their reputation.

Standing in silence in the middle of the living room, barely breathing, I was overwhelmed with loneliness. I missed the sounds and rustlings of

Madge and Carl and the aromas of appetizers and dinner fixings. I even wished for a knock on the door and the flippant entry of Hank. The thought of spending the night and all day Sunday in my same old routines depressed me. I was also spooked that the driver of the camouflage truck seemed to have it in for me.

"Well, you're a big girl, Billie. Break out of your rut."

Hearing my spoken advice galvanized me. Sitting at the bar with a tall glass of water, I booked a room at the Resort on Lake Lanier, calculating that behind its gates I'd be safe from the driver of the cammy truck. Within the hour, I'd showered, dressed, and packed overnight essentials and a bottle of pinot noir in the bottom of a large boat bag. On top of the pile, I balanced my laptop and Tony Wade folder, containing all the info on his life and death that I'd collected to date. I left a note for Carl and Madge on the bar and called Flo so she would know my whereabouts and not worry. As I pulled out of the marina, headed for the Resort, I suffered only a slight guilt pang that I wasn't running away to see Uncle Joe and Irene or at least sharing my destination with them, as the Resort was one of their favorite homes away from home. On the other hand, I'd only be there for the night.

After settling into my room and admiring a window-view of the lake, I changed into short-shorts, a tank top, and flip-flops and settled by the pool with my laptop and folder on Tony Wade. An array of young kids kicked and paddled in the shallow end, while older kids practiced belly flops at the deep end. Parents and grandparents, lazing in lounge-chairs, oblivious to the noise, interrupted reading or chit-chat to verify their charges had not drowned. A brave, elderly man, with glasses tethered to his nose, swam laps close to the edge of the pool. Food and drink service from the adjacent Bullfrogs Bar and Grill was in full swing. I joined the party by ordering a double gin and tonic.

"Shame you have to work on such a beautiful afternoon." The waiter set my drink on the table near my opened laptop.

I tipped him extra for the show of concern and reviewed contents of Tony's folder. I'd initially labeled it *Jake Wade.* I crossed through that name and wrote *Tony Wade.* Neither my brain nor my mouth was making the change easily. Nothing in the folder set off any light bulbs above my head, although I fingered the copy of the note that threatened Tony regarding a missing $250,000. What would I learn from Sylvia Wade on Monday? Would she know anything about the note?

Tired of contemplating questions I couldn't answer, I closed the folder and placed the laptop across my thighs. In the process, I surveyed action in the area. Adults and kids were thinning, the noise level decreasing. Inadvertently, I locked eyes with a fortyish man who was across the pool, clad only in bathing trunks and sporting a hairy chest. I looked away quickly after he raised a hand in greeting. For the next five minutes, I played solitaire on the computer and referred several times to contents of the folder that I had reopened. This show of dedication to "work" and refusal to look at him again sent the intended message. He disappeared without walking past me.

I ate dinner poolside, savoring a tasty grilled salmon Cobb salad and tall glass of iced tea. Back in my room, I stripped and luxuriated in a lengthy, lukewarm shower before propping in bed against plump pillows with a glass of wine. A to-do that I'd put off nagged me, and I dialed the cell phone number I had for Laverne, the woman who had befriended the man she knew as Jake Wade. A husky voice answered.

"Hi, Laverne. This is Billie Quinn. You must not be working tonight. I don't hear any hullabaloo in the background

"Worked six nights straight, so I'm off. Thank the Lord for small favors. You must know something about Jake." Urgency came through in her voice.

"I do. I've located a next of kin, and I know his real name. Tony Wade from Daytona Beach. He never used his middle name, Jacob, or the initial "J" in his signature, so posing as Jake Wade threw off every computer search."

"Jeez. *Tony.* I guess that fits. It's a sturdy name, but he'll always be Jake to me. What about his daughter? Whatever happened there, it tore him up."

"April Wade. There was something about her death that put Tony on the road, searching for what I'm not sure."

"Yeah. That's the way he seemed to me." She cleared her throat. "You mentioned next-of-kin. Who's that?"

For a moment, I considered and rejected giving Laverne a soft-pedaled answer.

"His wife, Sylvia. I'll deliver Tony's ashes to her Monday. She's taking it hard, of course, on top of losing her only child. On the phone, she comes across as totally supportive of Tony."

Laverne sighed. "Figures a nice guy like that would be happily married."

That response was my second clue that I needed to help her face a few of the facts that disturbed me. "Look, Laverne, I liked Tony, too, but he had a dark side. There's a strong possibility he came to Creeks County to confront somebody about April's death and that that somebody shot him to death. Who knows, maybe Tony meant to shoot first and, instead, was ambushed. I hope to find some answers when I see his wife."

Laverne fell silent. I adjusted the pillow in the small of my back and took another sip of wine.

"Well, all I know," she said, "is that Jake was a gentleman with me and a man of his word. That's the way I'll remember him. He wasn't like most of the bullshitting guys I deal with all the time."

"That's your choice. Just wanted you to be aware of the big picture." I wasn't surprised that Laverne clung to her idealized image of Tony Wade and would probably always call him Jake.

"Thanks for the call, Billie. I wasn't sure you'd keep your promise. Uh…"

I waited, aware that her breathing had quickened.

"Uh… I don't guess you can tell Sylvia how sorry I am for her loss."

"Don't think so. That would be awkward."

"Yeah. Sure. Well, thanks again for the call."

Laverne disconnected without waiting for a goodbye from me. My last sip of wine slid past the lump in my throat. I wasn't sure that my call had comforted her in any way.

Driving home Sunday afternoon, I made the mistake of thinking how smoothly traffic was flowing. Wrong. Ten minutes later, I shifted the Prius into ECO-mode and held my own in a stop and go line of cars and trucks. Twenty minutes later, on a curve, I pulled abreast of the culprit, an accident involving several vehicles and a truck tipped on its side. Scattered pell-mell across the highway were hundreds of rattlesnake-striped watermelons, some whole, but most in pieces, their red meat gleaming in the sunlight or smeared on the road. A state trooper waved cars past the mess in single file.

As I pulled into my marina parking space, I saw Carl and Madge's car. They were home ahead of me. I hoisted my boat bag to a shoulder and flip-flopped my way to the boat. By the time I opened the door, humidity had me in its clammy grip.

Madge turned to me from her perch on a barstool. "Hi and welcome home from your night out. We saw your note first thing."

Carl was slumped on the couch, earphones clamped to his head, watching a golf match. He acknowledged me with a slight hand wave.

"Don't mind Mr. Grumpy," Madge said. "He doesn't travel well. Thank the Lord he was in a good mood for my sister's birthday party. What did you do over at the Resort, besides drop fifty dollar bills left and right?"

I shortened the boring details and lingered over the details of my conversation with Laverne, knowing that Madge would relate to the human-interest angle. Why else would she devour every page of *People* magazine when it arrived?

Madge shook her head and sighed. "Laverne needs to get an office job. Not likely she'll meet another Jake in shining armor in that bar where she works."

I vacated the living room and left Madge to her cooking. By the time she called me to dinner, I had unpacked and showered. While we munched a lemon-flavored shrimp salad with crusty French bread and sipped a Spanish white wine, I entertained them with details of the watermelon-wreck I'd endured on the drive home.

"What's wrong with your get up and go?" Carl asked. "You could have snitched us a whole one for our dessert."

"Sure," I said. "You could have enjoyed it while bailing me out of jail."

We watched quietly as Madge cleared the dinner dishes and served us each coffee and a dollop of chocolate ice cream. While we ate and sipped, I shared what I had learned Saturday from Mr. Polk about a camouflage truck being spotted about the time Tony Wade was killed.

Madge showed little sign that she thought this information particularly pertinent. Carl, however, put his spoon down and leaned toward me.

"Correct me if I'm wrong, but didn't Pete complain that a cammy truck almost ran him off the road the morning he delivered Jake's, uh Tony's, box to you?"

"You have a good memory," I said.

"Then why can't he remember to take the garbage out?" Madge grinned and punched Carl lightly on the shoulder.

"This isn't funny, Madge. Billie's working up to telling us something else about a cammy truck."

I rewarded Carl with an exaggerated sigh. "Okay, smarty, you win. Flo has spotted a camouflage truck cruising the marina several times lately. The driver never stops, and the license plate number is either missing or slopped with mud. The first time she spotted the truck was the afternoon of the night some crazy tried to break into the boat."

"Oh, no!" Madge spoke into fingers that flew to her face and covered her mouth.

"Oh, yeah," Carl said. "Connect the dots and what do you get? Billie's got Tony Wade's killer on her tail. And he's not looking to ask her for a date."

"Well, the good news may be that he's only going to keep me in his sights and on edge."

"Don't bet on it. You better be on twenty-four-hour alert." Carl pushed his chair back from the table, stood, and stretched. "Let's go, Madge. I'm bone tired from all the driving we did, not to mention the birthday hullabaloo. Besides, I know I can't make any headway against Billie's hard head."

I walked them to the door. "Get a good night's sleep, Carl. I bought you a ticket to fly with me to Daytona Beach tomorrow."

He stopped, folded his arms across his chest, and shook his head.

"I know. I'm sorry. I had to make a quick decision when I bought my ticket. I could use your help."

Carl shook his head again. "What's so hard about delivering Tony's ashes to his widow?"

I tried a smile. No response. "That may be the easy part. I'm going to pump her for all kinds of information about Tony and their daughter. We're talking two murders here. Having her responses run through two brains and four ears couldn't hurt."

Madge looked back and forth from Carl to me. "Oh, he'll go with you, Billie. Won't you, honey?"

Carl unfurled his crossed arms and opened the door. "I'll sleep on it. Why would I want to aid and abet Billie's involvement in the law's business? She's playing with fire."

Chapter 23

The flight Monday from the Atlanta airport to Daytona Beach was short but definitely not sweet. Thunderstorms crackled through churning gray clouds, delaying takeoff for forty-five minutes. By the time Carl and I finally boarded, found our seats, and secured our small carry-ons overhead, I was glad I'd opted for first class. Once buckled in, I shoved a boat bag containing Tony's ashes under the seat in front of me. I had checked with the airlines and knew to place his cremains in a plastic container that could pass x-ray inspection.

Carl swallowed two aspirin without water, breathed deeply, and stretched both legs full length.

"Thanks for coming with me. I know you didn't want to." I hoped the overture would nudge Carl out of his non-communicative funk.

"Right about that, but you don't take no for an answer."

I sighed. "Think about it this way. I'd take someone with me if I thought a doctor was going to drop a health bomb. Four ears hear better than two ears."

"You think Sylvia Wade will drop a bomb?"

"Well, maybe that was overly dramatic, but you can take notes and help me assess the setting, body language, the more subtle stuff."

"Uh-huh." Carl fished the airline's catalog out of the seat pocket in front of him and began flipping pages.

I took the hint and immersed myself in a several-weeks-old issue of *People Magazine.*

When the captain announced, "Fasten seatbelts, prepare for landing," I initiated my ritual to ward off evil spirits that sabotage landings. I squeezed my eyes shut and held my breath. We bounced twice. At the end of the roar of reversed engines, I exhaled.

Reluctantly, Carl was escorted in a wheelchair to ground transportation. I could almost see fumes of embarrassment roiling over his head, although he had admitted that his bum knee wouldn't let him walk long distances. As we passed the luggage carousels, I marveled that *international* was a label for the Daytona Beach airport.

Curbside, we stood in a ragged line and waited for a cab. A warm, light breeze riffled the thinning hair of the woman in front of me, exposing pink scalp. I shifted the boat bag from one shoulder to the other. The weight of Tony Wade's ashes depressed me.

The cab driver, *Manuel,* according to his shirt badge, flashed a big-toothed grin and dropped our luggage in the trunk of his car. Once across the International Bridge and on the beach road, he drove at sightseeing speed. Sun-drenched, high-rise condominiums and an occasional McMansion, linked by palm trees, hugged the shoreline like a necklace. Several times, between the buildings, I glimpsed the Atlantic Ocean and frothy waves rolling onto white sand. I drifted into memories of childhood vacations when family homes and small mom and pop motels dominated the ocean view. Our rental house always had a pool, a rarity in those days, but a requirement of my father's.

"Aquí. We're here." Manuel turned the car on to a crushed-shell driveway and stopped at a modest two-story house perched on sand dunes between two condominiums, each at least fifteen stories high. By the looks of it, the Wades' lot could accommodate a third condominium of equal size or larger.

Carl whistled. "The house looks like the seventies, but someday, Sylvia will walk away with millions of sand dollars."

"Cute." I crossed my fingers that the witticism meant Carl was thawing.

I paid the cab fare and tipped Manuel generously.

"*Gracias*," he said, with a grin splitting his brown face.

I opened my cell phone and called Sylvia's number. After hellos, I said, "This is Billie. I'm just outside your house."

"Come inside and look for the stairs up," Sylvia's husky voice instructed.

We opened the only visible door and stepped into a cool hallway that dead-ended in an open area dominated by a floor to ceiling plate glass window that framed a view of dunes and ocean. Along the way, we passed an open shower, a half-bath, storage space, and a laundry area. To the right of the large window, a door exited to the outside. To the left, we found stairs that went up.

We stashed our carry-on bags under the stairs. I motioned for Carl to go first. He stepped up on each stair tread with his good leg and brought his injured leg up to the same level. He muttered once but otherwise didn't complain.

Carl opened a door at the top of the stairs, and we stepped into a large, multiuse room. Early afternoon sunlight spilled through a wall of glass that faced the ocean, a twin to the window downstairs. Two pelicans glided by, as if ordered for a photoshoot. Adjacent to a living room setup were a spacious kitchen and six-chair glass table. I assumed closed doors to the left led into bedrooms.

Sylvia Wade stood silhouetted against the glass wall, her back to us. When she heard the door open, she turned and walked toward us, a little unsteadily I thought. As she emerged from the sun's furnace, the silhouette faded, and her appearance sharpened. She was a handsome woman with a distinctive nose, full lips, and straight black hair that hung almost to her shoulders. There was no mistaking the resemblance to the woman who stood with a young girl in the candid snapshot Tony had left behind.

I introduced Carl, and we three shook hands.

"Let's sit at the kitchen table out of the sun," she said. As we settled, she offered drink options: iced tea, beer, wine, cocktails. "I'm having white wine," she added.

Carl opted for a beer, and I joined Sylvia in her selection. She poured my glass full and left the bottle of Chardonnay on the table.

"Shall we get right to it?" Sylvia eyed the boat bag still slung on my shoulder.

I unzipped the bag, removed the plastic container, and slowly pushed it across the table toward Sylvia. Tears flooded her eyes. With a nod, she cupped her hands around the gray box.

"Thank you both for bringing my husband home. I knew in my heart he might not come back." She dabbed her eyes with a cocktail napkin. "You mentioned you also have his personal belongings."

I reached deeper in the boat bag and withdrew a large manila envelope. "I don't actually have his belongings, Sylvia. They're in possession of the sheriff in Creeks County, Georgia. However, I brought photographs of everything that was in a special box that Jake, as we knew him, guarded zealously."

"Yes. I knew he was using his middle name—well, using the nickname for *Jacob*. I always teased him about his beautiful name: Anthony Jacob Wade. *A presidential name*, I'd say, and he'd wave off the compliment."

One by one, I placed the photographs before her. After stroking the margin of each photo with a forefinger, she reacted.

Photo of the traveler's checks. "I knew this was how Tony paid his way day to day. When he ran low, I sent a cashier's check overnight—usually five thousand dollars at a time. Most often, he was in a different state or town."

Photo of the forged driver's licenses, Social Security card and fishing license. "He always instructed me to make the cashier's checks out to Jake Wade. I made up some story that the bank accepted." She ran a finger over the image of his fishing license. "Tony was never without one. He loved to fish."

Snapshot of a woman and a young girl standing in front of a palm tree. "That's me and April, our daughter.

Those were happier times. Tony composed the shot and was upset when the developed picture showed the palm tree growing out of our heads." Sylvia sighed and dabbed her tearing eyes.

Photo of the unsigned, handwritten note, demanding repayment of $250,000. She studied the note and mouthed the words printed on it. "I didn't know about this particular note. Tony never showed it to me. There were other less threatening notes, so there's no doubt in my mind about who wrote it." She stopped, took several sips of wine, and looked past Carl and me to the ocean view framed by the glass wall.

Silence dragged on. Carl looked at me and shrugged his shoulders. I touched Sylvia's hand. "Anything you can tell us about this note would be helpful."

"That's right," Carl said. "Somebody tracked your husband down and killed him, possibly the person who wrote this note."

Slowly, Sylvia turned back to us. "Oh, I don't think so. Ralph couldn't squash a fly—well, at least until he flipped out. You wouldn't believe how his personality changed."

Sylvia refilled her wine glass. More silence.

"Who's Ralph?" Carl asked.

"Ralph Garrison, Tony's partner. They were in the construction business—homes and small businesses up and down Florida's coast. Then, about seven years ago, Ralph started flipping in and out of bipolar highs and lows. That…" Sylvia's voice trailed off, and she stared at the tabletop.

I cleared my throat, hoping to restart her memory. When that failed, I leaned toward her. "Go on, please, Sylvia. What else can you tell us about Ralph?"

"Oh…" Sylvia looked up at Carl and me, as if we'd suddenly appeared out of nowhere. "Oh, it was a hard time. In a high, Ralph spent money wildly, buying heavy equipment and stuff that Tony said they didn't need and couldn't afford. So Tony found a legal way to squirrel away $250,000—the only way, he said, to keep Ralph from blowing it. That's when Ralph began sending Tony all kinds of threatening notes like this one."

"Where is Ralph now?" I asked.

Sylvia fingered the stem of her wine glass. "Not sure. About the time Tony left home, I lost track of Ralph. I do know his wife, Katherine, divorced him, but she probably knows where he is."

"Where does she live?" Carl scribbled something on a note pad and looked up, pen poised.

"Jacksonville, I think. She got the house." A deep frown pulled Sylvia's dark eyebrows closer. "You'll let me know, won't you? I mean, if Ralph had anything to do with Tony's death…"

"I'll let you know," I said.

I hesitated before presenting the last photo, the formal photograph of April Wade. While Sylvia refilled her wine glass, I slipped the photo in front of her. She took one look at it, and her face crumpled.

"My baby, my precious baby." She hugged the copy of the photograph to her chest and cried softly. Carl and I stared at the tabletop.

Three or four minutes ticked by before Sylvia regained some control. I gathered the photocopies into a bundle and slipped them into the manila envelope. She kissed April's image before returning the photo to the envelope.

"I'm ready now to hear how Tony died." Her pale face was emotionless.

The moment I had especially dreaded had arrived. I took a deep breath, and without sharing the gory details, I recounted Tony's death by sniper fire and how his use of the alias *Jake Wade* had prevented proper identification until we found the link with April. I complimented Tony's caring nature by explaining his involvement in building a Habitat house for Sam and Ruby.

"That was like him. He was always helping someone less fortunate." As tears welled, Sylvia twisted the napkin she'd been fingering. "On the other hand, there was the stubborn side of Tony that probably got him killed."

"I imagine your daughter's death was a huge factor," I said.

"Yes. April's murder changed Tony. He became obsessed, and I couldn't reason with him anymore. What I'm about to tell you might lead to his killer."

I nodded. "Take your time, please," I said. "And if you find you can't go on, we'll understand."

Carl licked two fingers and turned to a fresh page in his note pad. He clicked a pen to expose the ballpoint tip.

Chapter 24

Sylvia excused herself and left us hanging. With some trepidation, I watched her walk an imaginary DUI line, Tony's ashes clutched to her chest. She disappeared through a closed door, to her bedroom I assumed. Carl and I used the break to visit the guest bathroom. Unexpectedly, he played the gentleman and let me go first.

I waited alone at the glass wall until Carl joined me. Silently, we stared at the scene spread before us. Beach and sea oats and ocean merged seamlessly in the harsh afternoon sun. I counted eight people in the water and one lone surfer who waited patiently for a wave he managed to ride a few feet. When I was a youngster, nothing could keep me out of the ocean, including crab bites and jellyfish stings. Paul and Nina had tolerated these hours in the sun by parking just outside the wave line under a large umbrella. I was a competent swimmer early, and they were comfortable letting me play in chest deep water, as long as my oversized truck inner tube was within reach. As an adult, I developed an aversion to jellyfish, and too many shadows in the water morphed into possible sharks, a fear I traced to the *Jaws* movie.

Carl broke the silence with a soft whistle. "Can you believe the number of cars parked on the beach? And it's not the weekend."

I sighed. "When I was a kid, cruising up and down the beach in my dad's convertible, the beach looked twice as wide."

"Yeah, and your dad probably looked twice as tall as he really was." Carl looked over his shoulder and inched closer to me. "You think Sylvia can finish her story before she passes out?"

"I think she's had a lot of practice self-medicating a boatload of emotions, so I don't know. It might be a coin toss."

A door click announced Sylvia's return. In semi-slow motion she detoured by the refrigerator, returned to the table, and deposited two things: an oversized scrapbook and a bottle of tonic water. Before sitting, she added a bowl of pretzels to the table clutter.

"More wine?" she asked.

Carl and I declined and poured tall glasses of iced tea before reclaiming our chairs. I ordered my fanny not to succumb to paralyzing numbness.

Sylvia sipped tonic water from the wine glass she'd been using. "I know you have many more questions," she said, "and I want to help you find Tony's killer." She pulled the scrapbook closer to her chest and breathed deeply, before continuing.

"For the first six months after April died, I cried when I thought of her or said her name or when anyone else said her name. Now, here it is eighteen months later. I still cry often, but I can talk about her. Thank goodness because I need room in my heart to grieve for Tony. Perhaps God hasn't abandoned me, after all."

"If telling us about April's death is going to be too much," I said, "Carl and I could look through the scrapbook and ask specific questions."

She shook her head. "No. Let me summarize for you so that you hear what I think is important. First, you have to see April as she was, as I remember her. She was pretty, yes, but her smile, her laugh, her vivaciousness—these were the qualities that endeared her to family and friends and served as magnets to all manner of young men."

Absentmindedly, Sylvia pushed the bowl of pretzels toward us. We declined.

"April stayed home all summer after her junior year at the University of Tennessee, partly to please us, but mostly to be around Ed Pace who had just graduated from UT. They had dated a few times at school, and she was smitten. More than once she said to me, *Get to know and like Ed, Mom. One day he'll be your son-in-law.* Unfortunately, someone forgot to tell Ed. April was one of three young ladies that Ed dated that summer. This prompted April to add Gary Nix to her date card, hoping to make Ed jealous."

Sylvia sipped the tonic water much slower than she had sipped the wine. I shifted to the other cheek.

"Soon Gary was head over heels for April. To complicate matters, both young men worked for Tony in his construction business. He built commercial and residential and could have separated them by work site, but he didn't see the need to. They worked within sight of each other every day and tensions built. Tony never forgave himself for that mistake."

Carl cleared his throat. "You're saying Ed and Gary vied aggressively for April's attention?"

I suspected Carl's interruption was an attempt to help Sylvia accelerate the story, a strategy I was all for. We waited. Absentmindedly, Sylvia patted the cover of the scrapbook but didn't open it.

"Aggressive… Yes, that fits," Sylvia said. "Once Tony had to break up a fist fight in our front yard. Both young men showed up, each thinking he had a date with April. Ed was correct that he was the one, but he couldn't resist insulting Gary, calling him a jerk. Gary tore in to him. After the fight, April was rewarded with increased attention from Ed, and she tried to cut it off with Gary. But Gary couldn't take no for an answer." Sylvia gently blew her nose on a crumpled cocktail napkin.

"Was it just too many phone calls, ringing the doorbell unexpectedly, or did he actually stalk her?" I fished for specifics.

"No. His behavior was short of stalking, but it was damned irritating and a little scary for all of us. And then. . . August fourth was a sweltering night. Tony and I had a nice steak dinner before attending a community theater production. We had drinks afterwards with the cast. April was home alone, inventorying her clothes for senior year at UT, making a list for an upcoming shopping spree in Jacksonville. We were looking forward to girl time together. Tony and I came home around eleven-thirty. All the lights on the first floor were ablaze. No lights were on in April's bedroom on the second floor."

Sylvia stopped again. She used the napkin she'd blown her nose on to wipe tears from her eyes. Carl and I glanced at each other. I focused on condensation clinging to my tea glass, remembering how inconsolable I'd been after my parents' death. Carl shifted his position. Sylvia struggled with her emotions another minute or so. She looked at us and pursed her lips.

"I'm sorry," she said.

"Please, don't apologize," I said. "If you'd rather not continue, we'd certainly understand."

"No. In a strange way, remembering and talking about the details helps me move on. Slowly, I grant you." And not without a little liquid help, I thought.

"We came into the kitchen from the garage and called April's name several times. We heard the TV droning in the den and thought she just didn't hear us. But she wasn't in the den. And she wasn't dozing on the couch in the great room. Then we thought she was already in bed, but we both remarked that it wasn't like her to leave all the lights and the TV on. We cracked her bedroom door and found the bed still made. At this point, Tony said, *Something's wrong. Her car is parked in the driveway. She has to be in the house.* I remember how my heart raced. I followed Tony downstairs. There was only one other place to look: the sunroom at the back of the house. During August, we seldom ran the window air conditioner for that room and rarely used it. Even at ten o'clock at night, the thermometer could register eighty-five degrees."

Sylvia trailed off again. She swallowed hard several times and blinked back tears. When she spoke again, her voice was so soft that Carl and I had to lean forward to hear every word.

"Tony switched the sunroom light on and stepped inside. I will never forget the terrible groan that shook his body and the way his knees buckled before he could regain his balance. He shouted for me to call 911. When I ran back to the sunroom, Tony was kneeling beside April holding her hand, saying *Oh, my God! Oh, my God!* Her head lay in a small pool of blood. Her eyes were open, staring into space. In that moment, I knew that my baby, my darling April, was dead."

Sylvia's last remnant of composure unraveled. She pressed her forehead against the scrapbook in front of her and sobbed softly. I touched her shoulder, and when she didn't flinch, I patted it gently. Carl cleared his throat several times before he pulled himself upright, walked stiffly to the glass wall, and stared at the ocean.

The sobs ebbed. Sylvia sat up and blew her nose. She rubbed both hands over the top of the scrapbook and then turned back the cover to reveal a lengthy newspaper article. I could read the upside down headline: Local Woman Murdered.

"I thought I could go through this scrapbook with you," Sylvia said. "But I can't. I'm exhausted. Please forgive me."

I fought a moment of panic. Details that might shed more light on Tony's murder lay between the scrapbook's covers.

Carl cleared his throat. "Could we possibly copy the pages?"

"Well…" Sylvia looked down at the newspaper article. "I suppose so. But I can't let this scrapbook out of my sight. There's a copy shop not far from here."

After parking Sylvia's big Lincoln, I steered her by an elbow into the copy shop and deposited her in a plastic chair in a waiting area. Her balance had improved on the tonic water regime. Carl detoured by the men's room. A young woman with a ponytail put our order in a short queue. Through an open door to the right of where we sat, several young people hunched over computers.

I bought three bottles of water for us from a vending machine. Sylvia sipped. Carl upended his bottle and guzzled half of its contents.

I rolled water around in my parched mouth before swallowing. "Earlier today, Sylvia, you said that to know April's story was to have a head start on finding Tony's killer."

"What did you say?" Sylvia cupped a hand around an ear. "It's so noisy in here."

I raised my voice over the hum of copy machines. "The rest of April's story. You said there might be a clue as to who killed your husband."

"Oh, yes. Definitely. You'll find out from the scrapbook that initially Ed and Gary were both suspects. But then, in a freak accident at the construction site,

Ed and another young man died in a fall from several stories up. The police then targeted Gary Nix and on, I thought, skimpy evidence took him before a grand jury. When Gary wasn't indicted and walked out of the courthouse—that's when Tony's obsession took root. He was absolutely convinced that Gary had killed April and, worse, gotten off scot-free. That's when he started hounding Gary."

Sylvia hiccupped and lapsed into silence again. She held the water bottle between white-knuckled hands.

Carl looked at me and tapped a finger against his wristwatch. I shrugged and mouthed, *Be patient.* The silence lingered and grew louder than the machine hum around us.

Carl pulled his chair closer to Sylvia. "What do you mean? Exactly how did Tony hound Gary?"

Sylvia's gaze shifted slowly from outer space to Carl. "Oh. Tony made threatening phone calls, followed Gary, and insulted him in public. Gary got a restraining order. Tony ignored it. I pleaded with my husband to give it up, but he took to quoting from the Old Testament: '*Vengeance is mine*'. Finally, Gary Nix left town in the middle of the night. Tony hired a private investigator to track him, but the trail never got warm. The detective was convinced that Gary was using an alias; otherwise, he'd have left some clues as to his whereabouts. Tony spent his nights on the Internet, trying to find Gary.

Then, about six months ago, he became *Jake Wade*, packed a small bag, and left. I didn't hear from him until July fourth. He was excited and talking fast. He must have been outside. I could barely hear him over all the fireworks explosions. He said he'd played a hunch and figured out Gary Nix's alias, that he knew where he lived and was on his way there. He wouldn't tell me any more. He was paranoid about revealing his mission."

"Mission?" I asked to keep Sylvia talking. Her eyelids drooped.

Sylvia looked back and forth from Carl to me, as if we had not been listening attentively. "Why, to find and kill Gary Nix, of course. That was always the mission."

"You think Tony finally located Gary Nix, and Nix struck first?" I asked.

"I would bet on it." Sylvia accented each word. "And that's made for a double tragedy."

"How so?" Carl asked.

"I don't think Gary killed April. It's true he saw her that night, but she was alive when he left. Now, God forbid, it looks like Gary has killed Tony in self-defense." She shrugged. "Violence begets violence. I warned Tony, but he wouldn't listen. He was a good man until all this happened."

My brain clicked around the details of Sylvia's theory. "Then you're thinking Ed Pace killed your daughter."

"Yes. But the truth will never be known because Ed died in that construction accident."

"I don't think you willy-nilly arrived at these conclusions," I said. "Something convinced you."

Sylvia nodded. "After the grand jury acquittal, Gary Nix asked to meet with me, which I did. But I never told Tony. He would have been furious. Everything Gary said to me that night rang true. He was distraught, even cried. He begged me to believe him so that he could leave town in some peace. He also told me that the police should look again at Ed Pace. People found Ed charming and fun to be with, Gary said, but there was a dark side." Sylvia paused and intertwined her fingers in her lap. The pause dragged on.

Carl and I exchanged looks. We waited.

"What do you mean '*dark*?" I leaned closer to Sylvia.

"Oh…" Sylvia turned to me. "I mean Gary told me some things, things that disturbed me. Like even after Ed told April that he wanted to date her exclusively, he continued at least one affair on the side. He even bragged about it on the work site. It could be that April found out, and they quarreled the night she was killed." Another pause that dragged on.

Carl shifted in his chair. "Then it's safe to say you believed Gary."

"Yes. I'm proud of my ability to judge people. Gary and I said goodbye on good terms."

Out of the corner of my eye, I saw the young woman at the counter wave to me. She handed me a large bag bulging with the scrapbook and the two copies I'd ordered. While I paid the bill, Carl helped Sylvia to the car.

After the constant hum of copy machines, the drive back to Sylvia's house was unusually quiet. Tires crunched on the shell driveway. I parked Sylvia's car where I'd found it and thanked her for sharing so much with us.

"You brought Tony home to me. I can tell you cared about him. Thank you again."

I carried the scrapbook under one arm, took Sylvia by an elbow, and escorted her to the top of the stairs, fearful all the way that she might stumble. She unlocked the door and turned to face me. I hated to drop another worry on her but saw no way out.

"I'll have to tell the Creeks County sheriff about our visit, so you can expect to hear from one of his investigators. I'm sorry you'll have to repeat so much that remains painful."

"It can't be helped. What will keep me going now is the search for Tony's killer."

"I'll keep you informed," I said.

I found Carl and our travel bags waiting outside in a patch of shade thrown by a rotund palm tree. I called for a taxi, and we slip-slid down the seashell driveway to the beach road to wait.

"Penny for your thoughts." Carl shoved a stick of chewing gum into his mouth. Peppermint.

"What about inflation?"

"Ha, ha. Make it a quarter."

"I'm thinking we're not done until Tony's killer is in handcuffs." I glanced sideways at Carl.

Carl's eyes widened and an angry flush painted his face. "Dammit, Billie. You said your goal was to identify Jake Wade and deliver his ashes to a family member. You've done that. And you promised that if I helped you, you'd back off and let the law handle everything else." His face was rust-red.

"I don't remember promising," I said, knowing in my heart that Carl's memory was closer to the truth than I would admit.

Chapter 25

Like an old married couple that had worn out the ability to chitchat, Carl and I dined quietly on fried shrimp and draft beer at a fishnet-draped shack with an ocean view. I decided not to aggravate the situation by rehashing what we'd learned from Sylvia Wade or by bringing up his angry reaction to my new goal: finding Tony Wade's killer. In silence, we walked back to the motel and rode the elevator to the fourth floor. Earlier, after the session with Sylvia, we had checked in on my credit card, a move that appeared to cause Carl some discomfort.

"Here we are." I slipped my key card into the lock slot and pushed the door open.

"So I see." Carl's voice reeked of grumpiness. On the third swipe of his key card, the door to his room opened.

"Breakfast downstairs at seven?"

"I guess," Carl said, as the door clicked shut behind him.

I dropped my purse on the queen bed, pulled the sliders open, and stepped onto the private balcony facing the ocean. I inhaled a gentle breeze off the water and registered an enticing mix of fish and seaweeds. What didn't go up my nose turned my lips salty. I closed my eyes and focused on the rhythmic slaps of waves against the shore, relishing the deep response I always experienced in the presence of any body of water.

A waft of cigar smoke drifted into my territory and cut short my musings. I couldn't see Carl around the concrete wall that separated balconies, but I knew he was treating himself to a forbidden smoke. Back home, Madge had put cigars on the endangered list.

I turned off the lights after the ten o'clock news and was still awake at eleven. Snippets of the afternoon spent with Sylvia flitted through my thoughts. I wondered if she was still up, had gone back to drinking. I hoped not. I had lived with the devastation alcohol brought to my mother-in-law's life and the heartbreak it dropped on Charlie and me. I enjoyed happy hour too much sometimes and was ever mindful of the dangers. I also muddled through half-asleep thoughts of loss.

Tony had lost a daughter, and the senseless loss had fueled an obsession that appeared to have led to his death. Sylvia had lost her daughter and husband to violent deaths. And, because Tony had vowed to kill a man, Sylvia said she'd lost her opinion of him as "a good man." I had lost Charlie to another woman and what I considered his skewed view of fatherhood. I drifted off to sleep with a lump in my throat and a Weather Channel musical snippet in the background.

Once airborne, headed to Atlanta, I relaxed; my white knuckles turned pink. I unbuckled my seat belt and pulled the photocopied scrapbook out of my carry-on. At first, Carl refused to help me review the stack of pages on my seat tray. Only after I appealed to his investigative talents and gave him a face-save did he grudgingly acquiesce.

"Look," I said, "you can help me make sense of the info in the scrapbook without aiding and abetting anything I'm up to that you don't approve of."

He took his time answering. "Okay, but only on that basis."

Together, we flipped through the pages to ascertain what was in store for later reading. There were numerous copies of newspaper articles detailing April's murder and a few police progress reports. We did read a number of letters randomly interspersed with the articles. Tony had written to various city and state law enforcement officials, demanding that more resources be put to finding April's killer. After a grand jury cleared Gary Nix, Tony's letters passionately accused the prosecutor of letting a guilty man go free.

At the bottom of the stack were two official reports, one displaying cramped handwriting and the other neatly typed.

Carl whistled softly. "We struck gold. It would take me weeks to come up with this stuff. I bet Tony hired a detective with solid connections." He handed me the police report and kept the autopsy report.

I began reading, but out of the corner of my eye saw Carl lift a flap of paper taped to a page of the autopsy report. He quickly lowered the flap.

"What's that?" I asked.

"Death photo of April. Not a pretty sight."

"If Sylvia and Tony looked, maybe I owe it to them to look also. Besides, nothing can top the sight of Tony's head and face blown away."

"I bet it was Sylvia who pasted this flap over the photo."

"Maybe." I could credit either of them with the desire to hide a reality they hated.

Slowly, I lifted the flap and involuntarily sucked in extra air. April in death, in color. White, smooth skin. Auburn hair shaved from half of her head. Head turned to display ripped skin and a deep, ugly gash along the temple. My stomach lurched. I looked away. Youth and hints of April's fresh good looks leaked through the horror depicted in the photograph.

Carl turned a page, read silently for several minutes, and then summarized: "Bruises on April's throat, but she died of brain trauma. Hemorrhage… Her temple struck the corner of a glass-top table. Cracked her skull." He resumed reading silently.

I shook my head to clear it of April's image in death. With difficulty, I focused on the police report, scanning the sections, making mental notes.

Carl placed the autopsy report under the stack of unread pages. "Nothing more here. What did you find?"

"Hold your horses," I mumbled. "Lots of details. But I think I spotted the kernels. April's body was found in the sunroom. Door to the back yard unlocked. No footprints in the yard. Front door locked. All doorknobs, inside and out, wiped clean of fingerprints. Nothing missing from the house, so robbery ruled out."

Carl shifted and rubbed his bad knee. "Bummer. No help there. What else? And how'd you learn to read so fast?"

"Took a course and practiced." I stifled a smile. It wasn't easy to impress Carl.

"Figures," he said. "So what else, smarty-pants?"

I flipped to a page that I had dog-eared. "Here's a section on suspects. Can't do this justice from memory, so bear with me." As I scanned paragraphs, I paraphrased police thinking. "Ed Pace and Gary Nix, April's suitors, were immediate suspects."

"Standard start," Carl said. "Most murder victims are killed by people they know."

"Ed Pace couldn't account for about one-and-a-half hours of his activities that night. He was seen in his seat up to intermission at a community playhouse performance. Had to be the same play Tony and Sylvia attended. And Pace was seen later at the reception for the actors. Under oath, he swore that he watched the second half of the play from the back of the theater. He was catering to an upset GI tract, needing to be near a restroom."

"Why didn't he just leave?" Carl asked.

"His date was in the play, so he wanted to tough it out. She was late getting to the reception, but Pace was there when she finally arrived." I looked up from the report. "I can see how homicide and Sylvia concluded he had time to commit the murder."

"Yep. On the other hand, grieving family members—and sometimes investigators—are famous for falling into a common trap." He unwrapped a piece of cinnamon gum and stuffed it in his mouth.

"I'll bite. What?"

"The trap is believing the first plausible story you hear or believing a theory concocted by someone you admire."

"I'm sure you'll keep me grounded," I said.

Carl turned his attention to the flight attendant and dropped an empty water bottle in the trash bag she carried down the aisle. "What's in the report about the other suspect? Gary who?"

"Gary Nix. No alibi. Telephone records reveal he called the Wade residence twice within two hours of April's murder. Short conversation both times. Initially, he admitted he asked April if he could come over, talk to her. But she turned him down. Claimed he was alone in his apartment, watching TV."

"Flimsy alibi for sure, but not enough to charge the guy with murder."

"Hang on. There's more." I turned to the next page in the report. "A neighbor of Sylvia and Tony's came forth. He was walking his dog around ten o'clock. Noticed an older pickup truck parked in front of the house. Remembered it because the right front fender, painted light gray, didn't match the truck's bright red finish. Truck was Nix's."

"Now we've got something to go on."

"We? Are you coming to my side?" I couldn't resist the dig, and he wouldn't let it roll off.

"Hell no! Some loony is out there with a high-powered rifle he doesn't mind using, and you won't back off. Your fairy godmother is no match, Billie."

I let Carl's warning go unanswered, although it seemed to me that the authorities could use all the help they could get. And I had the time and money to put to the task.

"To continue," I said. "Nix admitted he went to see April, hoping to renew her interest in him. She was upset about something, brushed him off, and made it clear that her romantic interest lay with Ed Pace. At that point, Nix said his pride kicked in, and he gave up. Wished her well and left her very much alive."

"Easy to say, hard to prove," Carl said.

I returned the police report to the scrapbook stack and stifled a yawn. "I agree, but then the grand jury found enough reasonable doubt not to indict."

"Bet that pissed the prosecutor."

Bells pinged and instructions to prepare for landing sounded over the intercom. I slipped the scrapbook pages back into the large manila envelope. Carl secured both of our pull-down trays. We clicked our seat belts shut.

"Poor Tony." I gripped the armrests, leaned my head against the backrest, and closed my eyes. "He couldn't accept that no one would pay for April's murder. He had to make someone—in this case, Gary Nix—responsible for her death. And this explains his state of mind when he told me he had something to do that involved honor. In his mind, to honor April meant he had to find and kill Gary Nix."

"It wouldn't be the first time a crazy obsession brought a good man down."

There were those words again: a good man.

The plane's nose dropped slightly, beginning the descent to the Atlanta airport. In an effort to calm my jitters, I looked out the window and studied a blue sky and puffy white clouds. A huge cloud in the distance formed a pig's snout.

A fresh thought came to me. I sat up straight. "Carl, do you think Tony's killer could still be in Creeks County? Or maybe he's in Atlanta or Gainesville or Athens where he could hide easier."

Carl's smile was tinged with smirk. "I've already thought through that possibility. If the sniper was Gary Nix and he's a local with responsibilities, I'd say he's still around. Probably using an alias, like Tony's detective concluded. If this Gary Nix is an itinerant, or if the sniper was Ralph Garrison, Tony's pissed business partner, then bye, bye, birdie. Either would have skipped right after the shooting. First thing I'd do is check area phone books for *Gary Nix* and the Jacksonville phone book for *Garrison*."

In spite of himself, Carl was helping me. I ran his scenarios through all I'd learned to date about Tony's actions. "So why did Tony hang around town for nearly three weeks? If he'd found Nix, why didn't he snuff him within a few days of checking into the motel?"

"Good questions with no answers here." Carl sighed. "You remind me of Mutt, a big, shaggy dog Madge and I rescued near a highway dumpster. No collar, obviously abandoned. Mutt could worry a big bone down to a nubbin that he'd swallow whole.

Every time, he'd nearly choke to death. Never learned a lesson."

I laughed. "Look out, or I'll take that as a compliment." I almost withheld the next thought. "Back to why Tony was around for weeks, my intuition— quit rolling your eyes—tells me that Gary Nix is still around. I have as good a chance to find him as the sheriff and GBI. Frankly, I think they've moved on to other cases."

Carl groaned. "You can't go there until you rule out Ralph Garrison."

"Sylvia said he couldn't swat a fly," I said.

Carl shrugged. "His bipolar diagnosis and the conviction that Tony owed him $250,000 is a volatile mixture in my book."

"Okay, okay. We'll rule him out."

"We? There you go again." Carl shifted in his seat.

I had lost track of the plane's descent and quickly transferred my focus to the landing. The wheels touched down and bumped the runway before I could break into a sweat.

As soon as we'd deplaned, I pulled Carl out of the flow of bodies headed for the luggage carousel and called Madge on my cell phone. I asked her to drop everything and check lake-area phone books and Athens, Gainesville, and Atlanta listings for a *Gary Nix*. "After that," I said, "check Jacksonville listings for a *Ralph* or *Katherine Garrison*. I'll explain later."

The airline go-cart, or whatever they're called, that I'd ordered pulled up and zipped us to the terminal front door. Carl waited curbside while I rescued the car.

Carl dropped his luggage on the foredeck and wiped sweat off his face. He followed me as I rolled my suitcase through the door. It was good to be home. I kicked off my flats and headed for the pitcher of iced tea on the bar.

"Welcome home, you two." Madge walked out of the kitchen and pecked me on the cheek. She grabbed Carl in a tight hug.

"Whoa." Carl smiled shyly.

Over a welcome-home dinner of London broil, wild rice, and steamed asparagus, I summarized for Madge our trip to Daytona Beach and what we had learned from Sylvia and the scrapbook pages. I knew Carl was listening, but he feigned disinterest by focusing on the newspaper TV guide, folded flat beside his plate. Madge reported that she had bombed out on finding a telephone listing for Gary Nix.

"I looked with a plan." She began stacking dirty dishes. "Little towns, big towns, and Atlanta in that order. Took nearly an hour."

"I'm not surprised," I said. "What about the *Garrison* search?"

Madge smiled. "That one was easy. I wrote the Jacksonville telephone number for a *Katherine Garrison* on the pad on the bar."

Carl met my gaze. "You got lucky. Like I said, it's rule out time."

Madge and I cleared the table and returned with small slices of key lime cheesecake.

"Poor, poor Sylvia." Madge's fork hovered over her cake. "First, her daughter was murdered, then her husband. No wonder she drinks too much. And poor, poor Jake—I mean Tony. It wasn't right, him setting out to kill Gary. But you can understand a father's grief. Imagine him sitting all alone in that grimy motel room night after night. He was itching to act, wasn't he? But he had to wait, and not so patiently, for Gary to show up."

I choked on the bite I had just swallowed, sending it into the wrong pipe. My eyes watered, and I coughed several times. Carl moved to pound my back, but I waved him off. Finally, I could speak.

"That may be it. Say it again, Madge."

"Say what again?"

"Tony was biding his time. Waited for days that became several weeks. Holed up in that God forsaken motel room. His only relief was working with Habitat, drinking beer with Pete, and seeking solace with Laverne. He couldn't act because Gary Nix wasn't in town for whatever reason, yet was expected to return. To me this pretty well proves that Nix is a local person and still around. We can find him."

Carl held up his hands and rolled his eyes. "This has to be what a one-track mind looks like. Rule out Garrison. Remember?"

"How about right this minute?" I walked to the bar and put my hand on the pad on which Madge had scribbled the telephone number.

"You're on your own." Carl pushed away from the table and stood slowly, testing his level of stiffness. "Come on, Madge. Let's abandon ship before Billie has us bailing more of her troubled waters."

"You want to go with me in the morning to drop our sleuthing results on Sheriff Farr? Should be fun, Carl."

Madge was ahead of Carl going out the door and missed the bird he shot me behind his back.

I formulated a strategy for approaching Katherine Garrison about her ex-husband Ralph, then settled at the bar and punched her telephone number into the boat phone. After six rings, disappointment gripped me. I decided to go for eight rings, and she answered on the seventh. My heartbeat perked up.

After giving my name, I asked for Ralph Garrison and was informed in a crisp voice that he no longer lived at that address, that in fact he had died earlier in the year. Katherine relayed this news in an emotionless voice.

"I'm very sorry." So much for an approach strategy. Instead, the words RULED OUT in caps flashed repeatedly on my mind's marquee.

"The end was not unexpected. May I ask what your business is… was with Ralph?"

"His business partner, Tony Wade, was shot and killed several weeks—"

"Oh, my God! How awful. I'm sure Sylvia is a basket case. I'll have to call her tomorrow."

This was the first time Katherine's voice had revealed any emotion and what was revealed was constrained.

"Yes, she's taking it hard. Your call would be welcomed, I'm sure. As for my business with Ralph, may I be frank?"

"Of course. I've never been one to pussy-foot around an issue."

"Found in Tony's possession was an unsigned, hand-printed note demanding repayment of $250,000. The person who wrote the note was automatically considered a suspect in Tony's murder. When I finally located Sylvia Wade, she knew immediately that your husband had written the note, but she had dropped contact with you two and didn't know that he had died. By the way, she was firm in her refusal to believe your husband had anything to do with Tony's murder."

Katherine sighed. "I gather this phone call was you on a fishing trip—just in case Sylvia was wrong about Ralph. Are you with the police?"

"I admit to fishing, but, no, I'm not with law enforcement. Tony was killed while working for me in North Georgia on a Habitat for Humanity build. Somehow I couldn't rest easy until I talked with his family." As I had hoped, the boatload of details I left out curtailed further questioning by Katherine.

"For the record," she said, "I didn't share Ralph's anger over Tony's move to protect the business's assets. If you've ever lived with someone on a bipolar high, you know how crazy, erratic actions and decisions bubble up and take on a life of their own. Ralph off his meds was impossible to reason with. He threatened Tony several times, but follow through just wasn't in Ralph's nature. I wonder why Tony even kept that note demanding $250,000."

"Perhaps he wasn't as convinced as you and Sylvia that Ralph was harmless.

"No. You don't understand." Katherine's tone bristled. "Shortly after April was murdered, the business was sold and Tony made sure that Ralph received his half of all assets, including his half of the disputed $250,000. Ralph was back on his meds, and he and Tony reconciled."

"I see," I said. But I had no clue as to why Tony had kept a defunct threatening note in the box that held memories of April and Sylvia and a happier time. And why, I wondered, had Sylvia not shared this information? Best guess: Her conviction that Ralph was incapable of shooting Tony overrode all competing theories.

In the background, I heard a two-note ding-dong and then heavier breathing in my ear.

"I'm sorry, but I must cut this short. My ride to bingo is here. I hope you consider your fishing expedition successful."

I chose not to take this as a dig. "Yes, very successful. Thanks for your time, Mrs. Garrison."

After hanging up, I dialed Madge and Carl's boat phone. She answered and, as she handed the phone to Carl over protests I heard distinctly, she said, "Don't pay any attention to Carl's mutterings. He's had an aura. We're in the midst of warding off another migraine."

"Sorry about your head, Carl, but you'll be glad you took this call," I said. "Ralph Garrison died earlier this year, so he's definitely ruled out as Tony's killer."

"Rooty tooty," Carl said.

I didn't take the bait. "Now we're back to Gary Nix as the numero uno suspect. Believe me, he's in the area. My gut tells me so. We can nail him, Carl. I know we can."

Carl's sigh was heavy in my ear. "I thought you were fueled by intuition. Now you've put your gut to work on this ridiculous scheme. And you keep saying 'we.' I don't want any part of 'we,' Billie."

"Well, let's take it one step at a time. The offer's still open for you to go with me in the morning to tell the sheriff we've discovered Jake Wade's identity."

"You're making my headache worse. Have fun without me." Carl's quick disconnect reverberated in my ear.

Chapter 26

Red in the face failed to describe Sheriff Rodney Farr's reaction when I told him, in what I thought was an ego-saving manner, that I had established Jake Wade's true identity to be Anthony Jacob Wade, Tony Wade to friends and for legal transactions. Ignoring his sputtering, I rushed through the rehearsed details of delivery of the ashes to Tony's widow, Sylvia. The crimson in Farr's face engulfed his ears and spread across the bald spot over his forehead and downward to his neck.

"Unbelievable." He jabbed a finger in my direction. "You can't run around the country concealing information that might lead to apprehension of a murderer. The window of opportunity to catch the perpetrator is shut tighter because you obstructed an ongoing investigation."

I marveled that the sheriff's anger failed to wipe out official terminology. Surely what he really wanted to say was, *Damn! You've one-upped me.* As for obstructing an investigation that appeared stalled big time, well, I kept that thought to myself.

"Look, I learned of Jake's identity last Friday, and this is only Wednesday." I sounded defensive to myself. "Besides, once you review the scrapbook pages, you'll know everything I know." I patted the large envelope I had put on his desk. I was giving him the second set of copies.

Farr ignored the envelope and leaned back in his swivel chair. He steepled his fingers under his chin. Red had drained out of his forehead and neck but still stained his cheeks. We glared at each other for several seconds. He broke first and rolled his chair back to the desk. He leaned forward—so close that I smelled musky aftershave.

"You've told me everything you know, Ms. Quinn? I won't be surprised tomorrow or next week to find out you forgot some vital detail?"

I considered stonewalling and then decided to fudge an answer. "I doubt you're interested in my theories," I said.

"Try me."

"Okay. I think Tony Wade tracked the man he suspected of murdering his daughter to Creeks County. I also think that man blew Tony's head off before Tony could take his revenge."

The fudge part was that I didn't name Gary Nix as the man. Let the sheriff come to his own conclusions. If I was now in a cat and mouse game with the sheriff, I preferred to be the cat.

Farr studied me for a long moment before responding. "That's not an unreasonable scenario, Quinn, and all the more reason you should disengage from this investigation immediately. That's what I'm ordering you to do."

"I hear you, Sheriff." I closed the door behind me, wondering what language he'd used when he'd proposed to his wife. Did he get on one knee, take her hand, and say "You are hereby ordered to appear with me at the altar?"

My next stop was the coroner's office. The funeral home parking lot was quiet, which meant that business was bad for the day. Albert Riggs's office door was open, and he sat at his desk, studying a file in front of him. I tapped on the doorjamb before I stepped inside. With a sweep of his arm, he invited me to sit down.

"Sorry, but I can't visit today," I said.

I handed him the signed and dated form that documented Sylvia Wade had taken possession of her husband's ashes. He scanned the document and tossed it into a wooden in-box on his desk.

"I'm glad, Billie, that you cracked the mystery of Jake Wade. A man shouldn't end up in an unmarked grave or an unidentified urn. How'd the sheriff take your coup? Pissed, I'll bet. Please, pardon the French." A smile crinkled his face.

"You nailed it." I returned the smile. "Well, this is goodbye, Albert. I certainly don't want to see you again in any official capacity. I'll remember you as an okay guy."

"Thanks, my dear. Take care."

He held the door open for me. After I had taken five or six steps down the hall, Riggs called my name. Had I forgotten something? The weight on my shoulder assured me my purse was in place. I turned to him and waited.

He cleared his throat. "Uh, I think you should know that anything you told Sheriff Farr is going to become general knowledge in the ranks and beyond. I'll learn of your conversation by sundown. He can't find the person or persons leaking info, and it's frustrating him big time. He's even searched his office for a bug. I hope you didn't tell him anything that could endanger you."

"I don't think so, but thanks for the tip." I smiled, despite the shiver that ran down my back. The frown on Alfred's face dissolved.

There was no need for Alfred to worry unnecessarily. I could worry for both of us and keep things in perspective. Nothing I told the sheriff could endanger me unless it got back to the sniper. And that possibility seemed highly unlikely.

I was about half way back to the marina, driving in light traffic, mulling over my conversation with the sheriff, when my cell phone vibrated. It was Uncle Joe, calling from the boat. He and Irene were on the way to Highlands, their favorite town in North Carolina.

"Hi, honey. We're at the boat. Hope you don't mind an impromptu visit."

"Great. Make yourselves at home." I hated it that I felt a bit put upon. Not that I didn't love Uncle Joe dearly. I looked at him, and, through tears in my eyes, I saw my father, Paul. Although fraternal twins, their physical appearance and gestures were eerily similar. Both had stopped growing at six feet two inches, their frames lean-muscled through countless hours of swimming and tennis. Both had wavy brown hair, tinged with red. Personality set them apart. Joe was steady, conservative, and practical.

Temperamentally, Irene was the perfect match for Joe. She was good to him and for him, and our relationship was warm. Over the years, she'd consoled me when my mother and I regularly fell out.

Irene was six years post-breast cancer surgery. If it turned out not to be a cure, it was cause enough for daily celebration.

I nosed the car into my reserved parking space and slid out of the seat. Why was I so stiff? God, I was too young to develop arthritis. I stretched on tip-toe and gently bent to touch my toes, falling short about three inches. Just as I stood, a black and white sheriff's car eased past me. Behind tinted windows, I thought I could see that the driver saluted me with two fingers to the forehead. After a U-turn, the car eased past me again.

Staring at the retreating cruiser, I resisted the urge to throw a bird at its rearview mirror. Except for the salute, I wouldn't have taken the episode personally. As it was, I connected the dots and con-cluded Sheriff Farr had sent me a message.

As I stepped down onto the foredeck, strains of Big Band music greeted me. I opened the door to find Uncle Joe and Irene in a dance embrace in the middle of the living room. Joe pulled Irene upright from a deep dip. She was dressed in an all-white pants suit and white sandals with thin straps. She wore her platinum hairdo short, every strand perfectly placed. Irene had simplified her ward-robe: ninety-five percent of the time she wore white outfits or black outfits; five percent of the time she branched out to black and white combinations. Joe looked crisp in tan slacks, a navy polo shirt, and loafers.

Their moment of oblivion reminded me of the sweet times when Charlie and I had stripped to our birthday suits and slow-danced our way to bed.

I clapped. "Practicing to dance with the stars?"

Joe winked at me before turning the volume down on the Bose radio perched atop the big television.

"Satellite radio's a wonderful invention," Irene said.

"Dancing cheek to cheek was a wonderful invention," Joe said.

We hugged all around, and they sat side by side on the couch. I poured tall glasses of iced tea for us and passed around a bowl of mixed nuts.

"So what's up besides a trip to Highlands?" I asked.

For the next thirty minutes, they entertained me with details of their gourmet cooking sessions with friends and their latest trips—a Caribbean cruise and a long weekend in San Francisco. When Joe looked at his watch, I suspected correctly that a change of subject was at hand.

"Billie girl…" He started with his favorite nickname for me. "I'm here to make my yearly plea, and you know what it is."

I shook my head. "Uncle Joe…"

"Hush now. I know you hate this conversation. But it's only fair that you listen. If I repeat myself often enough, maybe, just maybe, you'll finally hear me and take action."

He was right. I owed him the courtesy of listening once again. I sighed and folded my hands in my lap.

"That's better." He cleared his throat and glanced at Irene before turning back to me. "Billie girl, it's time you let me involve you in your finances, begin to teach you some of the things you'll need to know when I'm gone."

My heart skipped. "You're okay, aren't you?" Losing my only uncle was not a thought I often let into consciousness.

"Healthy as a horse. But I'm not many moons from having seventy candles in my cake. Who knows what the future holds?"

I said what I always said. "Uncle Joe, I'm happy with the way things are. I trust you completely. You worry about my millions. You're good at it and even enjoy the challenge. I'd like to concentrate on spending some of it to help others."

Joe sighed, stood, and pulled Irene to her feet.

"As for this stubborn fixation you have, setting up a foundation to help downtrodden women, well, Billie girl, it sounds like a headache you don't need."

"Women in need, Uncle Joe."

"That's me," Irene said. "Point me to the bathroom."

Uncle Joe and I laughed, and the tension between us evaporated. We chatted about how much cooler they might find Highlands, especially at night.

"There's some reason why, in the old days without air conditioning, folks from South Georgia made a beeline for North Carolina in the dead of summer." Uncle Joe bent and kissed my cheek.

"It's possible they were escaping mosquitoes and gnats," I said.

"Or running away from polio." Irene, every hair still in place, linked arms with Joe. "Whatever Highland's attraction, I'm game to find out in person. Let's go, honey."

I waved them goodbye from the aft-deck. Joe tailored his stride to match Irene's. They would have been pleased to know their backsides looked two decades younger than their ages.

I tuned the TV to CNN news and stared at the screen without comprehension. My nerves were on edge; I couldn't sit still. A check of my watch indicated that the mail had probably arrived. I slipped into boat shoes and pushed through heat waves boiling up from the dock. At the bank of mailboxes, I unlocked my box and extracted a stack of envelopes and flyers. In a quick shuffle, a letter from Pam surfaced. I put it on top of the stack and started back to the boat.

"Hey! What've you been doing to attract the fuzz?" Flo waved to me from the open door of the marina store. Her captain's hat was pushed back on her head, and she was barefoot.

"Hi. What are you talking about?"

"You know. That deputy sheriff's car you did the tango with earlier. He was parked over there with the stored boats and only cruised the area after you got here. Looks like he was waiting for you."

"Chalk it up to my magnetic personality," I said. "I'm more interested in that cammy truck your friend was going to check on."

Flo shrugged. "Haven't heard from him yet."

"Unfortunately, no news could be buillding to bad news."

A look of distress crossed Flo's face as I waved goodbye and slogged through wet heat to the boat.

After I read Pam's letter, my spirits sank. As an antidote, I ate a bowl of pistachio nut ice cream, followed by another bowl. I lost track of time and started when the doorknob turned.

"Whoa. Look, honey, it's gloom and doom hugging a couch pillow." Madge held the door open for Carl who stepped into the living room clutching grocery bags in both arms.

"I'm afraid to ask what's wrong, given Billie's colorful history." Carl placed the bags on the bar and hoisted himself onto a stool.

"The gloom part is a letter from Pam. You can read it later, but, bottom line, she's concluded the foundation I want to fund isn't viable, and she's sticking with her job."

Madge clucked her tongue. "Oh, Billie, I know how important this is to you. I'm sorry."

"And don't forget the flip side." Carl held his hands out and turned palms up. "Some things aren't meant to be."

"Thanks, Mr. Cheerful." I tossed the pillow aside and scrunched my fanny to the edge of the couch.

"Whoa, don't stop now," Madge said. "What's the doom part?"

Sometimes I thought Madge could read my mind. I considered keeping a gnawing anxiety to myself and then thought better of always trying to tough it out.

"My session with Sheriff Farr left him livid. He warned me to butt out of the investigation of Tony's murder. And I'm pretty sure I was followed home by a deputy whose face I couldn't see too well through the tinted windows."

Carl drummed his fingers on the bar top. "Could have been a routine security sweep."

"I thought of that, but the deputy slowed down abreast of my car and, I'm pretty sure, saluted me with two fingers."

"Hummm," Carl said. "Most of the time all the guys can be bothered to do is raise one finger off the steering wheel to acknowledge civilians. You may have a point."

"Oh, for heaven's sake, you two are worrying a bone with no meat on it." Madge gently stirred a pitcher of Martinis and filled three chilled glasses. "Here. Drink up while I fix dinner."

Chapter 27

After dinner, I tilted my recliner to raise my legs and hid behind a newspaper. I needed peace and quiet. Madge tidied the kitchen while Carl twiddled his thumbs at the bar. They left a little after eight o'clock, and I succumbed to yawns and tearing. I scrunched deeper into the leather of my chair, turned on the TV, and muted the sound. A headline in the "Living" section of the paper caught my eye: "101 ways to cool it in hot weather." After reading the first tip—float ice cubes in the bath water—I yawned again. Renewed tearing blurred the print. I gave up and closed my eyes.

I was in a semi-dream state, floating on a rubber raft on calm water, when chaos struck. Something exploded. I heard a crash. My head jerked up just as a forty-pound cannon ball slammed into my left shoulder. My legs lifted off the recliner and flopped back minus one shoe. Pain ripped a track from my shoulder into my neck. I ordered my left arm to move, but nothing happened. It lay limp and askew on the armrest.

Ringing in my ears mixed with footsteps that drummed the dock and then stopped. A hubbub of excited voices drifted into the boat.

"What the hell was that?" A man's rough voice.

"Damned if I know, honey. Sounded like it came from Quinn's boat."

"Look!" A third voice. "That whole fucking window's blown out!"

Knuckles, maybe a fist, banged on the living room door. I heard my name shouted. I tried to answer. My parched lips opened but no sound escaped.

"She must be in there. The lights are on. Shit! The door's locked."

A jumble of voices, then the order: "Stand back!" Somebody kicked the door. Once, twice, three times. The boat rocked gently. It was like a movie in slow motion. I blinked hard as three people burst through the door and stopped a few feet from me. Their images were blurred, and only a few details registered. A burly man, dressed in short shorts and flip-flops, stared at me. An older woman wore a short bathrobe and slippers. Her hair wrapped around jumbo curlers. A younger woman bulged in cut off jeans and a black T-shirt. She was barefoot.

"You okay, Quinn?" Burly asked.

"She looks glassy-eyed to me," said the woman. Wife?

I opened my mouth again and spoke, no, squawked.

"That was gibberish. I'm calling 911. I might need them, too, if I step on all this fucking glass." The younger woman pulled a cell phone from her back pocket and tiptoed into the kitchen.

"Look, honey. What's that thing on the floor? Is it what I think it is?" The older woman pointed to the floor near me.

I looked down. Neck hurt. Shoulder throbbed. Shimmers of glass surrounded a tiny, misshapened football studded with shards. Football?

"I'll be damned." Burly scratched his chin. "It's the biggest baking potato I've ever seen."

I closed my eyes. Odd. Why would Madge leave a potato on the floor? So tired. Shoulder hurt like hell.

I opened my eyes and looked into the face of a young man with peach fuzz on his cheeks. His EMT uniform came into focus. I was stretched out on the couch, and he was kneeling beside me. Behind him two men looked on. One was a second EMT. The other man's uniform was all too familiar—deputy sheriff. Peach Fuzz pressed two fingers against my wrist.

"You fainted. Probably shock," he said. "Can you talk?"

I swallowed; the effort scraped my parched throat. "Think so," I heard myself say.

"Good. How many fingers do you see?"

"Two—in a V."

"What day is it?"

"Still Thursday night, I think. Where are all the people who came?"

"I sent them home. You seem okay, ma'am, but to be safe, we'd like to transport you to the emergency room for a thorough check-up and some x-rays of that shoulder."

I struggled to sit up straighter. Pain jabbed my shoulder. "No. Don't want to go. I'm okay. See?" I asked my left arm to move toward the ceiling, but only the forearm lifted slowly to perpendicular. Not what I ordered, but it was progress.

Over Peach Fuzz's shoulder, I saw the deputy take a step forward. "Could I call someone for you, ma'am? Relatives? Friends?"

"Yes. Madge and Carl. They're on a boat near here." I gave him their cell number.

While the deputy placed the call, Peach Fuzz fumbled in a black bag and withdrew a folded item that, unfurled, became a sling. He secured the straps around my neck and gently eased my arm into the cocoon. I flinched but conquered a groan.

Peach Fuzz stood up and smoothed the front of his pants. "We'll head on then, ma'am. I suggest you see your doctor in the morning. And you'll need a good dose of OTC painkiller if you plan to get any sleep tonight. She's all yours, Owens."

With a foot, Deputy Owens pushed the ottoman to a spot along the length of the couch near my head. He lowered his short, squat body, and balanced an aluminum clipboard on his knees. He jotted notes on the top sheet.

"The friends you asked me to call, ma'am. They were real upset. They're headed home from the video store and should be here in a few minutes."

Tears welled in my eyes, and I swallowed a lump in my throat. Memories of times I'd been comforted by my parents or Lilly flooded my thoughts.

"I know you," I said. "You came to the Habitat shooting. And you came when somebody tried to break into my boat."

"Yes, ma'am. I'm beginning to think you're picking on me." He kept his focus on the form and whatever he was writing.

"What happened to me? I don't remember."

Any chance for Owens to answer that question was snuffed when Carl and Madge arrived. Madge barreled through the open doorway first and stopped near the deputy. Carl followed, walking stiffly with a cane. He whistled and jiggled the door, hanging by one hinge.

"Billie, honey! Are you all right? What happened?" Her eyes were wide and several rows of wrinkles creased her forehead.

"Not sure. I fell asleep in the chair. Woke up when the window shattered and something damned heavy slammed my shoulder. Heavy like a flying bowling ball."

"You were hit by a large potato launched from a homemade contraption. Spud gun we call it." Owens reached down beside the ottoman and held up a potato encased in a zip-top plastic bag.

I liked potatoes, but this one was twice the size of anything I would tolerate on my plate.

"A spud gun? But why? Who?" Carl asked.

"A loony, that's who," Madge said.

"You make anybody angry lately, ma'am? These guns are legal in Georgia, but they're dangerous even in a wide-open field. Put them together wrong and boom they'll explode. Shooting one near all these boats makes me suspicious you pissed somebody off. Pardon the language, ma'am."

"He's right, Billie," Carl said. "If that potato had hit you in the head, you'd be dead. Or have silly putty for a brain."

"Teenagers like to mess with these guns. Any chance you crossed a teenager lately?" Owens poised a pen over the clipboard.

"Not likely. I don't know any teenagers. But right now I need to stand up. Every joint in my body feels frozen. And water… I need some water."

Madge rushed to the kitchen. Owens and Carl stood close to the couch facing each other. They couldn't lift me by my arms, so they squiggled their hands under my fanny and on the count of three stood me on my feet. Carl draped my good arm around his neck. Blood that had pooled in my prone body surged free. I fought back dizziness.

"Here, drink this." Madge tipped a glass of water against my lips. Water dribbled down my chin while I downed three gulps.

Owens asked me a few more questions and jotted the answers on his report. "That's it, ma'am. Are you sure you don't need to go to the ER?"

"Maybe you should, Billie," Carl said. "You could have a broken collarbone."

"No. I'll be okay." I used the firmest voice I could muster.

"Your call, ma'am." Owens pulled his Stetson low on his head and brushed against the unhinged door as he left. I held my breath, fearing the door would fall off, but it held.

When Madge and Carl were convinced I could walk a straight line and keep my balance, Madge slowly walked me to their boat. Carl stayed behind to execute the plan we'd agreed on. He would seal the shattered window with a heavy-duty garbage bag and duct tape. Once outside, he would close the door as best he could and seal around it with duct tape.

It was midnight when Carl joined us at their breakfast nook table. Madge set three mugs of hot chocolate on the table. She had already overseen my double dose of aspirin and water.

"Hot chocolate in August isn't my drink of choice," I said. "But this is working a healing miracle."

Carl grunted. "You'll need the miracle in the morning. You're gonna be sore as hell."

"Thank God you're not in the emergency room." Madge was not Catholic, but she crossed herself.

I lapsed into scattered memories of the ordeal. Carl blew on his hot chocolate and sipped noisily. Madge added a plate of oatmeal raisin cookies to the table. My favorite cookie. I pinched a piece and rolled it around in my mouth. When most of the cookie had dissolved, I chewed on several raisins.

"What do you think this means, Carl? If I'm in somebody's way, why not just shoot me with a real gun and be done with it? Why a potato gun, for God's sake?"

"Not sure," Carl said. "Somebody shoots you dead with a gun, they're a murderer. And they leave behind a bullet that becomes evidence. Somebody who shoots at you with a potato gun, maybe they're out to scare you more than kill you. And unless I've missed the latest forensic tricks, a potato can't be run through ballistics."

"Can you aim a potato gun precisely?"

"Aim it, yeah. But *precisely* may be a stretch." Carl bit into a cookie. "Standing on the dock in the dark... maybe the shooter just hoped to get the potato through the window to make a statement." He paused. "Of course, the shooter knew that if the spud hit you, it could possibly kill you or at least do serious damage."

"So the thug who did this has mixed feelings about whether I live or die? Is that a fair conclusion?"

Carl shrugged. "That's one scenario. Who knows?"

"We're tip-toeing all around it, aren't we?" I bit off a chunk of cookie and mixed it in my mouth with hot chocolate.

"Yep," Carl said.

Madge set her mug down with a thump. "Well, if you sissies won't say it, I will. Billie, you snooped around, asked too many questions, and now you're too damn close to knowing who killed Jake, I mean Tony. It makes sense somebody wants to stop you. And I think you ought to listen."

Carl lifted his mug. "You know what I think. I'm just damned tired of saying it."

I downed the last, lukewarm sip of hot chocolate and licked my lips. "Yeah, I know. But I can't do that—back off."

"You need to reword that." Carl leaned toward me. "You can, but you won't."

I rubbed my injured arm. "Bottom line, whoever shot Tony Wade is a coward. And I don't cotton to cowards telling me what to do."

"More accurately, you don't like anybody telling you what to do. Especially me." Carl spoke through clenched teeth.

Madge rolled her eyes. "God, help us."

Chapter 28

Madge fussed over me, and I let her tuck me into their spare bed. The potato-hit had left my shoulder throbbing. Shooting pains coursed into my neck and jaw. By the glow of a night-light, I stared at the rotating blades of the ceiling fan until dizziness set in. Sleeping on either side was impossible. I lay for hours on my back and snorted myself awake each time I drifted off to sleep. At four-thirty by the dresser clock, Madge sat on the edge of the bed and fed me more aspirin, after which I conked out. The next thing I knew, eight o'clock sunlight filled the bedroom.

Carl's prediction came true. Slowly, I sat up and hung my legs off the bed. Every muscle in my body ached, as if I'd been run through a ringer forward and backward. I still wore the clothes I had on the night before. It took five minutes to climb down from the bed's perch, locate my sandals, and wash my face one-handed. I didn't check the mirror for fear it was true: my mouth was growing fuzz that had spread onto my lips.

After a breakfast of milk and dried apricots, the only thing that appealed to me, Madge drove me to my doctor for a work-in appointment. We plowed through *Southern Living* and *Cooking Light* while elbow-to-elbow with patients who looked to be in varying stages of sick or well or, perhaps, just there for lab studies or x-rays. A taciturn nurse with spiked hair ushered me through the weight and blood pressure routine and ordered me to wait on the edge of the examination table.

I was on the second reading of numerous medical diplomas and board certifications adorning the wall when Dr. Murphy tapped on the door and walked in. Underneath the starched white jacket, I suspected he was dressed for the golf course—his favorite subject of conversation, given an opening. He eyed my sling and laughed when I told him I'd been struck in the shoulder courtesy of a medieval contraption that shoots big potatoes.

"Too bad it was a raw potato, Billie. A baked potato would leave half the bruise you're going to have."

After a cursory examination, he sent me down the hall to the X-ray department. More waiting. I read the certificates backwards and tried to remember all the words of "The Star Spangled Banner." Served me right for failing to bring a magazine with me.

Dr. Murphy reappeared, smiling and humming off-key a tune I didn't recognize. "The good news is no broken bones." He manipulated my arm and shoulder and pooh-poohed me when I winced.

"Okay," I said. "What's the bad news?"

"Use the arm and shoulder several times a day and work up to swinging a golf club. Ignore me and your shoulder could freeze. That would be bad."

By four o'clock that afternoon, I had learned how to maneuver my extremities to accommodate soreness. Carl had fixed the living room door and installed a new lock. Offered a bonus for promptness, the glazier had installed new panes in the window before lunch. The longest, hardest job fell to Madge. Hands encased in thin-skinned leather gloves and knees protected by pads that buckled on, she crawled around the living room floor on all fours, picking shards of glass out of the carpet and dropping them in a small metal pail. She then vacuumed the floor twice, going first horizontally and then vertically.

While Madge vacuumed, I poured over the scrapbook pages again. For two days, something I couldn't pinpoint had gnawed on my brain. If Gary Nix had left Daytona Beach as Gary Nix, why had it taken so many months for Tony to track him down? And if Nix had adopted an alias, how could Tony have figured it out? I toyed with one of Madge's conclusions about Tony: A man addicted to Sudoku puzzles and skilled in the intricacies of construction would have enjoyed logic for the sake of logic. But what bit of information could have clued Tony to Nix's choice of an alias?

A phone call from Sheriff Farr broke my concentration. He identified himself curtly and jumped straight to the reason for the call.

"I just read Deputy Owens's report, Ms. Quinn. You're damn lucky to escape with a bruised shoulder. A hit on the head and somebody would still be cleaning up your brains. In fact, the person or persons who launched the potato from the dock are lucky. These guns—that's what I call them—are unreliable and can explode without warning. Most are a ragtag combination of PVC pipe and common sources of fuel and ignition. I bet my weekly poker money we'll find the cannon used against you in the water near the marina dock. And it won't tell us a thing we can use to go after the attacker."

"If I hear you correctly, Sheriff, you're saying that the person who did this will never be identified."

"Exactly. But the primary reason I called is to say I agree with Deputy Owens. Somebody fired a warning shot across your bow. You should think about what that somebody could do if he comes at you with a real gun."

"I'll think about that, Sheriff. But, honestly, who would want me dead?" Thank God I wasn't attached to a lie detector.

Silence.

"Let's cut the crap, Quinn. Tony Wade's killer is spooked by all the snooping you're doing. He or she doesn't know how much you know. And neither do I. If you're working on a theory, spit it out. I have resources you can't buy."

I was tempted for a moment but only for a moment. I had part of a theory. If I ever developed a theory with a beginning, middle, and an end, I might change my mind and share it with Farr. Until then, if resources boiled down to money, I was willing to outspend the sheriff's budget to bring Tony's killer to justice. This seemed the least I could do.

"No theory here," I said, calling on my most innocent voice.

Farr cut the connection without a goodbye.

After dinner, I asked Carl to stay and review the scrapbook pages with me since my earlier exploration had yielded no brilliant insight. Madge excused herself, saying that she would relish the peace and quiet of a blacked-out TV screen. Carl grumped and waved her out the door.

"Just so we understand each other, I'm helping you under duress. I don't approve." Carl spoke with his arms crossed.

"I understand. But on the plus side, you may keep me from arriving at some ridiculous conclusion or taking some ill- advised action." I smiled to soften the dig.

Carl shrugged. "That would be a first."

We sat at the bar, copies of the scrapbook pages stacked between us. After discussing each article and each report, I summarized pertinent information on three-by-five cards. We then sorted the cards by categories: facts established by the police, coroner, other law enforcement personnel; information (we hesitated to call them facts) relayed by reporters in newspaper articles; and information we had gleaned from Sylvia Wade.

Several pages from the bottom of the stack was an article entitled, "Two Die in Crane Accident." I picked it up and began reading.

"What's that about?" Carl asked.

I held my hand up and read several more paragraphs before answering. "Very interesting. Ed Pace... You remember him—the man April was head over heels for. He was an initial suspect in her murder. Well, he and another guy were working on the fourth floor of a planned six-floor office building.

Apparently, they were assigned to unhitch construction loads hoisted by an on-site crane. Witnesses reported everything was routine until, without warning, a load of steel beams that was being lowered slipped..." I glanced at the article to refresh my memory. "The load slipped in its sling, began swinging erratically, and swept Pace and the other guy over the edge of the building. Between being whacked by the crane and falling four stories, they didn't stand a chance."

"Bad dumb luck," Carl said. "Does the article mention OSHA's verdict?"

"Nope. Only that OSHA was investigating."

I was scribbling these facts on blank cards when I realized that the article never named the man who died with Ed Pace. *Name withheld pending notification of next of kin.* We looked, but found no follow-up article.

My scalp prickled. Some people smirk at women's intuition. Not me. Something transmitted to Carl. He swiveled his barstool to face me.

"Okay. What?" he asked.

"We need the name of the man who died with Ed Pace. I'm playing a hunch."

Carl sighed. "Here we go again. Sylvia probably knows since the accident happened on Tony's construction site."

I had added Sylvia to my cell phone address book. I punched her number. The phone rang eight times before the answering machine picked up.

"Sylvia, Billie Quinn here. Please call me ASAP when you get this message. I have an urgent question."

Chapter 29

Sylvia had not called by eleven Thursday night, so I climbed in bed, hoping to sleep soundly. No way. My thoughts drifted back in time, and I slipped in and out of spells of dozing. Another of my lucid dreams featured Lilly, looking not at all ghostly. She was in my bedroom, laughing the laugh that trilled upward at the end, moving in the cramped space with a slight limp. One leg was shorter than the other. From memory, I smelled her skin lotion, laced with a hint of spices.

Without Lilly, my nanny, I would never have gotten to know people who spawned the words "salt of the earth." When Paul and Nina traveled, and that was often after I started first grade, Lilly planned an intriguing mix of outings. She was careful to include visits to the zoo, the children's museum, approved movies, and mornings at the library for story time.

My parents were satisfied that I was being "enriched." I enjoyed all of these outings, but I was most fascinated by our "secret" excursions to her house.

"It's not a house, young lady. It's a home."

In my mind, visits to Lilly's home were visits to a dollhouse. My house was huge and some rooms were closed until Paul and Nina gave a big party. Lilly's house was small—kitchen, dining area, living room, a big bedroom, a small bedroom, and one bathroom. There was also a very small room she called "my bonus room," furnished with a table, chair, and an old, black sewing machine. Lilly taught me the word "knickknacks." We walked from room to room, each crowded with photos of people, plates painted with landscapes, glass paperweights, and animal and people figurines.

We spent extra time in the big bedroom, Lilly's bedroom. "Let's follow our ritual," she would say, teaching me another word. At that, she'd lift me onto her high bed, where I sat cross-legged in the center of a beautiful quilt made by her granny. Then Lilly, perched on the edge of the bed, showed me the framed photographs on a large bedside table. It became a game.

"Now, who is this, Billie?"

I would study the face of a man who looked directly at me. A little smile lifted one corner of his mouth. His face was as wide as it was long. His hair was short, dark, and wavy.

"That's your husband, George. He's in heaven."

"And who are these people?" Lilly held up another photograph.

"That's your mama and your papa. They're in heaven with George."

There were photos of her two brothers and a sister and an aunt and an uncle. Always, the last picture was of her daughter, Bertha, who sat between two little girls, Vassie and Myra.

"My precious granddaughters, all grown up now and on their own. Their mama's in heaven, too." Lilly always ran a fingertip across the images in the silver frame. "They're dressed in their Sunday best," she'd always say.

To close our ritual, Lilly boiled water on a gas stove until a whistle pierced the air. She made tea for us in dainty white cups and served the steaming brew with ginger snap cookies. Between sips of tea and nips of cookies, I talked about school, the good and the bad. Lilly always listened patiently. In later years, when I was in high school and vented my frustration with my parents, she never interrupted.

"I know it's hard, Billie. But remember, they love you. Never forget that." This was her standard answer, but she never trivialized my feelings.

Gradually, we branched out and visited Lilly's brothers' homes. On these trips, I learned about big men who wore undershirts around the house, ate pig's feet, drank beer and burped, and laughed loudly at stories I didn't understand. One memory stuck with me: The brothers and their men friends gathered around the bed of an old pickup truck, forearms resting on bed railings, talking and teasing each other across the narrow space between them. These men, so unlike my father and Uncle Joe, treated their wives and children in a gruff but respectful manner.

Years later, it dawned on me that, without Lilly's influence and the excursions she took me on, I could have graduated from college thinking all children and adults were as privileged as I was.

A tap on the door startled me. "Come in."

Madge pushed the door open and stood in the doorway. "Are you going to spend all day Friday in bed?"

"What good would it do? I can't sleep." I hunched myself to the edge of the bed and used my good arm to sit up. "Carl was right. Every muscle still hurts like hell."

"Poor, grumpy Billie." Madge shook her head. "Get up and move. You'll feel better."

"I'll feel better when Sylvia returns my call."

After a modified shower and a bowl of cereal, I collapsed in my recliner and stared at the Weather Channel. Madge bantered as she checked the refrigerator, freezer, and pantry and made a shopping list. To questions about my shoulder and this and that, I answered politely but in monosyllables.

"This place is depressing." She looked at her watch and stuck the shopping list in a side pocket of her purse. "Here's hoping your funk lifts before I get back."

I napped in my chair for twenty minutes and perked up. I nixed a walk to the marina mailboxes, as I wanted to be near pen and paper when Sylvia called. I compromised and settled under the canopy on the party deck with the telephone, a glass of iced tea, and a book I had been reading off and on, one that Hank had recommended. I missed Hank. Or did I just miss being the object of a man's desire?

Sylvia called mid-afternoon and apologized for the delay in responding to my message. She had just returned from Maryville, Tennessee, where she had held Tony's memorial service. Maryville was his birthplace and home to surviving relatives. Her voice was strong, and she spoke without slurring words. Either that was a positive sign as to her mental and emotional state, or she hadn't been home long enough to down much booze.

"Why did you call, Billie? You sounded tense."

"Sorry if I alarmed you," I said. "After reviewing the scrapbook, Carl and I have a question for you. What is the name of the man who died in the same accident that killed Ed Pace? In the article about the accident, that man's name was withheld pending notification of next of kin."

Sylvia sighed. "Tony and I didn't need the stress of that accident on top of April's death. I thought those two terrible events would put him six feet under. In the end, thank God, OSHA cleared our company of any responsibility. Can't say the same for the crane owners. It was just a terrible, freak accident."

"I'm glad you didn't have to spend months or years in court," I said. *Come on, come on. Tell me the name*, is what I thought.

"Ed's parents were devastated. You can imagine." She paused and breathed deeply. "Did I tell you that I think Ed killed April? Oh, I don't think he meant to. Whatever happened between them that night, he just went berserk."

"Yes, you told me. But that wasn't Tony's conclusion."

Bigger sigh. "No. But if he could have believed that, he'd still be alive."

"Sylvia, do you remember the name of the second accident victim? If you've wiped it out of your mind, I can understand. What a traumatic time for you and Tony."

"Of course I remember," she said, with a touch of indignation. He and Gary Nix lived in the same long-stay motel. Ed Pace lived at home with his parents."

I shifted the phone to my other ear and waited.

"His name was David Wayne Harris. We called him David," she said. "He moved around the country from construction job to construction job, never staying long in any one place. It took weeks to locate next of kin. A brother in Texas said he didn't have the money to get David's body home. So Tony paid for cremation and shipped the ashes to the brother."

I half-listened and nursed my disappointment. When Sylvia ended her monologue, I said, "I knew you'd know. Thanks."

"You don't sound very enthusiastic, Billie. Mind telling me why this information seemed important?"

"Just filling in the blanks. Nothing to worry about."

She accepted my disclaimer, and we chatted for a few more minutes. She asked about any progress in finding Tony's killer, either through my efforts or the sheriff's. I said there hadn't been any progress, feeling it best not to get her hopes up. I promised to keep her informed, and we said goodbye.

I wrote the name on the notepad on the bar: David Wayne Harris. What had I expected? Some kind of answer spelled out in fireworks to explain how Tony could track Gary Nix's cold trail, if Nix had used an alias? I said the name aloud. Then I wrote the name in bold, block letters: DAVID WAYNE HARRIS. Next I printed the initials: DWH.

"My God! It can't be!" My voice was loud in the silence.

I drew a circle around two of the initials and called Carl.

"I just talked to Sylvia," I said. "The name of the guy who died with Ed Pace in the accident was David Wayne Harris. Does that bit of info strike any bells with you?"

"No. Can't say it does, but you're obviously pumped. The only Harris I know is that deputy who's helping us with Sam and Ruby's house." He paused and then whistled. "Damn, Billie, I see where you're coming from. DW could be short for David Wayne."

"Exactly." My head spun with fragments of facts and memories. "Gary Nix—the man Jake wanted dead—is masquerading as DW Harris. What better alias could Nix have picked? A here-today-gone-tomorrow construction worker cut off from family but with a usable Social Security number. There wouldn't be a red-hot trail to follow, except that Nix didn't count on Tony using the same logic, coming up with the same alias. That was damned smart of Tony."

"Whoa! Slow down and think it through. You don't want to jump to a wrong conclusion. What else do you have?"

Various tie-ins were jumbled in my mind in no particular order. "Well, for starters, DW was in the vicinity when Tony was shot; otherwise, he couldn't have arrived so quickly on the scene. And he hight-ailed it when Deputy Owens told him to find the spot the killer fired from. Great opportunity to be sure he'd erased all evidence."

"Seems more like coincidence. And what about the camouflage truck that kid saw? He said it was up and down the road about the time of the shooting. You've been thinking that truck was the killer's."

That gave me momentary pause. I switched the phone to my other ear. "True, but remember Aaron also saw a deputy's car up and down that road. Maybe the cammy driver and DW Harris were in cahoots."

Carl sighed. "That's a stretch. Anything else?"

"Well, DW was back the next Saturday, volunteering for the build. It didn't seem odd at the time, but then I was desperate to find a new supervisor for the project."

"You told me it was Bernie's idea to volunteer."

"That's what DW said, but he could have used Bernie as cover. Considering the big leak in the sheriff's department, DW would have known within a couple of days that I was out to identify Jake Wade. Volunteering for Habitat would let him keep an eye on me."

"I don't know."

Carl lapsed into silence. I waited for him to pick up a thread or ask another question. Instead, he sighed again.

"Okay," I said. "I just thought of something that clinches my case. Remember when Madge speculated that Tony had to hang around town for several weeks, as if waiting for Gary Nix to re-appear after an absence?"

"Yeah. That's definite speculation."

"But I can tie it to something specific I learned during one of the Habitat breaks." My heart rate spiked. "Dawn told me that she had won a cruise and that she and DW were out of town for nearly two weeks. Tony knew this and hunkered down to wait for the man he knew as Gary Nix to return. After many months of tracking Nix, he wasn't about to miss his chance to avenge his daughter's murder."

"I can see you're convinced. But will Sheriff Farr buy it?"

"I'll soon know. Obviously, I can't go it alone from this point. You want to go with me in the morning to tell him?"

"Hell, no. This is your baby to wash or throw out with the bath water."

I laughed at the mangled cliché and thwarted a crying jag. I hadn't anticipated that someone I liked would become the prime suspect in the cold-blooded murder of Tony Wade. The unexpected development also dealt a serious blow to the pride I'd always taken in being able to accurately size people up.

Chapter 30

I called Sheriff Farr's office Friday morning and was transferred to his secretary, Eunice, who curtly informed me that he'd be out of the office most of the day.

"Would you care to leave a message? I could deliver it if he calls in." Curt had morphed into oh-so-accommodating.

"No message. But it's very important that I talk to him as soon as he's back in the office. It's about the Tony Wade case."

"I'll deliver the message; however, I cannot assure you he'll return the call today." Back to curt.

As aggravating as I found her mercurial manner, I bit my lip and responded politely. "I'll count on you, Eunice, to stress the importance of returning this call."

She cut the connection without responding.

Left in limbo, I considered options for distracting myself while waiting for Farr to call back. Out-of-hand, I rejected two major items on my to-do list: answer a list of financial questions Uncle Joe had e-mailed me and brainstorm other possibilities for helping women in need. Tackling either project would do nothing, I knew, but raise my anxiety level. I settled on a chore I'd put off for weeks, a chore to channel my nervous energy; I organized my bedroom closet and straightened my dresser drawers— no easy task with my arm still in a sling.

Farr called around three o'clock and interrupted the admiring looks I was bestowing on my closet. At my feet rested two paper bags bulging with clothes I'd salvaged for charity. I answered on the third ring and double-timed to the living room where Carl was stretched out on the couch, looking at TV. I put the call on speakerphone, and Carl slowly sat up. His face was gray, and a frown creased his forehead.

"If you have something to tell me, Quinn, spit it out, or you can come to my office." Farr's words were clipped and rushed. "I'll be here until at least six tonight."

Carl waved his hands to capture my attention. He mouthed *No. Stick with the plan.* Earlier, when I had taken a break from playing Martha Stewart, he had insisted that I shouldn't be seen again talking to the sheriff. "You'd just create scuttlebutt that would race through the rank and file. And if there's really a serious leak in the department, DW Harris would find out you're on to him."

"You still there, Quinn? I don't have all day," Farr said.

"Sorry. I was thinking." I cleared my throat. "I called to ask you to meet me this afternoon in a neutral place. Believe me, you don't want the information I have to get loose."

"And why would you worry about that?"

"Well, the coroner mentioned something about information leaking out of your department and..."

"Riggs is full of bs."

"Whatever," I said. "It's your call, Sheriff."

I heard a bump, as if a knee or chair had contacted a hard object. Farr muttered something indistinct.

"Okay, Quinn, but this had better be good. I'll meet you in forty-five minutes at Al's Diner. Eastside in the strip mall. There's a booth in the back where we can have some privacy."

After I cut the call, I turned to Carl and found him again stretched out on the couch, his eyes closed.

"You want to go with me?" I asked.

"No. I want somebody to cut my head off and soak it in pain meds."

"Another migraine?"

"Coming on. I just took a pill. Now I need some peace and quiet."

"You want me to call Madge? You're the color of sheetrock."

"No. She'll be here soon. Vamoose, Billie. You don't need me. You can manhandle the sheriff."

"How do you know I won't smother him in feminine wiles?"

"Don't make me laugh. It hurts." Carl waved me away, eyes still closed.

Al's Diner was unfamiliar to me, although I knew a roundabout route to the strip mall. If Farr had planned to be late, to let me know whose time I was imposing on, I took the fun out of it for him. As I parked, I saw the sheriff's uniformed backside disappear through Al's shimmering metal door.

The exterior of the diner was retro-shiny aluminum, matching the interior glitz. A blast of air conditioning greeted me. In the center of the room, a long counter snuggled with at least fifteen swivel stools that were bolted to the floor. Booths hugged all the walls, and scattered between the counter and the booths were tables with aluminum legs and trim. All the countertops were covered in orange Formica, and orange vinyl padding covered the counter

stools, chair backs, and booth seats. I needed the
sunglasses I'd left on the car dash.

Farr motioned to me from a booth in the back.
He was planted in the middle of a bench seat, clearly
establishing that any asshole that wanted to engage
him would sit opposite. Not that it would ever have
crossed my mind to sit beside him.

A top-heavy waitress in a starched uniform took
our orders. We watched her swivel hips retreat before
turning to each other. There was an awkward silence
before she returned with two mugs of coffee and a
small mountain of creamer and sugar packets. Farr
removed his Stetson and laid it on the seat beside
him. Sweat plastered a fringe of hair to his scalp.

"Okay, shoot," he said, looking at his watch. "I've
got thirty minutes at the most."

"First, have your people interviewed Sylvia Wade?
If not, we'll need more time than that," I said.

He studied me through half-closed eyes, no
doubt debating with himself about how much detail
to share with me.

"Yes, I've talked with her at length." Silence.

"And?" I asked.

"And what?" Farr clamped his teeth shut. A muscle in his jaw twitched.

"Did she talk about Tony Wade's reaction when a
grand jury failed to indict Gary Nix for the murder
of April Wade?"

Farr slowly ripped two packets of creamer, emptied them into his coffee, and swirled the concoction with a spoon. He sipped the blond mixture and set the mug down with a thump.

"I see I'll have to play along with you, Quinn. So, yes, Mrs. Wade told me her husband fixated on Gary Nix as the killer. Followed him when he left town, determined to take revenge."

I nodded. "Would you consider it plausible that Tony probably tracked Nix to our neck of the woods and that somehow Nix found out and got the first shot in?"

"The logic's there. But I'm ahead of you." Farr leaned back and stretched one arm along the top of the seatback. "Checked Gainesville, Athens, Atlanta and, especially, Creeks County. No sign of a Gary Nix. If he's trouble prone, thought I might find him in police databases. Nothing. I'd say this shoots a hole in your theory, Quinn. Unless Tony Wade knew how to track a ghost." A tiny smirk played on Farr's lips.

"There's another possibility." I allowed myself a half-smile.

"So go ahead. Entertain me."

"What if Nix assumed an alias that Tony figured out? It would explain how he could search for and find the man he intended to kill to avenge his daughter's murder."

Slowly, Farr removed his arm from the backrest and leaned toward me. A furrow split his forehead, and he pursed his lips. "This is the hot news—right? You've discovered an alias. Well, spit it out. I can tell I'm not gonna like it."

I took a deep breath. "From everything I've learned, I'm ninety percent certain that Gary Nix is one of your deputies. DW Harris."

"Shit!" Farr slapped open hands on the table and rocked the mugs. A flush rose from his neck to his face and disappeared into the receding hairline of his scalp.

"I don't buy that, Quinn. You're bottom fishing. DW Harris has been with the department a year. He's demonstrated a level head and catches on quickly in training sessions. Shows the right kind of initiative. I have him on a promotion fast track, for God's sake."

"What about your background investigation of him? Nothing suspicious there?" I asked when Farr stopped to breathe.

"Nothing to really raise my hackles, and they are easily irritated."

"Nothing?"

"Okay, well, he had moved around the Southeast a number of times, but I attributed the wandering to a young man's desire to see some of the world. A credit check upheld Harris' claim that he lived paycheck to paycheck. Hell, if I attached negatives to this stuff, I'd have a short supply of deputies some years."

The more Farr mounted a defense of Harris, the more sweat popped on his forehead. I suspected that his discomfort stemmed from having uncovered shoddiness in vetting a candidate for deputy sheriff.

Farr's defense petered out. He wiped his forehead with a napkin he plucked from a dispenser nestled between salt and pepper shakers.

"So what's your case for suspecting Nix might be using 'DW Harris' for an alias?" he asked.

I summarized the train of thought that had led Carl and me to uncover the name of the man who died in the accident with Ed Pace, the young man April Wade was attracted to.

"Believe me," I said, "when Sylvia Wade said his name, David Wayne Harris, and my brain processed it as DW Harris, I was shocked. I like DW. This shakes my confidence. I thought I was a better judge of people."

Farr drummed his fingers on the rim of his coffee mug and stared at something over my shoulder. At least two minutes passed before he refocused on me and spoke.

"So how is it that you know my deputy as well as you're claiming to? Am I about to receive another surprise at your hands?"

Farr's questions puzzled me, until I remembered that DW had said he wasn't in any hurry to tell the sheriff that he was working with me.

"I'm sorry," I said, and I really was. "I thought that, by now, DW would have mentioned that he, and Dawn, and Bernie are helping me build a Habitat house."

Farr shrugged. "Nope. This is news to me. I don't know why he didn't tell me, since it's a cause I believe in." He looked thoughtful. "So, now that you suspect he killed Tony Wade, what will you do about the build? Fire him?"

"I can't do that without good reason. And I certainly can't tell him what I've learned. But I don't plan to be on site alone with him."

"Make sure you follow that rule." Farr tapped a forefinger on the tabletop to emphasize each word. "As for the conclusions you've come to, Quinn— I know it looks bad, but it takes crazy coincidences to link my deputy to the man Wade was tracking. People walk free every day when circumstantial evidence isn't convincing."

"True. But here's another angle to consider. Carl told me to ask you about DW's proficiency on the firing range."

Carl's question hovered between us for a few seconds.

Farr sighed. "He has one of the department's highest ratings. The shot that killed Tony Wade was easily within his capabilities. But, hell, half the men in this county can shoot an eye out of a wild turkey at twenty paces."

"What about DW being the second deputy on the scene of the murder? Is that just a coincidence? Or would he have had time to shoot Wade and make his way to the Habitat site?"

Farr's shoulders slumped. "Even worse, Harris secured the sniper's hideout. If he's guilty, his report isn't worth a damn."

"Why was he on patrol alone that day? Is that usual?"

"He was serving warrants. Not unusual to do that solo or to be anywhere in the county."

I sipped on lukewarm coffee and watched a brown spider the size of a nickel crawl up the wall behind Farr's head.

"Something's missing in this scenario," he said. "What about the camouflage truck that was spotted near where the sniper hid? That kid, Aaron, kept connecting the shot he heard with a truck he saw. *Bang! Bang!* Remember?"

I had hoped Farr wouldn't highlight this hole in my theory. "I have the same question, but right now, I'm convinced DW Harris is really Gary Nix."

Farr slid to the edge of the bench seat and looked at me. "I'll investigate, of course, but I can't tip my hand. If Harris is spooked for any reason, he's a flight risk. I'll count on you keeping quiet, Quinn."

"Of course."

Farr set his Stetson on his head and automatically pulled the brim to a spot slightly north of his nose. He stood and dropped a crumpled five-dollar bill on the table.

"And, for the umpteenth time, butt out. If you keep on, Quinn, your reward will be a lot worse than a potato to the shoulder."

"I hear you, Sheriff."

I paid my bill at the front register and stepped outside into blinding sunlight. Ahead of me, I saw Farr marching to his cruiser.

Back at the boat, I found Madge in the kitchen, scouring the range top with a special cleaning pad and energetic circular motions. She stopped momentarily to acknowledge my arrival. Carl was slumped on the couch. He claimed his migraine was better, yet he was wearing sunglasses. I briefed him on my session with the sheriff, especially his reaction to my conviction that Gary Nix was posing as DW Harris.

Carl grimaced. "You have a talent for wounding men's pride. And how the hell can you butt out, with DW coming every Saturday to work on the Habitat build? He'll be there tomorrow."

"I told Farr about DW's involvement, and he understands I can't fire DW without cause." I paused.

"Anyway, I wouldn't fire him; he knows construction. We're so close to finishing the house. Sam and Ruby have waited too long. What's the harm in pretending a little longer that all is well?"

"Because all's not well. You're juggling fireballs, Billie. We have to assume DW killed Tony Wade and is behind the attacks on you. You better believe he's a roadside bomb—ready to explode if you step too close."

"Listen to Carl, Billie." Madge wiped her hands on her apron as she settled on the couch near Carl. "You're too pig-headed for your own good."

The bomb image gave me pause, yet I knew I wouldn't back off, not yet, anyway. "I know I'm playing it close, but what about the flip side? Think about it. I don't have any reason to fire DW. It would look suspicious, might even lead him to suspect his ruse has been discovered. Besides, we work Saturdays in a group. Pete, Neal, Sam… If there's trouble, I can count on them."

Carl sat up straighter on the sofa and winced at the effort. "Well, I'll be there, too. I can't do a helluva lot more than keep my eyes open for trouble, but I can do that. Had lots of practice for lots of years. I'll ride with you in the morning." He turned to Madge. "Don't let me oversleep."

Madge rolled her eyes. "I don't like any part of this."

Chapter 31

Madge called Saturday morning, as I was finishing a third cup of coffee and a banana.

"I know Carl promised he'd go with you to the build, but, Billie, he's in terrible pain with a migraine. Throwing up, too. Maybe he can come later. Will you be okay?"

"Sure. Remember, I told him I feel safe surrounded by all the guys."

Madge sighed. "He's really worried that DW might pick up vibes from you and figure out that you know who he really is."

"Tell Carl to relax and get better. I've been practicing innocent facial expressions that will keep DW from discovering his masquerade is over."

"Joking won't keep you safe, Billie."

"I know, but maybe it'll keep me sane."

I parked under the small oak tree, and Sam and Ruby waved to me from the picnic tables. As I approached them, Ruby stared at my arm, cradled in a sling.

"What happened, Miz Billie? You break yo' arm?"

"Nothing to worry about. I'll be out of this contraption tomorrow or Monday." I raised my arm at the shoulder to reassure them and hid a flinch.

"That's good then." Ruby's frown turned into a smile.

Sam grunted and handed me a cup of coffee. Ruby fanned herself with an empty sausage-biscuit box. At eight in the morning, high humidity wet the air. An unusual quietness enveloped us. Above, a hawk circled silently on extended wings.

I exchanged my coffee cup for a lemon-filled donut and munched on a big bite as I glanced around. Even without windows and siding, the house looked solid. I tried to imagine the finished site down to an asphalt driveway and parking area, the hard, clay yard loosened, enriched, and grassed.

The calming image of the house gave way to jitters that had been with me off and on all morning. I'd played down my concern when talking to Madge, but soon I'd have to interact with DW, displaying a poker face, if I couldn't manage a smile, pretending ignorance of his true identity. Whatever, I didn't want to tip him off that his charade was coming to an end. Was DW experiencing some kind of weird kick, walking around a murder scene he had orchestrated? Sweat peppered my forehead, yet I shivered.

"You mighty quiet, Miz Billie," Sam said.

I waved off his offer of another donut. "Don't mind me, Sam. Just thinking. I didn't sleep well."

"I been thinking too, Miz Billie," Ruby said. "Just look at it, a brand spanking new house me and Sam are gonna live in. Sometime I think I'm dreaming. It's got all the things I ever wanted and all new things, except…"

"Except what, Ruby?" I couldn't imagine what we'd left out of planning.

Ruby took a deep breath. "All else it needs is a clothes-line out back."

I failed to stifle a smile. "But you're going to have a new clothes dryer."

"Oh, mind you, I'm thankful. Real thankful. But… but can't beat the smell of clothes dried in God's sunshine."

I'd never experienced a clothesline and, on the spot, concluded I'd been deprived of one of life's joys. I patted her hand. "Then you'll have a clothes-line. My housewarming gift for you and Sam."

"Look." Sam pointed to the road. "They all here at the same time. Like they planned it."

Neal led the way in on his motorcycle and revved the engine before cutting the ignition. Pete's banged-up truck was next, followed by DW's SUV. Dawn and the baby stayed put in the back seat with the door open. DW slid out of the driver's seat and buckled a tool belt around his hips. He spoke to Pete and Neal, and the three of them waved in my direction before turning their attention to the house. Good. I wouldn't have to put on my friendly mask just yet.

Bernie eased his F150 to a stop and slid out of the cab. Sam and I walked over to lend a hand. Up close, Bernie looked like hell. A gray stubble-beard clung to his gaunt face. Gray eyes sat in black rings. He looked like he'd lost at least five pounds in the past week.

"You okay?" I asked.

"Bad night." He looked at my sling, but didn't comment.

We helped Bernie unload the truck and followed his instructions as to where to place things. Sam lugged a deep fryer to the shade of the big oak. Bernie hefted a large cooler and set it on the ground near the fryer. I deposited a gallon of peanut oil to the side. Two more gallons were still in the truck.

"What's in the big cooler?" I asked.

Bernie removed the lid, poked a hand down in chipped ice, and pulled out a floppy piece of fish.

"Cat fish fillets. Snagged night fishing on the lake. DW helped me catch them."

A shrill whistle split the air. DW waved us toward him. Everyone joined the huddle except for Bernie and Dawn, who sat with Tim in a director's chair

under the big oak. We circled near the spot where
Tony's blood had stained the ground. I swallowed
and put on my friendly face.

DW looked around the circle before he spoke.
"Looks like somebody was injured since last week.
What's with the sling, Billie? Hope it's nothing
serious."

His face was smooth. A slight, vertical frown
creased his forehead. He was playing innocent to
the hilt.

"Oh, nothing," I said. "One of those embarrass-
ing weekend warrior goofs. I'll be out of the sling
tomorrow or Monday for sure."

A murmur of "goods" and "greats" traveled the
circle. I thought I saw a questioning flicker disturb
DW's sympathetic expression. I hoped my face was
as hard to read as his, as this would protect me from
giving away the secret Sheriff Farr and I were guarding. Success also depended on never slipping up
and calling DW by his real name, Gary.

"A bum arm is one way to earn a cushy job
today." DW smiled. "Why don't you help Bernie
with the chow. As for the rest of us—from now
to lunchtime, we need to move like a cat with his
tail on fire. But remember to drink lots of water.
It's gonna be a scorcher today, so let's finish those
pesky trusses and see how far we can get putting
the windows in."

Sam, Pete, and Neal fell in line behind DW.

"Wait for me. I'm gonna help too," Ruby said.

I rejoined Bernie in the outdoor kitchen. He didn't seem too happy to have me assisting but let me set the picnic tables and establish a drink station.

"What else?" I came up behind him, and when I spoke he jumped.

"Damn! I didn't hear you." He wiped his hands on the tail of a stained towel stuffed under his belt. "I can handle it from here." Without waiting for an answer he turned, took several catfish pieces out of a milky fluid, and dredged them in a pile of flour.

"Okay, you're the boss."

I thought about cheating. Who would know if I sat in my car for a while with the air conditioning on? I'd know. A rivulet of sweat rolled down my neck and nestled in the front of my bra. I mopped my face with a bandana and sat on the tailgate of Pete's truck. Indistinct voices and sporadic hammering came from the direction of the house.

My cell phone vibrated in my jeans pocket and startled me. I flipped the phone open and saw that Madge was calling.

"Billie, is everything okay there?" Her voice was tense.

"Yes, for now. Where are you? How is Carl?"

"We're parked under a shade tree about a quarter of a mile from you. Carl's better, but he can't muster eating and socializing with people. I packed us a picnic lunch. We'll…"

A muffled voice interrupted Madge, and then Carl was on the phone. "Bottom line, we'll be close by in case DW tries any hanky panky. Just hit speed dial, and we'll be there pronto."

I was touched that Carl had left his sick bed out of concern for me. On the other hand, now I had to worry about his well being on another level.

"Go home and get well, please, " I pleaded. "You and Madge will expire sitting in your car in this heat."

"Don't worry. We've got AC, and we're in the shade. Remember—speed dial if you need us."

Before I could object further, Carl cut the connection. I knew better than to call back.

I stretched out on the bed of Pete's truck and dozed restlessly. Sometime later, three short blasts of a car horn roused me. I sat up and found my bum arm almost out of the sling and my fingers tingling. I repositioned my arm and flexed my hand.

"Soup's on," Bernie shouted.

I was in line behind everyone but DW, and he wasn't in sight. I loaded a sturdy paper plate with golden fried catfish, fried wedges of sweet potato, hush puppies, and cole slaw. I deposited my plate and tea at one end of the picnic table and went back for dessert. I was scooping the last of Dawn's cherry cobbler onto a clean paper plate when, from behind, someone gripped my good elbow and squeezed hard.

As I turned, DW released his grip. A half-smile played on his lips. "What gives? Usually you're in the thick of things. Today I spot you goofing off in Pete's truck."

A blush burned my cheeks. "I wasn't goofing off. Bernie didn't need me and neither did you."

DW held both hands up and leaned back slightly. "Whoa. Why so defensive? I was just kidding."

I swallowed against a wave of anxiety. DW might have been testing me in some way, and I had overreacted. My thoughts spun around the need to regain footing, but what to do? Unfortunately, I chose a bad option.

"Oh, yeah," I said. "I'm known in these parts as Billie, the one-armed wonder." I assumed a boxer's crouch and pulled my uninjured arm and fist into a defensive position. He was laughing when I jabbed him so hard on a shoulder that my hand was numbed.

DW's laugh morphed into a look of surprise. "I'm not sure what's gotten into you, unless it's just that time of month." He turned on his heel and marched to the serving table, where he fork-stabbed everything he put on his plate.

"You and Mr. DW got a mad on?" Ruby's brown eyes welled with tears, and she chewed on her bottom lip.

Sam, Pete, Neal, Bernie, and Dawn had stopped eating midstream and stared at me, the same question on their faces. I had overreacted again. Damn! Taking a deep breath, I forced a wide smile.

"Oh, relax everybody. I think this miserable heat has scrambled my brain."

Hunched around the table, we ate in unnatural silence for about five minutes before pockets of conversation developed. Sam and Ruby discussed where to put the clothesline. Neal went on and on to Pete and me about the new motorcycle he was saving up to buy. More chrome. More power. Fancy color trim. Bernie was left out of the conversation but didn't seem to mind. He avoided eye contact and picked at his food. Was he brooding about his diagnosis of terminal cancer? Who wouldn't?

When Neal got up to get more tea, I quickly turned to Bernie, hoping to lift his spirits and to redeem myself in my own eyes.

"Best catfish I've ever eaten," I said.

"Thanks." He bit off a tiny piece of hush puppy and chewed slowly. "Secret's in the flour and corn meal coating. Gotta keep it light."

Bernie fell silent, eyes on his plate. He dabbed his fork in a small pile of cole slaw. Most of the important men in my life were talkers—my father, Uncle Joe, Charlie, Hank, and Carl, when he wasn't peeved with me. I had had little experience with men who hoarded their words and thoughts.

I tried again. "You and DW do a lot together besides fishing?"

"Bowling, hunting, stuff like that." He shoved his plate away and looked at me. "You should try some icy ointment on that sore shoulder. And you should stay away from that weekend warrior stuff you do."

"Bernie, can you take Tim for a little bit, so I can finish my dinner in peace?" Dawn stopped at the table's edge. Without waiting for an answer, she thrust a fussy Tim on Bernie.

"Sure." Bernie pushed his plate away. "Come to Granddad, little man."

After kissing Tim's cheek, Bernie turned sideways on the bench and bounced the baby on a rocking-horse-thigh. The up and down jiggle quieted Tim. I watched them for a few minutes. Way down the line, Charlie would have a moment like this with a grandson or granddaughter. I had almost made peace with the fact that I was forever excluded from the world of mothers and grandmothers. It was the *almost* part that tightened my throat.

After DW hustled the crew back to the house to begin installing windows, I helped Bernie clean up and put things away. He needed help to empty the used oil from the fryer. With my good hand, I held a large funnel-strainer steady in the mouth of empty jugs that I steadied between my feet. Bernie poured carefully. Residual heat of the oil warmed the funnel.

"Tell DW I've gone on."

I watched Bernie's truck stop at the end of the driveway and then turn slowly onto the dirt road. A cloud of red dust rose behind him. I admired Bernie for soldiering on despite the toll cancer was taking on him.

Returning to my stay-out-of-DW's-way strategy, I hunkered down again in the bed of Pete's pickup truck, legs dangling from the tailgate. I speed dialed Madge's number. She answered on the first ring.

I fudged my message a little. "We're through here for the day, calamity free. I'll be sure to follow Pete out and stay away from DW. You guys need to go home right now."

"If you're sure…" Madge hesitated. "It's pretty hot here. I do need to get Carl to his recliner."

Carl grumbled in the background.

"Go now. No arguments." I cut the connection before Carl could undo the command.

To distract myself, I called Uncle Joe and talked, instead, to Irene. He was playing golf with "the boys," and she was expecting friends for a late afternoon of bridge. I could tell my call was an interruption, so I hung up after a few pleasantries and called Pam. She was painting her toenails and in a talkative mood. I half listened to a lengthy, glowing description of Mr. Hot Date, suspecting that, as on so many previous dinner-and-a-play excursions, she'd be taken home by Mr. Not-So-Hot. Pam always bounced back from dating disappointments, and, in a few weeks, tried again. She was in no way desperate to land a man and enjoyed "playing the game," as she put it. I, on the other hand, kept my psyche intact by avoiding "the game" whenever possible.

The heat and long talk with Pam brought on a yawning binge. I stretched out on the truck bed, knees up, and studied the leafy canopy above me. Blue sky peeked through. A fly buzzed me repeatedly and then lost interest in dodging my hand waves. I drifted into a light sleep and awoke to the sound of my name yelled from a distance. I sat up and slowly straightened my back, stiff from lying on metal. I licked my lips and tasted salt.

"Yoo hoo! Come and look, Miz Billie, Miz Dawn," Ruby shouted from the front stoop.

I looked around and saw Dawn sitting in a director's chair, Tim asleep on her lap. She touched a forefinger to her mouth and motioned for me to go on without her.

Slipping off the tailgate, I stretched on tiptoe and checked my watch. Three o'clock! How could I have slept so long? Ruby waved to me, and I joined her on the front porch. She led me into the combination living and kitchen area. Sam, Pete, and Neal were standing together just inside the door, drinking from sweating bottles of water. Their hard hats and tool belts lay in a pile near their feet, a sure sign that DW had declared the workday over.

"Whew, it's hot as Hades," Sam said. The bandana tied around his head was wet with sweat. "But look at what we did." He grinned and waved his hands around. "Got the trusses in place, and look here at the windows. Ruby's done tested them. They go up and down real easy. Next Saturday we can finish the windows in all the house."

Pete and Neal slapped high-fives.

I watched DW climb a tall ladder he had positioned near the sidewall of the kitchen. He reached up and pushed on a board that moved several inches. When he turned in our direction, he motioned for me to come his way.

"How's about handing me my nail gun, Billie. Right there at the bottom of the ladder."

"Nail gun!" I was taken aback. "What the... You know nail guns are no-nos on site. It's one of Habitat's biggest safety precautions."

"I know, I know. Don't get hysterical on me."

"I'm not hysterical. I just can't imagine why you brought it to the job."

Gingerly, DW shifted his weight on the ladder. "I was planning to stay behind today after all you guys leave, except you won't leave. If I spot places needing more nails, I can take care of it zap zap. We don't want Sam and Ruby moving into a half-nailed house."

"Yeah. I hear that, Mr. DW," Sam said.

"Amen," Ruby said.

"So, how about handing me the nail gun. Please."

"Under duress," I said.

The nail gun was on the floor at the bottom of the ladder, nestled in a carrying case. I picked it up and was surprised by its weight.

"Where does it plug in?" I asked.

"Doesn't," DW said. "It's cordless."

"Wish I had one," Pete said. "I've tripped over too many compressor hoses in my time."

DW wiggled fingers at me. "Hoist it up, Billie."

I hefted the gun to a straight-arm position and waited for DW to take it. He bent slightly and put one big hand around the gun and then straightened on the ladder.

Just as I turned to get out of the way, something heavy, heavy enough to shake the floor, landed beside my right foot in conjunction with a small explosion. Shouts echoed around me. I looked down at the nail gun and a dent in the plywood sub-flooring.

"Good god!" DW came down the ladder so fast that it skittered sideways. "Are you okay, Billie? I don't know how that happened."

Sam, Ruby, Pete, and Neal crowded around us. Ruby put her arm around my waist. Pete picked up the nail gun by the handle, his finger nowhere near the trigger.

"I think you've got a new part in your hair." Neal whistled softly. "And it's a miracle none of us were hit by the nail that shot out on impact."

"Yeah, this baby nearly beaned you, Billie." Pete bent and slipped the gun into its carrying case.

"We're talking concussion at the very least. On one job I worked, some bricks fell on a guy's head. He was permanently loopy after that."

"What happened, Mr. DW?" Sam turned to DW who stood to the side looking on, his face flushed.

DW shook his head. "Damned if I know. I thought I had a firm grip on the gun, and then it was like it was pulled out of my hand. I'm so sorry, Billie. That was too close—and you without a hard hat on. What've I harped on, folks? Safety."

DW offered the explanation and apology in what I thought was a half-hearted manner. And why wouldn't or couldn't he look me in the eye? Was I being hypersensitive to read something sinister into what others would judge to be a clumsy accident?

"First, my shoulder is nearly torn off my torso. Now, I barely missed having my brain nailed to my skull. If bad news comes in threes, what's next?" I posed the question to DW, but he looked away.

"Lordy, don't talk like that, Miz Billie." Ruby wrung her hands. "You're just asking for more bad luck. I got a rabbit's foot at home you can carry if you want."

Chapter 32

I awoke with sunrise Sunday morning but not because I was eager to meet the day. Anxiety about the nail gun episode Saturday had built through the night and left me feeling queasy and out of sorts. And it didn't help that in tossing and turning, I had aggravated my injured shoulder.

Sitting on the edge of the bed, rubbing my shoulder, I replayed happy hour the night before. I had told Carl and Madge about DW dropping the nail gun from his perch on a ladder and nearly splitting my skull. Carl had thrown his hands up and berated me for telling them to leave their roadside surveillance before I actually left the Habitat site.

Madge, always seeking to smooth things, expressed a different view. "Accidents do happen, you know. Sure DW is out to get you, but would he do it in front of witnesses?"

"Not so fast." Carl's expression tightened. "You want to hear about all the accidents I investigated that were covers for some nasty fires? I'm almost sorry that nail gun didn't hit you on the head. Nothing else has gotten your attention."

"Carl!" Madge shook a finger at him. "You apologize to Billie right now."

Carl didn't apologize, and Madge was still on his case when they left for their boat. Since Carl's remark was vintage curmudgeon, I had just laughed. I shook off memories of Saturday night and, standing by the bed, I debated whether or not to accept Dr. Murphy's advice. He had said I could come out of the sling Sunday or Monday.

"Bye, bye." I opened the closet and threw the sling to the back of the top shelf. As I lowered my arm, blood that had been trapped at splint-level spilled into my throbbing hand. I was pleased that my shoulder didn't detach from my torso.

Later, after a leisurely cup of coffee and a blueberry muffin, I dressed in shorts, T-shirt, and flip-flops, my usual boring fashion statement. My mood improved, and I decided to walk to my marina mailbox for the Sunday paper.

I opened the door, took a step, and kicked something with the edge of a flip-flop and my big toe. A stab of pain led into a one-legged dance. I looked to see what I had kicked. A large, grubby-skinned potato with a knife blade stuck through it. The knife handle reminded me of generic steak knives available by the gross at restaurant supply stores.

Goosebumps rose on my arms and on the back of my neck. The crazy who'd nearly killed me with a potato gun had returned in the dark of night, and I'd heard nothing. Was DW flipping out or pushing the panic button? Why would he so quickly follow up the nail gun episode with still another warning? According to Carl, a rookie criminal, not to mention a deputy sheriff, could easily jimmy the door and kill me in my sleep. I shivered.

I struggled to get inside DW's head. If he thought that I had not yet discovered his true identity, Gary Nix, and he could frighten me into dropping my investigation, then he wouldn't have to kill me. This seemed to me to be the reasonable explanation, in that DW would have already skipped out if he'd learned that his boss knew he was really Gary Nix. No wonder DW was on the brink of shifting from scaring the hell out of me to dispensing with me.

I stared at the speared potato and ran through my options. Involve the sheriff? No. What could he do, except slam me again for butting into law enforcement business? Could a potato be traced? I didn't think so. Was there a fingerprint on the knife? Not likely, unless DW was a dummy, and I didn't think that for a moment. Option two: seek advice from Carl and Madge. I should, I thought. But I rejected the idea. Sharing another threat would only upset

them. Option three: Make it my little secret. And
that's what I did. I pulled the knife out of the potato,
marched both to the aft deck, wound up my pitching
arm, and tossed the suckers as far as I could. They
landed with a splash that rippled the water. Bubbles
gurgled to the surface before the water quieted.
Even if the potato floated, the knife would sink.

Trying to calm myself, I proceeded as if the day
were routine. I walked to the marina for the newspaper, unable to keep my eyes from shifting left and
right, looking for what I didn't know. Back at the
boat, I locked all doors to the outside and settled
on the party deck with a thermos of coffee and a
handful of dark chocolates. From my post, I could
spot anything suspicious on the dock or near the
marina office. I read the paper in spurts and gradually relaxed.

As sleepiness took hold, I closed my eyes and listened to familiar sounds—a chorus of duck quacks,
muffled voices, and the gentle slap of water on the
hull. I stayed in a twilight zone until a hunger pain
nudged me to full consciousness.

After lunch, I caved in to anxiety. I loaded the
.22 pistol, checked that the safety was on, and placed
it on the floor by the couch. And then I reverted to
routine and stretched out on the couch for the nap
I'd fought earlier on the upper deck.

I dreamed about scuba diving. I had lost a fin
and was searching for it in murky water. Twice, I

mistook a dark object resting on sand for the lost fin and recoiled when the mystery thing wriggled out of my grasp. The underwater silence was broken by a series of musical notes—the same two tones over and over. I opened one eye and slowly focused on the ceiling light. Ding-dong, ding-dong, ding-dong. Somebody was pressing the doorbell rapidly. What was the urgency? My heart raced. The doorbell sounded again. My thoughts jumped to Madge and Carl. There must be an emergency. I ruled out the potato shooter. Too blatant.

As I sat up on the couch, my foot landed on the pistol on he floor. I eased it out of sight behind the couch skirt as the doorbell sounded again. I yanked the door open. Hank peeked at me around a bouquet of multicolored flowers. In his other hand, he gripped a bottle of wine. Damp blonde hair hinted at a recent shower. Various honey-tanned body parts protruded from white shorts, white T-shirt, and boat shoes.

"Hello, lovely lady. I come bearing gifts. Have you missed me?"

"Damn, Hank. What's with all the doorbell shenanigans? You scared me."

He lowered the bouquet and frowned. "Well, so much for missing me. You sure know how to dash a guy's hopes."

I blushed, remembering that recently I'd asked Madge to find out if Hank's boat was still in the marina. "He's still there," she had reported. "Your interest in Hank is news to me. And I'll bet it would be to him, too."

Hank cleared his throat. "Thanks, Billie. I believe I will come in."

Hank kissed the top of my head as he brushed past me. I smelled his citrus-scented aftershave, and his body heat mingled with mine. I blushed again. I followed him to the kitchen and found a tall vase under the sink. I filled it half full of water and Hank eased the flower stems into their liquid home.

"They're beautiful," I said.

"And so are you." He leaned down and brushed his lips across my cheek.

Through the aroma of aftershave I smelled booze. In my presence, Hank had never overindulged. He liked his wine and an occasional beer, but, often, I had seen him switch to water, Coke, or iced tea.

"You've been partying without me," I said.

"We can fix that."

He held the bottle of Pinot Grigio high, then set it on the bar so he could rummage for the cork-screw. He popped the cork, slid two wine glasses out of the holder above the refrigerator, and poured the glasses half full.

"Let's toast," he said.

"To what?" I sat on a stool across the bar from him.

"To my new business venture. *Knott's Solutions.*" He snapped his fingers. "Install my software and kiss the hackers goodbye—well, at least eighty percent of the time. Financing is in place, and I've signed for a prime location in Atlanta for headquarters and R&D space."

"Wow! Congratulations. That is something to toast."

"Not to mention it comes just in time to save my sanity. Selling my last business earned me my houseboat sabbatical. But a guy can't twiddle his thumbs forever."

We clinked glasses and sipped. I was genuinely happy for Hank.

"This sounds like you'll soon be abandoning ship—so to speak, unless you can run a mega-business from the party deck."

Hank sighed. "I'm leaving tomorrow. The transport truck will come later to move the boat to Key West. When business madness gets to me, I'll retreat to the island. Will you miss me, Billie?"

The loaded question hovered in the air between us, as I plumbed my feelings. I would miss Hank. He laughed easily and was fun to be with. And, face it, that he found me attractive turned my ego into a helium balloon. Since the divorce from Charlie and the HIV scare, I had held men off, as Uncle Joe put it, "with a very stiff arm" and, as Pam put it, "with a chastity belt worn on the outside." When Madge teased me about Hank, I always countered with my opinion: Hank's love life was too loosey-goosey. He had a reputation in Atlanta that had reached Uncle Joe. In my opinion, Hank had a crush on me. Easy come. Easy go.

"Madge and I will both miss you." Hedging seemed the best way not to lie and not to encourage. And then I succumbed to a bad impulse and jabbed Hank unnecessarily. "But you'll be in your element in Atlanta with all the lovely ladies clamoring for attention."

He studied me through narrowed eyes and sipped the last of his wine. His next move was so quick that I wasn't prepared to find him on my side of the bar, his body pressed against my knees. I was trapped. If I stood, I'd be chest to chest with him. He smoothed a clump of hair I didn't know was askew.

"Why are you so afraid, Billie? You have something against being thought of as a lovely lady?"

"I…" I looked past his eyes and focused on the ceiling fan in the middle of the room. "Your reputation is out there. From lovely lady to lovely lady. I just can't go there, Hank."

"For you, I can change."

"But I can't. Please, please, just drop it and go have a nice life. Send a postcard now and then. Let me know you're okay." I realized that my breathing had become shallower, and my heart rate had spiked. It had been a long time since I'd experienced a panic attack, and I didn't want to revisit the frightening experience. I took a slow, deep breath and exhaled even slower.

Hank placed warm hands on my thighs and squeezed gently. "You need to get over Charlie. The guy did you dirt."

"It's not just Charlie. But the other reasons are none of your business."

He looked down at me. Creases book-ended the corners of his mouth. For the first time, I noticed the bulge of a small jowl under the tanned chin. Was his carefree plunge through life becoming tiresome, the nights without lovely ladies more frequent? Was I witnessing the fabled midlife crisis?

"I have to leave tomorrow, Billie, but you haven't seen the last of me. For now, how about a goodbye kiss?"

As I was composing my retort, he leaned forward, planted both palms on the stool to either side of me, and glued warm lips to my closed mouth. His tongue moved lightly from one corner of my lips to the other. My scalp tingled. I put my hands on his chest to push him away but held back. I parted my mouth slightly and our tongues touched. An electric charge coursed into my arms. I pushed hard on his chest. Hank stepped back and stood straight. He licked his lips.

"Hummm... Did that mean anything, I hope?"

"It really and truly meant goodbye, Hank. Please, go now." I walked to the door, opened it, and stood aside.

Hank hesitated in the doorway. He started to say something and then closed his mouth. I was pleased that he didn't beg, that he was leaving with his pride intact. I closed the door and locked it. Unexpected tears stung my eyes.

Chapter 33

After Hank left, I slumped on the couch and dissected my reaction to his convoluted declaration of affection. I cringed, remembering what must have seemed to him a cold and high-handed dismissal of his feelings. On the other hand, he was probably oblivious to the panic that had washed over me. I was taken by surprise, and since the divorce, emotional surprises sprung by men had brought out my survival instincts. I had enjoyed his kiss and the warmth of his body. Yet, I'd sent him packing at a moment in my life when I needed all the support I could muster. I was walking around with a target on my back and no way to paint over it. Worst of all, I'd brought my predicament on myself.

The phone rang and interrupted my funk. Pam's agitated voice filled my ear.

"I'll be about thirty minutes late, if I'm lucky. I just cleared a bad accident that closed one lane of I-85."

"Okay. Just be careful." I cleared my throat.

"What's wrong? You sound depressed."

In spite of myself, I laughed. "How can you possibly conclude that, Pam? I only spoke four words."

"Know you like a book." She disconnected without a goodbye.

I sighed and looked around to see what needed tidying before her arrival. For starters, she'd freak out if she inadvertently discovered a pistol loose in the living room. I fished the gun from under the couch, double-checked that the safety was on, and returned it to the drawer in my bedside table. I stuck my head into the bedroom Pam would use. Madge had towels on the bed, and all else looked shipshape.

With nothing else to do, and to ward off further brooding, I settled at the round table on the fore deck and half-heartedly worked on a Sudoku puzzle. Every few minutes, I scanned the area, until, finally, I spotted Pam as she stepped onto the dock, rolling a small black suitcase behind her.

I slipped on flip-flops and padded toward her through shimmering heat waves that hovered over the dock. She stopped as I approached. In her right arm, she cradled a paper sack.

"What's in here?" I took the sack from her.

"Cracker assortment, Brie, and a yummy Spanish wine. If you're a good girl and tell me why you're depressed, I'll share."

"I'm not depressed." I tried and failed to sound chipper.

"Don't lie to me, Billie. We don't lie to each other."

We walked the rest of the way to the boat in silence. While Pam settled in her bedroom, I popped the cork on the wine and arranged the Brie and crackers on a round plate. Pam emerged, looking comfortable in shorts, a tank top, and thin-strap sandals. I put the edibles and two wine glasses into the dumb waiter, and pushed the up-button.

We climbed the rear steps to the party deck, unloaded the snacks, and settled in lounge chairs under the canopy. The three o'clock sun hung in a bright blue, cloudless sky. A light breezed stirred the air.

"Okay," Pam said. "Tell all."

I breathed deeply and decided to avoid discussing my endangered life, which Pam couldn't do anything about anyway. Instead, I focused on something she could bulldog.

"Hank is history. He came by unannounced this morning. And when I failed to succumb to his charm, he said adios."

Pam looked at me and shook her head. "Don't be flippant. What did he do to panic you? Propose?"

"Nothing so serious." I ran a finger around the rim of my wine glass, dislodging condensation. "It was pretty obvious he likes me and wants to get more involved. Well, more like under the sheet games."

Pam bit a Brie-topped cracker in half and chewed on it for an eon. "For God's sake, Billie. Hank's a handsome, brilliant guy who's worth scads more millions than you can claim. Why can't you bend a little and have some fun?"

"I was tempted, I admit. He smells good, and all that tennis keeps his butt nice and firm."

Pam laughed. "You don't fool me. You joke to avoid the painful truth. No man can replace Charlie, even after Charlie fell from his pedestal and cracked into a jillion pieces. The bum."

"Cut Charlie some slack, will you? I finally have. And think about it. If we could have agreed to adopt, we would never have gone the surrogate route. We'd be a happy family of three now."

"Balls! You can't whitewash what Charlie did. He left you for what's-her-name. I haven't checked the statistics, but how many men fall in love with the surrogate mother and divorce the barren wife?"

Barren. The word stabbed my heart. A wildfire of endometriosis in my late twenties had cost me my uterus and damaged my ovaries. While I grew used to the fact I'd never have children, Charlie fixated on becoming a father. I wanted to adopt so we'd be on equal footing as parents. Charlie wanted a child from his sperm which—I was ashamed to admit—caused me to panic. I would be a second fiddle parent, a stepmother, for God's sake. I got stuck there, in irrational thinking. Finally, I agreed to a gestational surrogate, but my hostility to the idea created such tension that Charlie gravitated to Ellen. I didn't blame her for the breakup. I blamed myself.

"Hello." Pam waved a hand in front of my face.

"Enough about Charlie."

"Fine," Pam said. "He's only half the reason you can't warm up to Hank. Let's dissect the role of shithead." She lifted her wine glass in a mock toast.

I sighed. "Well, how would you like it if the first man you bedded after losing the love of your life called you and said, '*Oops! I just learned I'm HIV positive*'?"

"I admit that was damn scary. But you have to get past this phobia. You could live to be eighty-five. Wouldn't you like to walk the walk with a soul mate?"

My throat tightened. "What I'd like to do is drop this conversation. The goal was to ease me out of my funk."

"Well, help me out. What can we do to cheer you up?"

Mentally, I reviewed options that would ordinarily keep me engaged. Watch a DVD movie. Too sedentary. Take the Sea-Dos for a spin around the lake. Too active and too hot.

"Well?" Pam pointed to her watch. "Time's a wasting."

I wiggled to the edge of the lounge chair, stood, and stretched. "We need a change of pace. Follow me, ole buddy."

"You're not going to give me a clue?"

"One clue. You won't need a raincoat."

"This is it? A car wash? This is what will cure your funk?" Pam asked incredulously.

"Gonna wash that funk right outta my hair," I sang, off key.

I deposited money in the meter, and on the green light eased the Prius to the required stop and engaged neutral. Slowly, the car moved forward behind two other cars, and gyrating foam ribbons rhythmically slapped the car's surfaces.

"And I thought you couldn't surprise me," Pam said.

"I feel safe here. No sniper can get to me."

"Whoa." Pam reached across the seat and squeezed my shoulder. "What haven't you told me? I've never seen you so jittery."

I couldn't remember which details I had shared with Pam, so the floodgates opened and memories and fears tumbled out. The awful sight of Tony Wade dead, his skull broken like an eggshell.

The attempted break-in at my boat. The mysterious camouflage truck cruising in and out of the marina. The attack with a potato gun. Escalation of threatening phone calls. Identifying DW Harris as Gary Nix, a suspect in the murder of Tony's daughter and most likely the sniper who killed Tony. The strain of waiting while the sheriff investigated DW/Gary and collected enough evidence to arrest him.

I stared at the soap rivulets covering the windshield, wondering why we were progressing through the wash so slowly. "To boot, Sheriff Farr doesn't have enough men to give me protection, and I'm walking a tightrope by working with DW at the Habitat build, a little fact the sheriff doesn't approve of."

"Damn." Pam shook her head several times and squeezed my hand. "If the sheriff can't protect you, why don't you just leave the scene? Come to Atlanta and stay with me. Don't even tell Madge and Carl where you're going. You'll be out of danger."

"I'm tempted, but copping out would only be a temporary fix. Besides, Sam and Ruby have waited too long for their house. I have to see this through, but I'll take special safety precautions."

"I'm not sure that answer is good enough. We're talking life and death." Pam's expression was dubious.

"It's the only answer I have right now, and I don't want to talk about this stuff anymore."

Pam folded her arms and leaned against the headrest. "I know that tone of voice."

The car rolled through spurts of clean water and into a blow dryer before stopping. On the green light, I pulled forward and drip-dried the Prius on the quiet ride home.

We walked in silence back to the boat. I opened the door and stepped into a blanket of air conditioning. Carl looked up from the couch where he sat with earphones clamped to his head. The five-thirty news anchors mouthed silently as we walked by the TV. Madge hovered over a chopping board, rendering a large head of broccoli into florets. A plate of small filets mignon sat next to the countertop grill.

Madge held up a hand to stop Pam and me at the bar. "Carl," she yelled. "Take those damn-fangled earphones off. You need to hear this with Billie."

Carl grimaced, struggled to his feet, and joined us.

"This call must have come in after you gals left and before we got here." Madge wiped her hands on her apron and pushed the playback button on the answering machine.

You have one old message, Sunday 4:10 p.m. "You ignored all my warnings, Quinn." The agitated voice was male and altered, as if the speaker pinched his nostrils and pitched his voice higher. "But you just couldn't keep your stinking nose out of who killed Tony Wade. I can't let you keep on and ruin innocent lives. You hear me? I can't let you do it. You brought what's gonna happen on yourself."

"Oh, my God!" Pam spoke into hands that flew to her mouth. Carl's shoulders slumped. "Shit."

Madge's face crumpled.

Prickles crawled on my scalp. I replayed the message. I don't think that's DW's voice," I said.

"Who cares? Somebody wants you dead," Pam whispered.

Chapter 34

Monday morning, I poured a second cup of coffee and settled at the bar. Pam sat at the breakfast table under orders to stay quiet since she had insisted on listening in. I put the phone on speaker mode and called Sheriff Farr's office. Eunice answered and grumpily transferred me to him with only a two-minute wait.

"Somehow, I don't think this is a social call, Quinn. Be careful what you say."

I wondered if Farr had buried his pride and concluded he had a gigantic leak in his department, but I didn't say anything.

"I do need to talk to you in private. Can you step outside your building and call me on your cell phone?"

Silence. "Well, obviously, I'll have to humor you, although I don't share your distrust of the security of my department's communications. What's your number?"

I gave him my cell phone number and disconnected. He waited ten minutes to call back, no doubt indulging his passive aggressive relationship with me. Pam closed the magazine she'd been reading and motioned for me to return to speaker mode.

"Okay," he said. "What's so urgent? It better be good."

I heard the blast of a car horn and was satisfied that he had left his office building.

"You be the judge, Sheriff. Listen to this phone call I got last night."

Holding the phone close to the answering machine, I played the threatening message, and returned the phone to my ear.

"Well, crap," Farr said. "Play it again."

I complied and then interrupted Farr's silence. "It doesn't sound much like DW's voice to me."

"Agreed. But you'd be surprised, Quinn, how easy it is to disguise a phone voice."

"Well, whoever's shadowing me, he thinks he knows exactly what I'm up to, what I've learned about Tony Wade's killer. And, frankly, if I'm not overreacting, he sounds bent on sending me to join Tony."

"You're not overreacting. Problem is, like I told you, I don't have enough men to give you round the clock protection. Take my advice and hole up for a while with relatives-preferably out of town."

"I'll think about it," I said, knowing I wouldn't go to Uncle Joe and Irene. "What's new with your investigation? Have you discovered any incriminating evidence about DW? Can't you arrest him?"

Another, deeper sigh. "Nothing concrete. We can't tip our hand, or he might bolt. I have the GBI checking the information you gave me. I'll keep you posted. Meanwhile, for God's sake, draw your neck in. Hang out with that Carl guy. Don't do anything stupid."

I laughed. Not because there was anything funny about my situation but because Farr was close to begging. I couldn't resist a closing shot. "Why, Sheriff, I didn't know you cared."

Pam tossed the magazine to the end of the couch, stood, and began pacing the living room.

"Billie, you aren't safe enough staying in the marina, not even staying with Carl and Madge. No, close your mouth and listen, for God's sake." She stopped pacing and shook a finger at me. "You told me the sniper killed Tony from a hundred-plus yards. You'd be the old sitting duck walking the dock to and from the boat. You're going to pack some duds and follow me back to Atlanta this afternoon. You can camp out in my condo for as long as necessary. Don't argue, you ninny."

Pam's plan flooded me with a mixture of relief and resistance. "Okay, I'll do it. But no matter what, I'm coming back Friday, so I can be at the Habitat build Saturday. I can't let Sam and Ruby down."

"We'll tackle that later." Pam's face was set in stone. "Just remember, if DW made that threatening call last night, Billie, he's through playing games with you."

There was no answer for that.

Against Pam's advice, I walked her to her car. After she started the engine and turned the air conditioning fan on high, she slid off the seat and stood with me while the car's interior cooled.

"I expect you to be no more than twenty minutes behind me." Pam shook a finger in my face. "And for God's sake, check your rearview mirror now and then for the nutcase who's after you."

"Yes m'am," I said, saluting. "And thanks for caring about my safety."

Pam smiled. "Call me selfish. Good friends are hard to find, much less keep."

I hugged Pam and waved her off. She stuck her arm out of the car window and shot me a bird.

Back at the boat, I packed a small travel bag and called Madge and Carl to relay the plan.

Madge sighed. "Thank the Lord. You're not safe around here."

"I set several table lights for auto on and off, so it will look like I'm here. I'll be back Friday afternoon, and, if it's okay, I'll spend the night with you guys."

"Better than okay. You have to."

I settled into Pam's guest bedroom and after a quick shower joined her on her condo's enclosed balcony five stories above the bustle of Atlanta traffic below. We were surrounded by night-lights of surrounding buildings of varying heights and exterior finishes. The effect, so different to life on the lake, was magical. We wolfed Chinese take-out reheated in the microwave.

Back in the living room, sipping on a robust red wine, Pam casually mentioned that she'd be flying to California the next day for a three day conference, returning Friday late evening.

I laughed. "You didn't want to tell me this before I said I'd come, did you?"

Pam grinned. "I thought you might turn me down."

"You know I love your company, but, truthfully, I could use absolute peace and quiet. I've been obsessing over Tony's murder. I need to chill."

And that's what happened. I zoned out Tuesday through Thursday. Mornings I spent with coffee and the Atlanta paper on the balcony. The condo was within walking distance of Piedmont Park, where I strolled and watched other people indulge their park behaviors. If there were deviants around, I didn't see them. Once, walking back to the condo, a police cruiser pulled abreast of me just as the driver activated a siren. Startled, I jumped up and landed on the grass beside the sidewalk, my heart thumping. As the cruiser sped away on squealing tires, I hugged my chest and berated myself for overreacting. Lunches were leisurely, consumed at neighborhood eateries. Dinners I had delivered and ate on the balcony before wallowing in one or two movies from Pam's growing collection of DVDs. I gravitated toward courtroom dramas and romantic comedies.

Friday morning, I ate a banana for breakfast, washed linens, and left Pam a thank you note written on a paper sack. I detoured by the Botanical Garden where I wandered around, enjoying nature's luxurious, asymmetric beauty and views of Atlanta's nearby geometric skyline. The odd juxtaposition always raised goose bumps on my arms.

I stopped by my boat long enough to see that everything was normal and in place. No knife-speared potatoes appeared underfoot, thank God. I stuffed my work clothes, boots, and clean pajamas and underwear in a boat bag and proceeded to Carl and Madge's boat.

I tapped on the door and stepped into the living room. Madge whirled from where she was working at the kitchen counter. She wiped her hands on an apron and held her arms wide for a hug.

"Thank the Lord, you're home safe and sound. Flo called us, all worried when you didn't answer your phone. That camouflage pickup cruised the marina several times while you were gone."

Carl's reaction surprised me. He got up from the sofa, turned the TV off, and walked to me. He opened his mouth to speak and then closed it. I could almost see wheels turning behind his pained expression. Finally, he stuck his hand out, and I shook it.

"I was worried about you, Billie. You made the right decision, hiding out in Atlanta. But it would be the wrong decision to go to the Habitat build tomorrow. Please, don't do it." I had never heard such concern in his voice, and the word "please" had never crossed his lips when talking to me.

I resisted the urge to reach out and touch his arm. "I have to go," I said. "I've come too far to disappoint Sam and Ruby. Will you come with me? I'd feel safer."

A flicker of something I couldn't read passed over Carl's face. "Absolutely," he said. "You can't go by yourself."

After a light dinner featuring Madge's famous tuna salad and a dish of Greek yogurt topped with fresh fruit, Carl excused himself and went to bed. Madge and I settled at the breakfast table to play gin rummy.

"Carl's head still isn't right, is it?" I asked. "He looks so pale. Is it usual for him to suffer so many migraines so close together?"

"It's weird, really. He can go for months without a migraine and then hit a stretch like this when the headaches are so frequent they're almost continuous. Carl takes his medications, but nothing seems to help. He's pretty pitiful in this state, but he's determined you're not going to the Habitat site by yourself in the morning. That's why he turned in early, hoping he can sleep this off."

We settled into a quiet game of cards. My concentration was off, so Madge won most hands. She wasn't one to gloat over her lopsided success, for which I was grateful.

Madge dealt the cards. "This is your hand, Billie. I can feel it."

One by one, I checked my dealt cards. "Yuk. Your ESP is broken. This definitely isn't my lucky night."

Madge checked her cards and maintained a poker face. "Correction. This isn't your lucky year so far. We have to figure out a way to get you out of this scrape alive."

"Amen." I checked the kitchen wall clock and yawned. "Please, win this hand, so I can go to bed."

I was one card from gin when a pajama-and-robe-clad Carl shuffled to the table. His hair looked like it had been spiked.

"Honey, are you okay?" Madge pushed her chair back.

"Couldn't sleep. Keep your seat, Madge. I've come to tell Billie something I should have told her weeks ago."

"Hallelujah!" Still clutching her cards, Madge raised her hands toward the ceiling.

I held my breath and watched Carl lower himself gingerly into the chair at the head of the table. His face was pale and pinched.

He cleared his throat. "Billie, you're just like my kid sister, Jean. I close my eyes and the two of you are staring at me." He shifted on the chair and leaned forward. "None of my warnings and arguments swayed her when she'd made up her mind about something I disapproved of. Stubborn to the nth, she was. Just like you. I could see trouble coming. Could smell it. And sure enough, she fell for a no-good motorcycle lunatic. Unemployed to boot. I begged her to dump the guy, but she just laughed." Carl's voice cracked.

Madge left her chair to stand behind him. She squeezed his shoulders.

"My worst fears came true." Carl's voice had dropped to a hoarse whisper. "She waved to me that night from the back of the motorcycle. I begged her to stay home. It had rained all day and was still drizzling when they took off." Carl's voice dropped another notch. "Jean died with that bum on a lonely road in a slippery curve he overdrove. Dammit, she wouldn't let me protect her. I was her brother, but she wouldn't listen to me. She'd be about your age now. I'm standing by like a dummy, knowing you may get yourself killed, and I can't stop anything." With the backs of his hands, he wiped tears from his cheeks.

"It's okay, honey." Madge squeezed his shoulders again.

I was flabbergasted. I reached out slowly and covered one of his hands with one of mine, feeling the wetness of shed tears. The lump in my throat swelled.

"Thank you, Carl, for caring. Looks like I could have learned a lesson in stubbornness from your sister. I can tell you loved her a great deal. Let me get this Habitat house built and Tony Wade's killer in jail, and I promise I'll take your advice more often."

Madge was first to laugh, and then the three of us vied to see who could laugh the hardest.

Chapter 35

Saturday morning before daybreak, I eased into my Habitat work clothes and tiptoed to the kitchen. I had forgotten to have Madge leave the coffee maker ready to brew, so I fished around in the cabinets until I found instant coffee. Try as I might not to bang doors, I was only half successful.

Madge shuffled into the kitchen in a short nightgown and well-worn slippers that threatened to fall off with each step.

"Oh, it's not a big rat out here after all."

"Ha! Ha!" I said. "How is Carl feeling? I need to head out early."

"I left him in the bathroom throwing up. He's too sick to go with you this morning."

"Poor Carl. I know he has a hard head, but how does it hold up to so many bad migraines?"

Madge shrugged. "One thing keeps him sane—me too. The headaches will stop soon, thank God, and he may go months before another attack. Unfortunately, he's suffering rebound pain now."

I peeled a banana and ate it while sipping anemic coffee. Madge stationed herself at the bar across from me and leaned forward.

"Carl sent me out here to see that you stay away from the build this morning. It's not safe, he said, because that last threatening phone call shows DW is desperate to get you off his tail at any cost."

That was the gist of Carl's argument, but Madge went on and on, embellishing with her own fears for me and insisting that I call Pete and let him stand in for me. She followed me to the bathroom and stood in the doorway while I brushed my teeth, her monologue droning on.

Back in the kitchen, I retied a loose bootlace. When I plucked my car keys off the wall hook and slung my purse over my shoulder, she stopped talking and put her hands on her hips.

"I'm sorry, but I have to go," I said. "Sam and Ruby are counting on me. Besides, DW would be foolish to try anything with Sam, Pete, and Neal milling around. I can keep myself out of DW's path. And, think about it, if I don't show up, DW could conclude that I'd cracked all his secrets, that the game was up for him."

"Okay, I give up." Madge threw her hands skyward. "The word 'stubborn' was invented just for you, Billie Quinn. Promise me you'll call me every hour on the hour. If you don't, Carl will drive me crazy, and I'll worry myself to my sick bed."

I promised. But, to hedge my bet, and without Madge seeing me, I made a last trip to the bedroom and transferred the .22 pistol from my bedside table drawer to the boat bag I always took to the site. I was stubborn, but I wasn't suicidal.

Leaving early gave me time to detour by Lowe's and check systems for drying clothes outdoors. I bought the deluxe model with facing metal T-poles drilled to accommodate multiple wires or ropes. I imagined Ruby smiling and humming as she pinned clothes to air dry. I threw in packages of pinch-pins and a pin bag designed to hang and slide on the line. I requested delayed delivery to the site.

I turned off the paved highway and slowed on the dirt road. Recent scraping by a maintenance crew had left ribbons of red clay outlining the edges of the road. A pink dust cloud tracked my car. I wondered what North Georgia had looked like in the early 1800s, before crummy farming practices and erosion had ravished rich and loamy soil.

Still running ahead of schedule, I bumped into the driveway and pulled past Sam and Ruby's Cadillac to a spot that I thought would be shady most of the morning. I left car air conditioning and stepped into an invisible wet cloud. As I scanned the picnic tables and adjacent spaces without spotting Sam and Ruby, my upper lip sprouted a sweat mustache. They were probably inspecting their home-to-be. I climbed the steps to the house and walked through the dim, stuffy interior, leaving shoe prints in a film of sawdust. No sign of either of them. Standing on the back stoop, blinking against bright sunlight, I scanned the lot to the tree line. Nothing. I cupped my hands around my mouth and shouted their names. Silence answered me.

I checked my watch: eight o'clock. Where were Pete and Neal? And DW and his family? Something didn't compute. Or was it a weird coincidence that everyone was late?

Walking up to the picnic table, I found two half-full cups of cold coffee. A third cup, probably bought for me, had the lid on. A box of donuts looked unopened. Now, I was worried. I walked to the edge of the woods, aware that the T-shirt under my work shirt was sticking to my back. If Sam or Ruby had had an urgent bathroom call, a trip into the woods or to the portable toilet was understandable. But would both of them get a call at the same time?

After a few minutes, I checked my watch again. Eight ten. There was definitely something wrong. Wrong enough that my scalp crawled. I jogged toward my car and my cell phone. As I opened the door on the driver's side, a heavy blow to my left shoulder, the one hit by the potato, dropped me to my knees. A stabbing pain exploded in my head.

"Stay right there. If you try to get up, you're dead. I have a knife."

A cold, sharp pressure on the back of my neck convinced me that the knife was real. I couldn't see who spoke, but I knew the voice.

"Bernie? What the hell…"

My shoulder throbbed. I struggled to move my arm even a few inches. The pain was worse than multiple blows to the funny bone. A hand grabbed the back waistband of my jeans and yanked me to my feet. He stood behind me, maintaining a firm grip at what felt like arm's length. Knuckles dug into my spine.

"You should've listened and butted out. I never wanted to hurt you. Now, it's too late." His breathing was shallow, his voice raspy. "And don't hold your breath that help is coming. I called everybody and said you cancelled the workday. Except Sam and Ruby, they didn't answer."

"That's crazy. Why would they believe you?"

"Easy. I'm the food guy. You had to stop me from buying stuff. And you had to leave town all of a sudden. Family emergency."

Ka-ching! Ka-ching! Ka-ching! Disjointed thoughts skidded into perfect alignment. "My God! It wasn't DW. You shot Tony!"

I flailed my good arm, hoping to jab him where it would hurt. No such luck. I squirmed against Bernie's grip on my waistband. He tightened his hold, digging his knuckles harder into my spine.

"Yeah, it was me. I didn't want to, but had to. DW don't know nothing about it. And he's not gonna find out. Jake's face was so tore up nobody could've thought he was Tony Wade. DW don't know how close he came to getting his ass killed." He hesitated. His voice dropped to a whisper. "Yeah. I know he's really Gary Nix. He told me all about it before he married Dawn. I believe him. He didn't kill Tony's daughter."

Bernie shifted and tightened his grip on my waistband, pushing me toward the house. Panic flooded my thinking. I jerked against his grip and dug my heels in. No use. He punched me between the shoulder blades. I stumbled several steps and stopped again before sinking to my knees. He didn't lose his grip and quickly yanked upward, forcing jeans fabric into my crotch. I was dead weight. His move.

"Stand up, bitch, or I'll end it right here."

The cold, sharp edge I'd felt earlier was again pressed to the back of my neck. Gingerly, in slow motion, I rose to my feet and didn't struggle as

Bernie propelled me toward the house. I scanned the yard, the woods, the road, praying for something or someone to help me. What caught my attention was the faded, banged-up Cadillac hunkered in half-sunlight.

"Sam and Ruby. Where are they? If you've hurt…"

"Sneaked up on them from the woods. Little chloroform did the trick. Wore a ski mask. They never saw my face. They're tied up in the back of the car. Like I told you, I don't like killing people. But I do what I have to do. Timmy needs a dad. I never had one. Dawn needs a husband. I'm gonna die soon. I'm doing all this for them."

Bernie stopped babbling and pushed me forward. I had to keep him talking, distract him until I could see a way to escape.

"How did you know that Jake Wade was really Tony Wade and that he was in town?"

"Had something in common, we did. That shaved head and beard didn't fool me. I seen his picture in the newspaper stuff DW showed me from the trial. 'Course he didn't know me from Adam. But I knew he came to get revenge on DW. I was sorry for the poor bastard. How would I feel if some shit-ass murdered my daughter? But DW didn't kill Jake's girl."

Something in common, but what? Factoids about Tony flashed through my thoughts. Construction background. Married with one child, a daughter. A sportsman in his spare time. Hunting…

"Fishing," I blurted. "The fishing rods in Tony's motel room... You bragged about catching fish you cooked for us. That's the connection."

Bernie pushed me ahead. "Yeah, that's it. Met him in a bait shop. Talked awhile about the best lures for big mouth bass. I liked the guy. Fished and drank beer with him a couple of nights. Hated like hell to shoot him."

Bernie tugged me to a stop near the steps to the small front porch of the house. He released his grip on my jeans belt. Without thinking, I wheeled to face him. He breathed in shallow gulps, exhaling stale alcohol across the space that separated us. His face was pinched and gray-white. Stubble-beard glistened with sweat. His eyes burned in deep sockets. Fear pressed on my chest, robbing me of oxygen. I gauged the distance between us—more than arm's length.

"Whatever it is you're about to do, Bernie, don't do it."

"Can't back off now. Like I said, you brought it on yourself, poking your nose in none of your business. And the damn last straw... You went and told the sheriff that DW is really Gary Nix. But I'm gonna fix it right now so that nobody can think DW shot Jake, uh, Tony."

A shiver chilled my sweat-soaked body. Whatever his plan, I was obviously the star. I judged the distance between us again. I'd have to rush him to make contact. I was trapped front and back between Bernie's body and the house. I eyed the narrow openings around him, left and right.

Bernie's eyebrows bunched in a straight line.

"Don't even think about it." He yanked on something in his back pocket and dangled a shiny metal object from one hand. Handcuffs! "Turn around and hold your arms straight out," he ordered.

I turned around but kept my arms tight by my sides. Staring me in the face was one of the posts supporting the porch roof. My heart thudded against my ribs. Damn! He was out to handcuff me to the post. Then what? Club me to death? Shoot me in the back of the head?

"Goddamn it! Do what I say. Put your arms around that post."

Bernie moved closer to my back, but I couldn't sense how close. I stood still, stiffened my arms straight by my sides, and curled fingers into fists. I fought through panic. I'd keep him talking, make him lose focus. I might have only one chance to get away. I couldn't blow it.

"How is killing me going to help anything? Think about it, Bernie. And how the hell did you find out the sheriff knows DW is Gary? Did you bug the sheriff's office? No, that's crazy. There'll be one pissed sheriff if he discovers a leak as wide as Lake Lanier. You can't get away with this. For God's sake, use your head."

"Shut up. You're driving me crazy. I told you. I don't want to do this, but I can't confess. I can't let Timmy grow up knowing his granddaddy was a killer."

"You can't get away with it. Maybe the ski mask didn't fool Sam and Ruby."

"Shut up, goddammit! If I have to, I'll take care of them, too."

A new spurt of adrenaline flooded my body. My heart beat in my ears. "You're not thinking straight. Face it, Bernie, you're dying. You can confess and clear DW. You probably won't even stand trial."

"You don't listen, do you? Just like a woman. I told you I can't 'cause of Timmy." Bernie held the cuffs up and jangled them. "You won't feel a thing. Just like Tony didn't feel a thing. After I handcuff you to the post, I'll shoot you from where I shot Tony. Then I'll come back and take the cuffs off. They'll find you laying on the ground. Dead just like Tony. The perfect alibi for DW since he's on duty today with a partner. They'll say the nut who killed Tony is still loose."

My brain squirmed with jumbled memories. Lilly sitting on the quilted bed, showing me photos of dead George. Standing beside Uncle Joe staring through tears at the urns bearing my parents' ashes. Hearing the chill in Charlie's words: *Billie, I want a divorce.* The HIV scare. Why couldn't at least one of my last memories be positive?

An unexpected blow between my shoulder blades took my breath and forced me forward a foot or more.

"Put your arms around that post, or I'll do it for you."

Bernie's hot, sweaty body pressed on my back. He grasped both of my wrists in hands slippery with sweat and forced my arms around the post. He held the loose cuffs in his left hand. Metal bit into flesh as he snapped a cuff around my left wrist.

"Shit!" He spit the word.

I saw his problem at the same time. The right cuff wasn't open. He lowered my left arm, released my right wrist, and kept his body smashed against mine. Quick, smelly breaths peppered my neck. I felt his body shift slightly and then heard a soft click. I couldn't see but assumed he had opened the right cuff. It was now or never.

I commanded my whirling brain to focus. Bernie held fast to my left wrist but my right arm was free. The pressure on my back eased slightly. The hot breaths on my neck receded. He was repositioning to cuff both of my wrists around the post. I had to use the only weapon I had—my body.

I dropped my chin to my chest and jerked my head backward with as much force as I could muster. A crack sounded as the back of my head rammed into Bernie's face. I ignored a sharp pain that cut into a dizzying curtain of stars. I jammed my right elbow into his ribs. He released my left wrist and with a loud grunt fell away from my back. I wheeled, heart hammering, afraid I'd only stunned him. I danced on my toes and punched the space around me, hoping to connect if he was standing. But he wasn't. Sprawled on the ground, he gasped for air and held his nose. Bright red blood poured past his fingers and ran down his chin.

"Bitch," he growled between gasps.

He rolled on his side and pushed up on a forearm. I swallowed the cotton in my mouth. *Damn! Now what?* And then my next move came to me like a scene in a movie. I raised my fists in fight position and danced closer to Bernie. I stopped, took careful aim, and kicked him squarely in the balls. An ear-splitting yell trailed off into pitiful moans and groans. He didn't give a damn about me. His eyes were squeezed shut, and both hands were cupped around the family jewels.

Thank God the key was still dangling in the right cuff. I shook head to toe as I fumbled the key into the cuff around my left wrist and freed myself. While Bernie was still grasping his crotch, I snapped the cuffs around his wrists and jumped back to a safe distance.

I ran at top speed to my car, grabbed the cell phone, and slipped the .22 pistol out of the boat bag. Thank God, I'd left it loaded. On the run back to Bernie, I dialed 911. In a calm voice, the operator repeated my plea for help and asked me to stay on the line.

"Can't... Need two hands."

I slipped the phone into a jeans pocket just as I stopped a few feet from Bernie. He struggled to sit up, but didn't try to get up. His face was gray. Lingering pain tugged the corners of his mouth. He pulled the hem of his T-shirt up and pressed it under his nose. Quickly, bright red blood soaked through the fabric. I pulled the hammer back on the pistol, gripped it with my trembling right hand and pointed it at Bernie. Left-handed, I recovered my cell phone.

"Hello... hello... Don't hang up." A calm voice spoke in my ear. "We need directions. Hello. Are you on the line?"

"I'm here." I gave the 911 operator directions and pocketed the cell phone. I gripped the pistol with two hands, steadying my aim at Bernie. "Like I said, if you've hurt Sam or Ruby..."

"Jesus, be careful with that gun. They're okay. Tied up in the back of the Caddy."

"I don't trust you." I took a deep breath and shouted, "Sam! Ruby!" I waited to the count of fifteen. Silence. I yelled again. Still no answer. "You're lying, Bernie."

I gripped the pistol more firmly and sighted his chest—in the heart area. He held up his cuffed hands. The nosebleed was less profuse. Brown blood was caking on his upper lip.

"No! Look!" He pointed behind me.

Was this a trick? I took two steps to the side so that I could keep Bernie in sight and still see the Cadillac. At first glance, I saw nothing, and then something round and dark moved side to side in a back window. Sam's head. Sam's wonderful, brown, kinky-haired head.

I smiled. "You may not believe it, Bernie, but this is your lucky day."

Minutes later, a deputy's car skidded to a stop in the driveway. Two deputies I'd never seen jumped out of the black and white, leaving the blue light flashing. One deputy ran to me and pried the pistol from my hands.

"What's going on, lady?"

"He tried to kill me. Gotta help my friends."

I didn't wait for permission. I flagged the second deputy, a pudgy man, who was jogging slowly toward us, talking into a shoulder radio. He followed me on the run to the Caddy. We opened both back doors. Ruby lay curled on the floor. Sam had maneuvered himself upright on the seat. On his side of the car, the deputy turned Sam so that he faced out, legs dangling. With some help from Ruby, I pulled and tugged her to the same upright position on my side. She was wringing wet with sweat. We untied their hands and feet.

"Thank God you two are okay. I'd pull that duct tape off your mouth, Ruby, but I think you guys will be happier to be the ones ripping it off when you're ready. And don't try to stand too quickly. Just sit here, please."

I motioned to the deputy and took off at a run for the cruiser. I arrived slightly ahead of him. He had been a blur in uniform until that moment. Now, under the Stetson, I saw a square-jawed face with a five o'clock shadow and bushy black eyebrows. His pocket badge read *Hardy*.

"What now, lady?" He struggled to control rapid breathing.

"I have to talk to the sheriff. Can you patch me through? It's a matter of life and death."

Hardy studied me for a minute, weighing his options. He made the decision I would have made in his shoes: a positive response could be a career booster. He asked for my name, moved away a few feet, and spoke into the shoulder radio. All I heard was mumble. He reached into the front seat of the cruiser and came out with a cell phone. When the phone trilled, he handed it to me.

"Sheriff Farr?"

"This better be good, Quinn."

"How's this for good: Bernie Satterfield just tried to kill me. He claims he killed Tony Wade. But I'm not sure. He's DW's father-in-law, so he may be covering for DW."

One, two, three seconds of silence. "Bernie? I know him. He's Eunice's, my secretary's, boyfriend.

This is bizarre. The guy's dying. Does he know DW is Gary Nix?"

"Yeah, he knows. It's complicated. I'll fill you in later. Right now, Gary Nix, DW, whatever, needs to be in custody."

Farr sighed. "Consider it done. He's on patrol. It'll be easy enough."

"Thanks." I handed the phone to Hardy, and, for the first time in an hour, filled my lungs with hot and humid air.

Chapter 36

Dorothy Longview and I had scheduled the dedication of Sam and Ruby's new house for a cool afternoon in late September. The absence of humidity and a pallet of leaf colors were energizing.

Madge, Ruby, and I bustled around the kitchen and then stood back to admire the goodies we'd arranged on the dining table: pink lemonade, oatmeal raisin cookies, carrot cake, and mini-pizzas the size of saucers. I brewed some coffee for those of us who couldn't eat sweets without caffeine. I tuned the Bose radio, a housewarming gift from Carl, Madge, and me, to a gospel music station favored by the new homeowners. Carl surveyed the scene from the living room, his bad leg hoisted on a small ottoman.

At two o'clock, Sam propped open the front door, and he and Ruby greeted each guest with non-stop smiles. First to arrive were the subcontractors for plumbing and electrical. They looked almost formal in khaki slacks and crisp, long-sleeve shirts. In their footsteps loped Sam and Ruby's pastor, a tall man with graying hair and oversized glasses that continually slipped to the end of his nose. Pete and Neal arrived together, followed shortly by the other volunteers who had worked the day Jake was killed—Gloria with one of the twins and Fred, who had begged us to pray for Jake that awful Saturday. They loaded paper plates with food and gravitated to the porch and front steps. I couldn't look at the porch posts without shivering.

"Wearing out the floor boards ain't gonna make him come." Ruby wiped her hands on an apron emblazoned with the word *welcome* in various colors and sizes.

I hadn't realized that I was pacing.

"She's right," Dorothy said. "DW, uh Gary, is probably too busy helping Bernie cope to care about us."

I sighed. The man I'd known as DW Harris had reverted to his real name, Gary Nix. He had been invited to the dedication by snail mail and follow-up e-mails but had not responded to either. Obviously, I needed closure more than he did.

Dorothy dumped an empty plate and cup into a plastic bag hanging from the doorknob of the tiny pantry. "It's past time to start the formalities," she said.

I helped her gather every one in the living room and quiet the hubbub of conversation.

"Everyone, please, form a circle, and join hands."

I stood between Pete and Sam, my hands swamped in their rough-skinned grasps. A mix of shaving lotions, deodorants, and perfumes glued us together, shoulder-to-shoulder.

"Reverend, please, lead us in prayer and bless this house," Dorothy said.

Heads bowed. Breathing quieted.

I gave the Reverend virtual thumbs up. From "Gracious God, thank you for being with us today," to the actual blessing of the house, he kept it short and focused on Sam and Ruby's future in their new surroundings. When he said, "Amen," hand-squeezes traveled the circle.

"Wait." Sam held up his hands, closed his eyes, and tucked his chin. We all followed suit.

"And thank you, Lord," he said, "for all the good folks here who sweated to help us get a new start. And a big thanks to Miz Billie for sharing what's hers. And most of all, Lord, thanks for the life of Mr. Jake. Maybe he wasn't all good, but he died in your service. We pray all this in Jesus' name. Amen."

The circle broke into small groups and conversation resumed. The minister apologized for having to leave early, but an elderly woman in his congregation had died, and the family needed him.

I was standing alone, fighting disappointment that Gary hadn't come, when Gloria and Fred joined me.

"You two look great," I said. "Thanks for coming."

Gloria grimaced. "I've been battling guilt—wimping out like I did. I still have nightmares. And today, when I walked near where Jake died, my stomach flip-flopped."

"I'm past nightmares," Fred said. "But every day I get on my knees and thank God for giving me one more day."

I looked away without acknowledging Fred's statement. On one level, I wholeheartedly appreciated that I'd been given more days to live, that I hadn't died at Bernie's hands. Still, rock bottom, I couldn't believe in a God that rolled dice, sparing one person's life and killing another person.

"Listen up, everyone." Dorothy raised her voice and waved her hands. "We're not through. Follow me out the back door, please."

I lingered in the living room. Three o'clock by the wall clock. I opened the front door and surveyed the newly sodded lawn. No sign of Gary. I was the last person out the back door. Dorothy stood with Sam and Ruby on one side of a newly installed clothesline on which a piece of white paper hung by a clothespin. The rest of us stood on the other side of the line.

Behind me, I heard the back door close. I turned my head and watched Gary Nix descend the steps and walk to my side.

"Sorry to be late," he whispered. "The baby is cranky. I had to help Dawn settle him down."

We focused on Dorothy, who cleared her throat and waited for quiet. "So we've come to that special moment." She lingered over *special.* "It's the moment of pay off for all the sweat equity Sam and Ruby put in on this house."

In slow motion, Dorothy pinched the clothespin that gripped a white paper to the line. She held the paper high before holding it out to Sam and Ruby.

"This is a letter from me on Habitat stationery saying it's okay for you two to start living in and enjoying the house. In another two or three weeks, the official paperwork will be completed. Oh, and here's something you'll need." From the clothesline, she released pins that held two house keys on rings. With a big grin, she handed one to Sam and one to Ruby.

Pete and Neal whistled, and everyone applauded.

"Thank y'all from the bottoms of our hearts." Sam's voice cracked.

"And more thanks to Miz Billie for my beautiful clothesline," Ruby shouted above the fracas.

Later, amidst the jumble of goodbyes, I asked Gary to join me for a Coke or coffee, and, somewhat hesitantly, he agreed. We slipped our vehicles into the exodus from the Habitat house. Sam and Ruby waved to us from the front porch. Light rain from the previous day had dampened the surface of the unpaved road and prevented the usual cloud of clay dust kicked up by tires.

On the drive to the coffee shop that Gary had selected, I reflected on happenings of the past two weeks. Dorothy had supervised completion of the Habitat house. I stayed busy answering a thousand questions about the what, how, and why of Bernie's attack on me. All evidence pointed to him as being solely responsible for Tony Wade's death, motivated by determination to save Gary Nix, posing as DW Harris, from the murderous wrath of Tony. Bernie viewed it as his dying gift to his daughter and grandson; they would not be robbed of a husband and father. Sheriff Farr had fun haranguing me for running around the county with an unregistered pistol. In the end, when I showed him my belatedly acquired permit, he dropped the matter. On his own, Carl signed up with Flo to learn how to navigate a houseboat on Lake Lanier, a move that let me know he and Madge would stick with me.

Gary and I parked side-by-side in spaces reserved for customers of Java Cup. We walked together to the door, commenting on black clouds that boiled in the western sky and the noticeable drop in temperature. A skinny waitress seated us at an out-of-the-way table and brought two mugs of coffee. Gary doctored his with a spoonful of sugar. I sipped mine black, savoring the taste and aroma.

"I can't stay long, Billie. Dawn really needs me to help with Tim. The baby is miserable and can't get comfortable. Doc said it's a bad cold—just keep him calm and his nose unclogged."

"Okay," I said. "Is it true that Bernie kept tabs on the investigation through the sheriff's secretary?"

"Yep. Farr's face turned a permanent red. He never suspected her as the source of the leaks. Eunice is drawing unemployment now." Gary checked his watch. "What else is on your mind? I really have to go."

"Speaking of unemployment, Farr told me he gave you a choice—resign or be fired."

Gary shrugged. "Resign. What else? I couldn't argue with his beefs. I managed to get hired as a deputy, used an alias, and never mentioned I was a suspect in a murder case. The grand jury's exoneration cut no slack with him. Didn't matter either that I was being stalked by an enraged father hell bent on snuffing me."

"If it helps, Sylvia Wade doesn't think you killed her daughter. She's convinced Ed Pace did it in the grip of warped passion. Some version of we always hurt the ones we love."

"That fits my theory. It sure as hell wasn't me. Too bad Ed died in that freak accident and took the truth with him."

A crack of thunder nearby startled us. Gary checked his watch and pulled his ball cap low on his forehead. "I really need to go."

"Give me a few more minutes. It's important."

He hesitated. "Okay. Shoot."

"So what will you do now? Sometimes no job can mean big opportunity."

He laced his fingers around the coffee mug and studied a spot on the tabletop. Rain pelted the metal roof. "I'm going back to college. Bernie signed over his savings to us. Poor guy. He'll die in prison. And I can work part-time. We'll scrape by."

"Have you decided on a course of study?"

He grinned. "Criminal justice."

I rolled my eyes and laughed. "Into the frying pan, huh?"

"Why not. Dull moments would be hard to come by."

Silence fell between us. After thirty seconds or so, Gary squinted at me and cocked his head. *He's wondering what I'm about to say.* For several days, I'd mulled ways to help Gary and Dawn, and now I had my answer.

"Gary, watch your mail carefully for the next week or so. Open anything with a return address of Joseph Quinn, Attorney at Law, Atlanta."

"Damn! How could I be up shit's creek with one of your relatives?"

I laughed. "No. It will be an offer to help finance your education with only a few strings attached. You can talk it over with Dawn and decide to take it or leave it."

Gary leveled an earnest gaze on me. "You're full of surprises. Why would you do this for me?"

"Did you see the movie, *Pay It Forward?*"

"Yep. It was a winner with Dawn and me."

"I like the thought of sharing some of my good fortune with you, because I think you'll use it wisely and, when you're able, you'll pass the baton to another worthy person."

"I can see you mean that." He smiled and reached for the bill the waitress had left. "In that case, coffee is on me."

Gary paid the tab, and we stood in the wind lock as the rain pelted harder on the roof.

"Gotta go," Gary said. "See you, Billie. And thanks."

Gary sprinted toward his SUV; I splashed behind in his wake. While I fumbled to open the car door, a driving rain soaked me from sandals to scalp. I slipped onto my leather seats as water puddled under my butt. I turned the wipers on full speed and eased out into a line of traffic moving by at a few feet a minute. My cell phone trilled and vibrated; I pressed it to my wet ear.

"Where would I live?" Pam asked.

For a split second, comprehension failed. "Wow! You wouldn't joke about this, would you? You're signing on? You and me fighting for women in need?"

Pam laughed. "I'm too old to wear a cape and a mask, Billie. And no houseboat. I'm not the house-boat type."

"That's a deal. Get your petite butt over here, and we'll find you a proper house or condo. Meanwhile, I can't see five feet in front of me through a sheet of rain. I'll call you later."

We clicked off. I thumped the steering wheel with a palm and shouted, "Yes! Yes! Yes!" at the top of my lungs. What a way to end a perfect day and jump into the future. Well, maybe one more thing would add to the perfection. I'd call around and see where Hank had landed in Atlanta. I would apologize, in person. And if the sparks that had once jumped between us were still there, I'd do the hard work to start a fire.

The End

ACKNOWLEDGEMENTS

Over more years than I care to admit, many people helped me to bring this book to its final formats—print and digital. To each thank-you, I wish I could attach a photograph and a short bio, for only then would it be clear that each person is a fascinating character worthy of starring in his or her own story.

For their technical help, many thanks to (their titles reflect their status at the time I consulted them): Spencer Frye, Executive Director, Habitat for Humanity, Athens (GA) Area; Jennifer L. Swartz, D.O., Assistant Medical Examiner, Bergen County (NJ) Medical Examiner's Office; Rebecca Broxton, Detective, Police CSI Unit, Athens-Clarke County (GA); and Andy Garrison, Director, Northeast Georgia Police Academy.

Additionally, a raft of family and friends provided much appreciated love, encouragement, and moral support:

- Writers Support Group: Genie Bernstein, Dac Crossley, Paige Cummings, Jim Murdock, Janice Pulliam.
- Readers who provided invaluable input: Harriette Austin (my writing instructor), Nancy Graham, Sarah (Sallie) Krickel, Ted and Gay Miller, and John Songster.
- For their friendship in specific times of need: Don Carver, Barbara and Charles Dawson, Nancy Graham, Sarah (Sallie) Krickel, and Anne and Chester Lee.
- Susan Torrant, who reads voraciously and coaches me by recommending authors and books to sharpen my craft.
- Ray McGinty, my brother, who, through incessant teasing (Will *I ever* read a copy of your book?), kept me plugging toward The End.
- Nancy Graham, my great friend and companion, who saw me through the first draft (50,000 words in 30 days), many subsequent hours of frustration, mixed with elation (progress!), to the 78,000 final product you hold in your hands. Without her, the kernel of a plot/protagonist would never have popped and made a book.
- Finally, without my talented and empathetic editor, Lizz Bernstein, you, dear reader, would be skimming the pages with red pencil at the ready.

January 2012

Habitat For Humanity International (HFHI)

HFHI, generally referred to as **Habitat for Humanity** or simply **Habitat**, is an international, non-governmental, non-profit organization devoted to building simple, decent, and affordable housing. The international operational headquarters are located in Americus, Georgia with the administrative headquarters located in Atlanta. There are five area offices located around the world: United States and Canada; Africa and the Middle East (located in Pretoria, South Africa); Asia-Pacific (Bangkok, Thailand); Europe and Central Asia (Bratislava, Slovakia); and Latin America and the Caribbean (San Jose, Costa Rica).

Community-level Habitat offices act in partnership with and on behalf of Habitat for Humanity

International. In the United States, these local offices are called Habitat affiliates; outside the United States, national offices manage Habitat operations. Each affiliate and national office is an independently run, nonprofit organization. Affiliates and national offices coordinate all aspects of Habitat home building in their local area, including fundraising, building site selection, partner family selection and support, house construction, and mortgage servicing.

The mission statement of Habitat for Humanity is to "seek to eliminate poverty housing and homelessness from the world and to make decent shelter a matter of conscience and action." Homes are built using volunteer labor.

(Wikipedia entry 9/2011, edited)

Example of How a Local Habitat for Humanity Affiliate Operates

Athens (GA) Area Habitat for Humanity, an independent affiliate of Habitat for Humanity International, is an ecumenical, not-for-profit organization dedicated to the elimination of substandard housing in Clarke, Oconee, and Oglethorpe counties in the state of Georgia. Our organization was founded in 1988 based on our strong belief that everyone in the Athens community deserves the opportunity to live in safe, decent, affordable homes. As of August 2011, Athens Area Habitat for Humanity has served more than 73 families in partnership with businesses and countless volunteers.

Habitat for Humanity is unique because our service is made possible through volunteer labor and donations of money and materials. Significantly, the way we pursue our mission is just as important as accomplishing it. Habitat builds simple, decent houses with the help of the partner families and sells them to qualifying families at no-profit and no-interest. A Habitat home is a hand up, not a hand out. Habitat homeowners work side by side with volunteers, cutting the cost of building the house. Homeowners must repay the cost of building their home with no interest charge and 100% of the mortgage payments going towards the funding of future Habitat houses.

Made in the USA
Middletown, DE
23 April 2016

ACKNOWLEDGMENTS

First and foremost, we want to thank all of the contributors to this book. Our vision to share the stories of those of us in the middle would not have been possible were it not for each of the writers in this book sharing a piece of their heart and soul with us. We would also like to thank Glenn Murray and 220 Publishing for making this book a reality. Thank you also to Christina Sanders for her fabulous designs and Tina Kobisa for her expert editor's eye. We can't thank our spouses enough, who encouraged us as we navigated the rough terrain that is the path of publishing a book. And, of course, thank you to our parents and our children – we are privileged to be sandwiched in the middle of such strong, beautiful and courageous people.

CPSIA information can be obtained
at www.ICGtesting.com
Printed in the USA
FSOW01n0627011216
27848FS